FLY ME TO PARADISE

FLY ME TO PARADISE

CATHERINE ANDORKA

FIVE STAR
A part of Gale, Cengage Learning

 GALE
CENGAGE Learning™

Detroit • New York • San Francisco • New Haven, Conn • Waterville, Maine • London

GALE
CENGAGE Learning

LIBRARY OF CONGRESS CATALOGING-IN-PUBLICATION DATA

Andorka, Catherine.
    Fly me to paradise / Catherine Andorka. — 1st ed.
    p. cm.
    ISBN-13: 978-1-59414-953-5
    ISBN-10: 1-59414-953-4
    1. Pregnancy—Psychological aspects—Fiction. 2. Self-actualization (Psychology)—Fiction. I. Title.
    PS3601.N549F57 2011
    813'.6—dc22   2010048193

First Edition. First Printing: March 2011.
Published in 2011 in conjunction with Tekno Books.

To the memory of Marino Campagna, my father and my forever hero.

And to my mother, Stella Campagna, Dad's heroine and mine.

No daughter could ever be more blessed.

And in memory of Roger Nelson, Founder of Skydive Chicago.

May you soar with the angels, always.

ACKNOWLEDGMENTS

I would like to acknowledge the following people with a huge debt of gratitude for their input, patience, and help with this book. Any mistakes are mine:

Greg Andorka (for always being in my corner), Kris Bagwell (for taking so much time with me to explain the fundamentals of skydiving), Jo Banias (for a litany of reasons), Mark Banias (for rescuing me from the depths of pro rally ignorance), Sherrill Bodine, Kim Brooke (for helping me undo my skydiving errors), Brit Brown, Laurie Brown (Where would I be without your input and support), Jack Churchill, Val and Dave Corderman (for your friendship and proactive encouragement), Linda R. Delunas, PhD., RN, CNE, Alice Duncan (my editor at Five Star), Arlene Erlbach, my amazing agent, Michelle Grajkowski (for persevering with me all this time). Much appreciation to Rosalind Greenberg, of Tekno Books, for publishing a book that is truly of my heart. Bill Hottinger, Jr., and Cheryl Jefferson. Enormous thanks to Edward H. Kaplan, M.D. (for your infinite patience and attention to my questions—and for so much more.) Jody Lowenthal, Carmen Mallory, Tom Mallory, Jude Mandell, Jennifer Mathis, Lisa Mondello (my long distance angel and voice of reason), Mike Mucha (for letting me witness the thrill of your first skydive experience, and then sharing it with me in such an articulate way), Lance Muscutt, (for all the great flying information), Sue Myers (for all of your medical input and ideas), Michael John Obos, Rosemary Paulas (for a great idea), Patricia Pinianski, Laurie Powers, Keith P. Rojek, D.D.S., P.C., Andrew A. Ruiz, M.S., Embryologist/Andrologist. My heartfelt thanks to Tiffany Schofield (Acquisitions Editor) for your help, your support, and your limitless patience with my unending questions. Elaine Sima, Suzette Vandewiele, and Marilyn Weigel. Finally, a special thanks to someone who wishes to be anonymous, but who shall always be acknowledged.

PROLOGUE

Madeline Holt crossed her fingers. *Please let this work,* she prayed.

"Would you like some magazines to read, or are you feeling tired?" the nurse asked, adjusting the pillows beneath Madeline's knees.

"I am a little groggy, but I always sleep on my side."

"In order for the procedure to be successful, we need you to lie on your back for several hours." The nurse opened the nearby storage cabinet for even more pillows and tucked them all around Madeline's sides. "This way if you doze off you won't turn over. Are you comfortable, Mrs. Holt?"

"I'm fine," Madeline answered, with a smile and a trace of sadness.

"I'll be back in a little while to check on you." With that she disappeared.

"Mrs. Holt," the nurse had called her. A lump formed in her throat as Madeline glanced at the ring on her left hand . . . the wedding ring she wore when she needed to feel close to her husband, despite the fact that it had been nearly a year since the car accident had taken him. "Oh Charles," she whispered, fighting back the tears. "Right now I miss you so much. Please be as happy about this as I am."

He'd never wanted children during the course of their seven-year marriage, but she hadn't been as sure. Nonetheless, she'd gone along with his wishes, rationalizing that with Charles operating his own insurance company and Madeline running her own accounting firm, the moments they'd managed to steal for each other were precious. Had a child been in the picture, those private moments would have been practically nonexistent. It wasn't until Charles had mentioned getting a vasectomy that Madeline had raised objections.

"It's so permanent," she'd cautioned. "What if we change our minds?"

Somehow she'd managed to convince him to contact the reproduction clinic. "Frozen sperm can last indefinitely," they'd been counseled. "That way if you ever decide you do want children . . ."

Madeline never thought she'd be making that decision solo, though at thirty-one, the tick of her biological clock was getting too loud to be ignored. Her firm was doing well, and as long as she continued to work, finances wouldn't be a problem. But there was a gaping hole in her world, a void that she very much wanted to fill by having a child with whom she could share her existence.

Charles was gone now, the result of the one time he'd chosen speed over caution in order to be punctual. Yet she took comfort in knowing his life force traveled through her at that very moment. Carefully, she laid her hands over her abdomen, fearful the slightest disturbance might interrupt the magnitude of the protocol. For if that journey met with success, her child would be the ultimate gift from the man she'd once married and loved.

CHAPTER 1

Mindful of the radar detector on his dashboard and the radio blaring Aerosmith, Kurt Williams sped through all the back roads on his way to the DuPage Airport in Illinois, where he kept his plane, a four seat Piper Archer II. Though over twenty years old, the aircraft was in mint condition and worth every penny he'd saved to buy it.

Scattered clouds dotted the afternoon sky. Coupled with fair visibility, the conditions weren't the most ideal for recreational flying. But Kurt was a seasoned pilot who made his living transporting corporate bigwigs all around the country. And after the morning he'd had, he planned to take advantage of his first day off in more than a week. Besides, he was in the mood to celebrate.

A short time later he sat behind the control panel. Logic made him take the time to do a thorough preflight inspection, especially since he'd just gotten the plane back from his mechanic.

Instinct told him nothing bad would happen to him on this day. Not after the false alarm that had propelled him out to Skokie a few hours earlier. Once he'd heard Doc Kaplan's reassuring words, a weight had been lifted. He could breathe in the air of relief. No, relief was an understatement. Things would probably be even better come the New Year. He could hope. He would pray. But he'd been conditioned not to think in terms of guarantees.

He checked with ATIS for weather and airport information, then got permission to taxi out to runway THREE THREE. There were two planes ahead of him, and he waited his turn with eager impatience, anxious to get moving. Moments later, after tower clearance for takeoff and due diligence to all the last minute prerequisites, he pushed the throttle forward to gain enough speed to pull back on the yoke. The Archer was airborne. The engine roared loudly enough to render an adjustment of his headset. Yet the noise was a comforting alternative to the baneful messages that constantly vied for play space in his head.

As the plane rose, so did his spirits. Kurt had found his spot—the one place where the demons couldn't reach him. He had a relationship with the sky and a regard for its majesty. He soared higher until he reached a level safe above the clouds, a level that offered him total solace. The rugged, high performance machine could only climb to an altitude of 13,000 feet. But today that plane would fly him to the moon.

One Month Later

Madeline felt her knees crumble as she sank to her living room sofa. On the drive home from the doctor's office, she had not allowed herself to think about what he'd told her for fear of having an accident. Now, in the privacy of her home, she began to replay his words. "I'm so sorry, Mrs. Holt. I wish this hadn't happened, but I assure you it did. I thought it was imperative to inform you while there is still time to do something about it."

Madeline sat there, too stunned to move. Could it be true? After all the agonizing over the decision she'd made to have Charles's baby. Could she possibly have heard correctly? The baby she now carried—the child with whom she had already begun to bond—was not Charles's child, but that of a complete stranger.

An entire hour passed before she could compose herself

enough to pick up the telephone to call her attorney. "I want to talk with the donor," she insisted, after explaining her dilemma. "I refuse to take any sort of action until I meet with this man."

Kurt Williams paced back and forth, finally throwing up his hands in frustration. "How the hell does a mistake like this happen?" he demanded, waiting with his lawyer, LeeAnn Schaefer, in the conference room of her St. Charles office.

Before she could answer, they were interrupted by a knock on the door. "Mrs. Holt and her attorney have arrived," her secretary announced.

"Escort them back here," LeeAnn instructed. "Then if you wouldn't mind, could you bring us some extra cups for the pot of coffee I made? We seem to be out."

The secretary motioned to the affirmative, and LeeAnn got up to adjust the window blinds. Seconds later a man and a woman walked through the doorway.

"Good morning, Dan," LeeAnn said. The two attorneys shook hands while Kurt scrutinized the shapely redhead who stood nearby. So this was the other potential plaintiff, he thought, trying to swallow the resentment that threatened to choke him—the widow and supposed mother-to-be of his child.

Introductions were exchanged, and Kurt stood out of politeness, though shaking hands with Madeline at this point seemed too awkward. "Hi," he said.

Madeline nodded brusquely but remained silent.

The secretary returned. For a couple of moments, voices and coffee cups blended into the background while Kurt continued to eye Madeline with the lack of subtlety that went right along with his frame of mind. She was about the leggiest piece of work he'd ever seen, and not a button out of place on her designer silk suit. He judged her height to be close to six feet. Even though he stood five foot eight, he straightened his posture to match her stance.

She shifted her weight and looked downward. His eyes followed to her shoes. Navy, to match her outfit, with heels that were high enough to insure a chiropractor lifetime job security. No wonder he had to look up at her.

"Why don't we all sit down?" her attorney, Dan Renda, suggested.

When they did, Madeline took her place directly across the table from Kurt. She opened her purse, and he could see the carefully organized slots that held her credit cards and other items. She reached for a tissue and gently dabbed at her nose. All prim and proper. It figured. A chick like that wouldn't know what to do with a good head cold. A curly mop of thick, long hair seemed to be the one hint of unruliness about her. And he couldn't help noticing how the sunlight coming through the open blinds made it the color of burnished copper.

"Would you like some coffee, Mrs. Holt?" LeeAnn offered.

"If you have hot water, I brought my own herbal tea," Madeline answered.

That was the first time Kurt heard her speak. It stood to reason her voice would be all silky and smooth, just like her expensive clothes.

"How about you, Kurt? Would you like something to drink?"

His tension level was nearly over the edge now. He hadn't come down here for a fucking tea party. "What I'd like are some answers. I want to know how this happened. The Lynwood Fertility Clinic is supposed to be a reputable institution. In fact, I'd been told it's the best in the Chicagoland area."

Dan Renda responded. "The way we understand it, the lab takes careful steps to identify the sperm vials. Aside from client names, they assign unique lab numbers, and they even color code them. Apparently, Mr. Williams, you and Charles Holt came into the clinic around the same time," he noted, studying some papers in his hand. "Let's see now, it was approximately five years ago. Evidently the last three digits of your lab numbers were identical, and somehow so were your color codes. Even more coincidental," he added, removing his glasses to address the group, "Mr. Holt's middle name was William."

"Are you telling me they mixed up the paperwork and listed that as his last name?" Kurt asked, struggling to keep a lid on his temper.

"That's exactly what happened," Dan answered. "But it's only part of the story."

"Maybe I can explain the rest," Madeline interjected.

"Do that," Kurt snapped.

She glared at him, and for a minute he thought she might shut down.

"A few weeks ago," she continued, "at six o'clock in the morning, a woman was robbed at gun point at a cash station. She'd been on her way to work. She wasn't injured, but she was terribly shaken. Still, after she gave the police her report, she decided to go on to her job. She felt it was the responsible thing to do since lots of people were depending on her that day."

"I don't see what that has to do with . . ."

"I was one of those people," Madeline interrupted in a taut voice, eyeing Kurt as if he were a serial killer. "The robbery victim was the lab technician who provided the vial for the procedure I had, which ultimately resulted in my pregnancy. The doctor told me the woman was so distraught, she simply couldn't function well enough to do her job properly. That seems to be how the vials got mixed up."

Kurt muttered an oath and folded his arms over his chest.

"It's a mess all right," LeeAnn Schaefer agreed. "And we certainly have grounds for litigation. More importantly, Mrs. Holt, we still have time to resolve this dilemma."

Kurt watched as Madeline's eyes began to ignite, darkening

them to an emerald green. For one millisecond, he allowed himself to acknowledge her beauty.

"At this stage of the pregnancy," LeeAnn continued, "we're simply talking about an embryo. So it really wouldn't be difficult to eliminate the problem."

Madeline bolted upright from her chair. "Excuse me, but I believe we're discussing my baby here! I don't think of this life growing inside me as a problem that should be eliminated."

You tell 'em, Spunky! Kurt could hardly deny his rage over the situation. Fatherhood was the last thing on his present agenda. Yet suddenly he couldn't seem to keep his bitterness from mingling with a need to form some kind of alliance with this woman he'd met only moments earlier. After all, they were talking about the fate of his kid too.

"Hold it," he said, signaling with an outward motion of his hand. "I think the lady and I are entitled to some time out. Alone. So the two of us can consider things before we come to any major conclusions here." He turned to Madeline in silence, waiting for her response.

"Yes, I suppose you and I should speak privately," she agreed, her face still contorted with anger.

"Oh, I'm not sure that's advisable," LeeAnn said, looking to Madeline's attorney for support.

One glance at his client seemed to tell Dan Renda the issue was already out of his hands. "How much time do you think you'll want?" he asked, posing the question to Madeline.

She said nothing, but the expression on her face went from anger to trepidation, forcing Kurt to remember that she was a victim too. He couldn't help feeling a little protective. "Why don't we call off this meeting for today," he suggested. "The lady and I will get back to you when . . . when we're ready."

"How does that sit with you, Madeline?" Dan asked.

She nodded her approval.

"I still think this is a mistake," LeeAnn said.

But Dan Renda had already begun ushering her out the door. "Come on, LeeAnn," he said. "It's lunchtime. Your secretary is around. Why don't you let these two use your office, and I'll spring for a pizza at Ginos."

Suddenly Madeline was alone in the room with the man who'd supplied the sperm for her unborn child. She'd been told very little about him, other than he was single, had no arrest record and no traffic tickets. He owned his own home, and there were no creditors chasing him. By all accounts, he appeared to be the model citizen.

Nonetheless, she couldn't bring herself to think of him as the baby's father. Not this stranger who stood before her, with his muscular frame and his wavy, chestnut hair. His ruggedly handsome face suggested an inner strength—which wouldn't be a bad thing to pass on to an offspring. Despite his striking good looks, his posture thundered fury. And the icy blue stare of his eyes told her he resented the situation as much as she.

Well, she wouldn't allow herself to be bullied, and she rose to speak. "I suppose you're in agreement with your attorney as to what I should do. Let me tell you, Mr. Williams, as distressed as I am about this mix-up, I have no intention of terminating this pregnancy. No one can make me. You don't have to worry though," she continued, without giving him a second to reply. "I won't turn it into your problem. I'm the one who opted for the insemination process, and I'm perfectly willing to shoulder the responsibility. I'm entirely capable of caring for and providing for this child, so I won't ask you for financial support—or any kind of support, for that matter. I'll even sign papers to that effect. You're off the hook. Of course, what you decide to do regarding a possible lawsuit is entirely . . ."

"Excuse me a minute," he said, leaping out of his chair and walking toward the corner of the room.

His interference annoyed her to the point of spiking her adrenaline. She watched as he grabbed a step stool and set it down in front of her, so close he almost perched it on her foot. Then he stood, anticipating her response.

Careful, Madeline. He wasn't exactly decked out in a power suit, but his short-sleeved casual shirt and khaki pants emphasized a distinctly male physique that intimidated almost as much as the cocky look on his face. She knew he was waiting for her to speak. Instead she scowled at him, holding her silent ground.

Finally he gestured with a sweeping motion of his arm. "Thought you might need a little help climbing down off your high horse. I wouldn't want a lady in your condition to get herself hurt."

What colossal arrogance! "I beg your pardon."

"No problem, I wasn't planning to make you beg. Not today, anyway. I would appreciate it if you'd cut the diatribe. We could get through this a lot quicker if I could get a word in edgewise."

She did a slow burn that refused to confine itself to her insides, and within seconds she could feel her skin flaming from the front of her chest right up to the roots of her hair.

He flashed her a smug little grin that made her bristle all the more. Worse still, she was getting light-headed and queasy. The nausea had been coming in waves as of late, and she reached for the edge of the stool to steady herself. If only she had some crackers or something to quell her stomach. She felt sick and vulnerable—and faint.

The next thing she knew, his arms were around her. He'd caught her right before she hit the ground. Though she was still conscious, her legs had given way and her limbs felt like cement weights. He carried her toward the sofa at the opposite end of the room with about as much effort as if she'd been a twenty-pound bag of feathers.

"Stay put," he instructed, after laying her down and propping a pillow under her knees.

Instinct made her shift, trying to get her bearings.

"Don't try to get up!" he said. "You're whiter than snow. The idea is to get the blood flowing back to your brain."

She took a breath and tried to swallow, but her mouth was cotton. "Maybe if I had some water," she said as he knelt at her side.

"Can I trust you to be on this couch when I get back?"

"Scout's honor."

"I saw a water cooler out in the lobby," he said. On his way out the door, he had the audacity to grumble, "Girl Scout, my ass."

She would have been more irritated, but he'd called it. So what if she'd never been a Girl Scout. Then again, if he hadn't caught her, she and the baby could have been seriously injured. Pompous as he was, she supposed she owed him some measure of gratitude. Once she calmed down.

A moment later he returned with a paper cup full of water. "Drink this," he said, placing his hand behind her neck to help her sit up." Then he gently tacked on, "Please."

With trembling hands she took the cup from him and sipped. "Thank you," she said, as she felt herself stabilizing.

He studied her face. "Good, your color's coming back. You had me worried there for a minute. You know," he added, with a look of contrition, "I was just being a smart-aleck. I didn't mean to upset you like that."

The sincerity of his tone made her smile, and the grin he flashed made her blood flow accelerate. His liquid blue eyes met with hers, and for a second she forgot who he was. But only for a second. Kurt Williams was the prospective enemy. It wouldn't do to lose her wits.

"You don't get all the credit," she said, after clearing her throat. "I'm new at this pregnancy thing. But judging from what I've heard about how each woman is different and from the way I've been feeling recently, I gather this is all part of the package."

"How long has it been since you've had some food?" he asked.

No sooner had he asked, her stomach growled. She looked at her watch. "I'm guessing it's been too long. I am hungry. I've heard that if you eat frequent small meals, it helps to keep the nausea at bay."

"You feel well enough to sit in a restaurant for a while? Maybe we could both think better over some lunch."

"Yes," Madeline agreed. "I suppose that does make sense. There's a little cafe down the street. We could actually walk there."

"Sure you don't want me to grab my car? It's close by, and I'm a good driver."

"No," she insisted. "I need some exercise, and the fresh air will be good for me."

It was unseasonably cold considering the sunny spring day, and by the time they reached the restaurant, she felt chilled. In between spoonfuls of the steaming hot minestrone soup that started their meal, Madeline warmed her hands around her bowl. Kurt made small talk as she ate, almost as if he sensed she needed to get a few bites of nourishment into her system before she could handle any more heavy conversation.

"Look," he finally said, "I can imagine how upset you must be. But it's obvious you've had more time to think this through than I have. I heard about it for the first time yesterday, and I have to say, I'm pretty much in shock. Fatherhood wasn't exactly in my game plan this week."

She laid her soupspoon down at the side of her bowl, slowly and deliberately. Once again she eyed him squarely, struggling to stay calm. "I thought I made myself clear when I told you the child is my responsibility. I want nothing from you," she emphasized, "with the possible exception of your medical history. You never know when that might come in handy."

"You seem to be forgetting something," he said, with enough authority in his tone to warn her that he wasn't going to disappear from the scene merely because she commanded it. "You're not the only victim here—and you're not the only parent. Even though neither of us planned this, the kid happens to be mine, too, and I have rights."

The word "rights" jolted her. "Rights" implied legalities, attorneys, more talk of lawsuits and a host of other problems she didn't want to dwell on. All she really wanted was to be left alone so she could plan for her unborn child and the future they would have together. A future that did not include a father figure. But one look at Kurt Williams's determined face told her she'd better hear him out.

"What kind of rights are you talking about?" she asked, unable to mask the apprehension in her tone.

He must have noticed because his face immediately softened as he folded his hands underneath his chin. "I can't even pretend I know. Like I said, I'm still in shock. But I'll tell you this much, I would never try to talk you into terminating your pregnancy."

"I'm glad to hear that," she said, feeling some relief that at least he wasn't going to start in on her the way his attorney had earlier.

"I was six years old and halfway through the first grade when my dad walked out on my mom and me," he said. "My mother raised me by herself, and it wasn't easy on either of us. There were times when I really missed my dad, times when I needed a father. I give my mom a lot of credit. She worked long hours to keep a roof over our heads and food on the table. She had enough love for two parents. So I did okay."

Madeline couldn't help noticing the pride in his voice when he spoke of his mother, which, as far as she was concerned, served to better illustrate her point. "Well, see, there you are. The baby and I will be fine on our own. It's what I'd planned on all along."

"No, you don't understand, Madeline. Is that what people call you? Madeline?"

"Most people," she answered, unwilling to add that her father had called her Maddie up until he'd dropped dead of a heart attack shortly after her tenth birthday. She'd adored him. Though, no doubt, it was his death that caused her to be so independent. She'd been the one to raise her younger sister while their mom had suffered a breakdown. In fact, Madeline had nursed her mother back to health. Now her sister was married with two kids and living in Arizona, with Mom only two miles from them. While the move had been good for her family, she missed them all.

"Most people?" Kurt said. "So, would you mind if I call you Maddie? It's a little less formal, and considering the circumstances . . ."

"I'd prefer you call me Madeline," she answered.

"Fine," he said with an upward turn of his eyes. "Getting back to my point, I said I did okay. I didn't say I did great without a father. In fact, I swore up and down I would never do that to any kid of mine—walk out on him or her. I won't. You're having a baby. My baby—Madeline," he emphasized. "And I plan on being part of that process."

The skin on the back of her neck prickled. "You know, that almost sounds like a threat. What exactly does 'part of that process' mean, if you would do me the courtesy of being more specific?"

"Now there you go, gettin' on your high horse again. You want to pin me down to answers when I don't even know all the questions yet. I've never been an expectant father before. If you're worried I'm gonna follow you around all day with a bucket in case you have to puke . . . well I'm a busy guy."

"You needn't be crude, Mr. Williams."

"And you needn't be so formal. Call me Kurt," he added, after the waitress had left their sandwiches.

Madeline let out a sigh of resignation and took a bite of the turkey burger that had been placed in front of her. This discussion was going nowhere. "All right, Kurt. Let's change direction for a minute. If it isn't too rude to inquire, what do you do that keeps you so busy?"

"I'm a corporate pilot. I work for Cromwell. They make high performance transmissions and components."

She almost choked as the burger made its way down her throat. "I hate flying," she said. "The last time I was on an airplane, I wasn't sure whether we landed or we were shot down."

She couldn't have been more serious, but her comment prompted him to laugh out loud, which made him far less intimidating. And also rather appealing. In fact, his expression brought out captivating crinkles at the corners of his eyes—eyes so dark they were almost navy. Would her child look like him?

"So, the lady has a sense of humor after all. I take it the trip was a little bumpy? You'll have to come flying with me sometime. My landings are slicker than axle grease."

"No thanks." But she couldn't help returning a smile. "Next time I get a notion to go bounding through the sky in a pressurized crash rocket, I'll resist and call Greyhound."

"Ouch," he said with a wounded look. "A bus is okay if you're in no particular hurry. But what if you need to get somewhere fast?"

"Fast isn't the issue. At least bus wheels stay on the ground."

"Do I take that to mean you don't like heights?"

"Well . . ." Despite the fact that it was true, she hated to admit any weakness to him.

"So that's it?" he pressed. "You're afraid of heights?"

"Let's just say you don't want to get stuck behind me while I'm working up the nerve to board an escalator."

"Whew! That bad, huh?" He caught her gaze with a flicker of amusement. "I'll bet I could take you to some heights you'd enjoy."

CHAPTER 2

Kurt turned the key in the ignition of his 4Runner and headed for his home in suburban Geneva, still cursing himself for that shot he'd thrown Madeline back at the restaurant. The look she'd given him stayed etched in his mind, and he'd regretted his words the second they'd come rolling out of his mouth. Yet he couldn't seem to step on the brakes. Of course, his interest in her was purely out of concern for the baby she carried. On the other hand, a blind man running for his life in a hurricane would have a hard time missing the fact that Madeline Holt was downright gorgeous.

Since there was no way he'd let her cut him out of his child's life, it only made sense that he would have to start communicating with her. Wasn't that exactly what they'd been doing?

She sure had a knockout smile. He'd caught her looking at him—the way a woman looks at a guy when they're connecting. Okay, maybe for no more than a second or two. But the look had been there. *Before you made that moronic attempt to melt the rest of the frost.* He'd tried to cover his blunder with some nonsense that started with, "I only meant." But she'd reacted to his innuendo with a shocked expression and a blush that had traveled right down her neck. There had been nowhere to go after that. Except home. At least they'd exchanged addresses and phone numbers before they'd parted.

Time for a reality check, hotshot. You hardly know this chick, and she's pregnant with your kid. An acrid taste at the back of his throat rose up to make him cough. The concept of fatherhood was complicated enough without having the whole thing forced on him. He resented it. And for some reason he couldn't understand, he was also in awe of the prospect.

He tried to wash down his bitterness with empathy for Madeline's reaction. Imagine thinking you were being impregnated with the sperm of someone you had loved and then finding out later that . . . Jesus! She probably felt violated. Though he knew he wasn't responsible, he wondered if she hated him. Whether she did or not, didn't she realize he'd fallen prey to the whole mess too? Okay, so his Joe Cool act hadn't helped. In truth, he was scared, and his brash comment had flustered them both. The end result was a lunch cut short, but that wasn't necessarily bad. The way the conversation had been going, it was clear they weren't going to make any major decisions in one day. Better they each had a chance to think by themselves, before they met again.

Trouble was, neither of them had all the information. There were plenty of unanswered questions. Hell, she'd never even gotten around to asking him why he'd donated his sperm. He made a turn onto his street while reason continued to badger him. *Maybe the woman doesn't care why your sperm wound up in the lab.* In fact, considering how clear she'd been about not wanting any part of him or his help, he figured it was logical to assume any personal questions she might have concerning him would be minimal.

Still, he felt guilty for putting that thunderstruck look on her face when he'd told her he intended to be part of the process. Under the circumstances, he supposed he could understand her attitude. All the same, a little empathy from her would go a long way in helping him decide the best course of action for the good of everyone concerned.

The one thing she had asked for was his medical history, and the recollection of it made his neck muscles tighten. Up to the point where she'd mentioned it, he hadn't even considered whether or not the baby could be in any medical danger. Now the possibility was at the forefront of his thoughts, and he planned to call Doc Kaplan to get that question answered the minute he got home. In the meantime, he'd keep his concerns to himself. Madeline seemed high strung enough without giving her something else to stress over.

Madeline went charging up the back stairs of the building that housed her office, cognizant that she'd already lost a good portion of the workday. As it was, she would have to stay late to make up the hours. She was in no mood to get stuck in an unpredictable elevator that had already been fixed twice during the past week.

By the time she reached her reception area, she was actually breathless. Far more breathless than a woman her age should be after climbing two meager flights.

"Are you okay?" The question had come from Elsie Carlisle, her office manager, who'd already left her desk to walk to Madeline's side. Not waiting for an answer, the woman grabbed Madeline's briefcase and led her to a nearby chair. "You look like you're about to faint. Honestly, child," the woman scolded, "with all the hours you've been putting in recently, I'll bet you haven't even taken the time yet to have your lunch today."

Madeline glanced up and tried not to look culpable, considering the older woman was only half-right.

"Well?" Elsie pressed.

"I had some soup earlier, but my meal was cut short."

"It's no wonder you're as thin as a rail and looking so peaked lately. In fact, you haven't seemed healthy to me for days. I'm beginning to worry about you."

Elsie had been widowed nearly ten years and was like a

second mother to Madeline. Without her, Madeline knew the office would fall apart. Elsie'd been working for Holt and Associates since the day Madeline had started her business. Four years now.

Normally the two of them were close. But once she'd made up her mind to become pregnant, the possibility of disapproval had kept her from allowing anyone, even Elsie, to discourage her from having the insemination procedure. Eventually she would get around to confiding her predicament to Elsie. For the moment, she could not bring herself to share the secret of her pregnancy or the amazing story surrounding her child's paternity.

"Elsie, you fuss too much. I'm fine, truly. It's just that I took the stairs instead of the elevator. These shoes weren't made for climbing." But they were designed to make a statement. The taller she appeared, the more powerful she felt. Today, especially, she'd needed to be in charge.

Elsie looked down at Madeline's narrow, four-inch heels, and clucked her tongue in the disapproving way that always forewarned of a lecture. "Those shoes weren't made for anything other than to ruin your feet. It's a wonder you haven't fractured something yet. I know you young people have to dress in what's fashionable. Me, I'll take my walking shoes over a backache any day."

Madeline wasn't about to admit out loud that she felt as though her vertebrae had been rearranged. Or that she hadn't been sleeping well and was downright exhausted. She had work to do and clients who needed her. She stood and gathered her things for the short trek down the hall to her office. "Were there any messages?" she asked respectfully, ignoring any reference to her feet or her health.

Elsie gave her that familiar *I'm backing down, but this reprieve is only temporary* frown, and Madeline sighed with relief. "Mason

Products called. They want to be sure you'll be out there first thing tomorrow morning. That audit you've scheduled is very important to them."

Madeline groaned. "Yes, I know. I'll be meeting with the company president and their lawyers. This is my least favorite part of the job. As it turns out they've got an embezzlement problem, and they're waiting on me to hand over the evidence I've been compiling for the past month."

"Oh, dear. That puts you in an unenviable position."

"It certainly does. I'll call them back myself," Madeline said. Mason Products Corporation was one of her most important clients, and she'd worked hard to bring them on board. She couldn't afford to lose them. But they were out-of-state. Ohio, to be exact. It would be at least a nine hour drive, even if she only stopped once. Considering the current state of her pregnancy-altered bladder, one stop every four hours would be woefully insufficient. She would have to leave soon in order to be there on time. All she really wanted to do was nap.

Kurt had been shooting baskets into the hoop mounted over his garage door for the past hour. He felt restless and needed to keep moving. He'd been scheduled to fly the CEO of Cromwell, Inc. to Michigan the following morning. But the trip had been cancelled at the last minute, and it looked like he would have the next couple of days off. That's the way corporate flying was. Sometimes you had to be ready at a moment's notice. But the advantage to working for one company, albeit a huge corporation, was that most flights were scheduled a week in advance. Not that he minded a little down time, even though he loved his job.

He should have been tired instead of wired. His brain refused to cooperate. He looked at his watch, noting it had barely been three hours since he'd left Madeline. He took her business card from his wallet. What the hell, why not phone her and apologize? He couldn't resist the urge to sink one final ball before going inside to make the call.

It took a while for someone to answer, and then he was put on hold. He drummed his fingers impatiently on the kitchen counter. Finally the receptionist returned and told him Madeline had left for the day. *Leave it alone,* reason advised. *The woman needs a chance to sort things out.* Instead Kurt dialed her home number.

Madeline was packing for the trip when the phone rang. Packing and eating saltine crackers out of the box. She'd heard of women who'd gotten sick during pregnancy, but she'd always been the epitome of good health. With daily exercise, proper nutrition and vitamins, she'd had no reason to fear that would change once she was carrying a child. Besides, she thought morning sickness happened in the morning. But here it was late afternoon, and she was nauseous. This didn't fit into her schedule at all.

With her mouth full, she waited to grab the handset till the sixth ring. "Holt residence," she struggled to say.

"Madeline, is that you?"

She immediately recognized Kurt's voice. "Hold on a minute, please." She ran to the bathroom for water to wash down the remaining food, then hurried back to the phone. "Sorry, you caught me eating," she explained.

"Well, I'm not surprised you're hungry. Lunch was kind of a bust."

"I wouldn't exactly say I'm hungry. In fact, food is the last thing I want. I'm trying to keep my stomach calm with some dry crackers." But now that she'd forced all that water down, her insides felt like they were gearing up to launch like a rocket on a space mission. With no warning, and no way to stop it, she emitted an ear-splitting belch. Right into the speaker!

"I can't believe I did that," she said, appalled and profoundly embarrassed. "Please excuse me. You must think I have no manners whatsoever."

She heard what sounded like a muffled laugh. "Hey, it happens," he said. "Don't sweat it."

She sat down on the edge of the bed to get her bearings. Surely she could keep herself from giving in to this nausea. "Well, I'm not a rude person. I would never think to do something so offensive, except that . . ." She had to lie down a moment.

"Madeline? Are you okay?"

"I'm a little dizzy, that's all. I guess it's going to take a while for my body to get used to being pregnant."

"You're not going to faint, are you? Are you sitting somewhere?" His voice sounded genuinely concerned.

"I'm fine. I'm about to take a short nap, and then I'm leaving on a trip. I'm really tired, so did you call for a specific reason?"

"Trip? What trip? You don't sound like you're in any condition to travel."

Now she was getting annoyed. "Not to be rude twice in one conversation, but I don't think that's any of your business."

After a loud sigh from Kurt, there was a prolonged silence. "Sorry I bothered you. Actually, I wanted to apologize for that remark I made in the restaurant today and to see if we could get together again soon to work some things out."

"Oh," she said, regretting she'd snapped at him. "Well, your apology is accepted. I'm sure when I get back from Ohio we can decide on a time to meet." Her stomach didn't feel any more settled in the prone position, and she sat back up in the bed. She was definitely going to vomit. "I'm leaving in a couple of hours," she said, sucking in short breaths. "So, I need to hang up now."

"Wait! You're leaving tonight? What time?"

Without answering, Madeline dropped the phone on the floor and ran to the bathroom, finally giving in to the urge to be sick. With her head over the toilet bowl, retching until her muscles hurt, she prayed she wouldn't have this to look forward to for the next eight months. When it was over, she remembered Kurt waiting on the line. Maybe. She rinsed her mouth, blew her nose and went back to the phone.

"Are you still there?" she groaned.

"You're sick, Madeline. You shouldn't be traveling. What time is your flight?"

"I told you I hate to fly. I'm driving."

"By yourself? Where in Ohio?"

"Canton. Kurt, I appreciate your concern, but . . ."

"Look, I'll gas up my plane and fly you there myself," he said. "It'll be much quicker than if you drive. You're in no shape to be on the road all night."

"I'm in no shape to be in an airplane either. Now, stop fussing over me. I'm a grownup, and I'm used to taking care of myself. I'll be fine. I'll call you when I get back. Goodbye." With that she slammed down the handset.

Oh, God, she was ill. She really hadn't meant to be so cranky. She was used to dealing with people, and even though she resented his meddling, she certainly could have gotten her message across in a more polite way. But she would have to think about Kurt Williams's hurt feelings later. Right now she had other problems.

Kurt rubbed his ear in disgust. That woman was a tight ass, hot-tempered, control freak! Obviously pregnancy had clouded her thinking, or she wouldn't be planning to go off like this when she was so sick and needed rest. He'd have to be deaf not to have heard the gut-wrenching proof over the phone.

Despite her bad manners, his sympathy came unleashed when an unwelcome flash of déjà vu ran through him, sending him to the closet for his duffel bag. Not that he had any feelings for Madeline, other than he hated to see anyone suffer. Underwear and an extra shirt. Jeans. What kind of guy would let the mother of his unborn child drive all night long, by herself, in her condition? She'd be lucky if she didn't fall asleep at the wheel. His shaving gear was always packed. She lived in St. Charles—a mere ten-minute drive. A quick trip to the kitchen cabinets, and he'd be on his way. That was his kid she was carrying, and he planned to step in whether she wanted him to or not.

Kurt parked in front of Madeline's townhouse and turned off the engine. He sat there, trying to come up with a strategy. Up till this point, he hadn't cared much that he might have been overstepping his bounds. Sometimes you had to do that in order to help.

He made up his mind to try and reason with her, even though as he left his vehicle, he realized she might slam the door in his face. Shrubs and early spring tulips lined the perfectly manicured walkway to her front porch. He rang the bell twice before she emerged—no longer the essence of designer perfection he'd left earlier that afternoon.

"Oh, no!" she shrieked, covering her face with her hands. "Why are you here? I'm not dressed for company."

A spark of hope shot through him. She wouldn't be so damned worried about her appearance if she didn't care, at least a little bit, about what he thought. Not that there was anything wrong with the way she looked in those sweat pants. Her blue T-shirt hugged her slender torso like a second skin, belying her pregnancy. When he saw she wore no bra, he swallowed hard.

"I don't even have any makeup on."

"So you're a little pale," he countered, not really understanding the reason for her humiliation. She had flawless skin—and curly, wild hair that suggested she'd just crawled out of bed. That air of soft, girlish innocence was giving him a hard, grown man reaction. One he couldn't afford to indulge in right now. Maybe she'd be too worried about her looks to be pissed off when he tried to dissuade her from leaving by herself.

"Listen, Toots, I didn't come here to take you to the prom. Anyway, you look fine. I, uh, brought you something that might help you feel better," he said, waving the bag in his hand like a peace flag.

"What's that?" She pursed her lips, and he couldn't decide if her expression was a show of skepticism or more queasiness.

"Something to settle your stomach. Mind if I come in for a while?"

"You know a pregnant woman has to be very careful about taking any sort of medication."

"It's candied ginger. I swear it's harmless, but it might help to relieve your nausea. So, can I come in?"

She stood there like she hadn't heard the question, which he'd posed twice now. This tentative approach was new for him, and his patience wore thin. Why couldn't she just open the fucking screen door?

Suddenly she turned the lock and pushed the door out. "Only for a little while," she said. "I told you I'm leaving for Ohio tonight.

He stepped inside the foyer and opened the bag, offering her some of the candied treat. "It's an acquired taste. A little spicy, but it usually works."

She took a small piece and bit into it while he waited for her reaction. Then she took another piece and managed to smile. "It's different, but it tastes okay. We'll see if it stays down."

"Let's hope."

"Why don't you come into the living room for a minute?" she suggested, with more emphasis on the word minute than he would have liked.

He followed her, and for what seemed like an eternity, neither of them spoke. *Make your point before she kicks you out.* "Look, I take it you haven't changed your mind about this trip?"

"It's business. One of my most important clients. They're depending on me, so I have to go. I made reservations at the Best Suites in Canton. If I leave within the next half-hour, I should get there between three and four o'clock in the morning. I can grab a few hours of sleep before I drive to my client's office. That's the plan, and I'm committed to it."

It was an impressive speech followed by a series of yawns as she sat on the sofa. Suddenly she put her hand over her mouth.

"Sick again?"

"I'm fine!"

She sure didn't look fine. "How long do you plan to be gone?"

"Probably not more than a couple of days. Why do you ask?"

He checked his watch. "It's five-thirty. If you let me fly you there in my Piper, we could be airborne before seven. That includes the time it will take me to file a flight plan, drive us to the airport and gas up the plane. We could be in Ohio by ten o'clock, and you could be all tucked in before eleven. Plus you could sleep on the plane. Doesn't that sound better—and safer—than driving there by yourself?"

She raised a brow. "You're ignoring the fact that I'm terrified of flying. And I'm feeling queasy. I don't think you'd want me for a passenger."

"Let me worry about that," he said, in his most reassuring tone.

"No!" She leapt from the sofa like an angry bobcat. "Which word don't you understand? Why do you have to keep badgering me when I've already made up my mind?"

Before he could even think of an answer, she went sprinting down the hall, and he heard the slam of a door. By the unmistakable sounds that came next, it had been the bathroom door. Apparently it was going to take more than candied ginger to solve her problem.

He paced the room trying to figure out what his next move should be. Women were usually more susceptible to his charm. Not that he'd had a woman since Christie Reed had walked out on him during the midst of the worst crisis in his thirty-four years. Oh, he'd dated here and there, but he hadn't allowed anyone to get close enough to dump him on his butt the way she had.

He studied his surroundings. The first thing he noticed was the Steinway upright. He was drawn like a magnet to the piano with its honey oak finish, and he ran his fingers over the keys. It wasn't the type of instrument a beginner would own. He wondered how long Madeline had been playing if, in fact, she played at all. Maybe her dead husband had been the musician.

He couldn't see a speck of dust anywhere—not one fingerprint—not so much as a sofa pillow out of place. No surprise considering her impeccable appearance at the attorney's office. The furnishings were more formal than his taste, yet he had to admit the place felt comfortable.

His eyes turned toward the brick fireplace at the far end of the room where he noticed the wedding picture on the mantel. He walked nearer to get a better look. The bride and groom were facing each other and smiling, but there was no spark in Madeline's eyes. Not a hint of the fiery passion she'd exhibited in just the short time he'd known her, even allowing for the heat of their battle. It made him curious about the kind of marriage she'd had with Charles Holt.

He turned at the sound of her cough.

You didn't have to be a rocket scientist to see she was in bad shape. Her arms hugged her tiny waist as though her ribs hurt from the vomiting. It was an image that dredged up memories that were all too familiar, and he felt for her. Plus, he couldn't help wondering what all of this was doing to the baby. Their baby. He didn't know much about pregnant women, but it seemed to him that if she kept tossing her cookies, the kid wouldn't get any nourishment either. Considering her attitude toward him, he was starting to feel helpless.

"Look, I'm short-tempered, tired and sick," she said. "And I seemed to have turned into a raving shrew. Being pregnant might have something to do with that. In any case, I apologize. Though it doesn't change the way I feel."

"Are we talking about flying? Because I can respect that."

"I'm talking about this whole situation," she countered. "It's not that I don't appreciate your concern, but I'm used to making my own decisions, and not having them challenged at every turn. Yet, you insist on insinuating yourself into my life. You don't seem to grasp that I don't want your interference. I never planned on sharing this pregnancy with anyone. Certainly not with a perfect stranger."

He stood, staring at her in silence, fighting not to react.

She stared back at him, and those pouty lips of hers began to quiver. Were those tears welling up in her eyes?

"Well, I'm sorry. That's what you are to me," she sputtered at his lack of response. "A perfect stranger."

Oh, man. She was bawling. It served her right for the way she'd rebuked him. Still, he never knew what to do when a woman cried. "Well, nobody's perfect," he said under his breath.

"What? What did you say?" she demanded.

"I disagreed with you," he answered louder. "I'm not perfect. I'm just trying to figure out what I can do to best serve everybody's interests—including our child's. Because, lady, whether you like it or not, I am involved in your life now."

He reached over and handed her a couple of tissues from the box on the end table. "Here, blow your nose."

To his surprise, she did as he'd told her. Then she sat back down on the sofa and shot him a menacing look. "You should leave now."

His head hurt with the realization of how difficult she was going to make it for him—for both of them. "You want me out of here? I'm gone." For the moment.

She looked at him with her brows raised. He couldn't tell if it was an expression of surprise or hopeful expectation. "Fine, then I guess we're in agreement about something," she said. "Thanks for the ginger."

He walked away from her and headed toward the door at the same time her phone rang. Instinct made him turn to watch her as she rose and made her way to the kitchen. She hugged her sides again, as if she were having trouble standing. *Should I wait? Should I go and let her fend for herself?* He waited. Seconds later she appeared back in the living room. "Wrong number."

"You know, you are one stubborn piece of work. Why can't you admit you're too sick to make the trip and cancel?" he lashed out.

"I told you my client is depending on me. It's an emergency situation, and I have to go. Besides, I can't afford to lose the business. Especially not now that there will be two of us to support."

"Can't you send one of your employees?

"The only other person who's qualified is on vacation."

"Then let me drive you to Ohio."

Her eyes widened with a definite look of surprise. "I couldn't ask you to do that."

"You didn't. You're in no condition to be behind the wheel of a car. It's irresponsible of you to even consider it. You know I'm right." He expected to have to follow that statement with a full-blown speech about how a sleepy driver on the road is worse than a drunk driver. But he didn't expect her to agree to the plan.

"All right . . . if you're sure," she said. "My bags are packed. I'll need about ten more minutes to change my clothes and get ready to leave."

The look on Kurt's face had almost been worth her giving in to him. Not that Madeline would allow him to take advantage of her weakness for very long. This nausea was temporary. She was positive. As soon as it passed she would be in full control again, and she wouldn't be needing him to run interference. She didn't really need him now.

She would never allow herself to become as vulnerable and dependent as her mother had been. What had the woman gained? In the end, Madeline's father had gone away from her mother—exactly the way Charles had gone away from Madeline. No, she could manage without anyone's help. If she wanted to.

Nonetheless, for now and for the sake of her baby—*"their baby,"* as he'd so eloquently reminded her—she would put up with Kurt Williams. And his arrogant behavior. And his misguided medical advice, however well intended.

She hurried into some loose fitting slacks and a comfortable sweater for the long ride. A look in the mirror convinced her to dig her makeup bag back out of the suitcase. Not that she would primp for the likes of this man. But a little cover stick couldn't hurt. If she hid the circles under her eyes, maybe he'd stop harassing her about needing sleep. That done, she noticed her face had taken on the color of library paste. She supposed a little blush was in order too. As for the mascara, it would make her feel better, never mind if he noticed she hardly had eyes without it.

She looked at her watch and saw that she'd already used up the ten minutes, and she rushed to finish the job. It was exceptionally generous of him to volunteer to chauffeur her all the way to Ohio. She wished she could get over her hostility. It really wasn't Kurt's fault that he'd been dragged into this. All the same, he couldn't simply come waltzing into her life and into her womb, and expect her to be welcoming.

The baby she now carried should have been Charles's. She couldn't help being angry and hurt that it wasn't. Part of her wanted to hurt back, and maybe that's why she was having so much trouble being civil to Kurt. All things considered, she wondered why he didn't seem more resentful toward her.

After all, he'd made it clear fatherhood had not been in his game plan at this time. Which made her wonder why he'd donated his sperm. They'd never gotten around to discussing the issue. She made a mental note to ask him about it at some point—and a resolve to try to be more tolerant during their journey to Ohio. It seemed like she owed him that much in response to his gesture of good will.

"I'm ready," she announced, rolling her luggage into the living room where Kurt waited. "Don't you need to go home and pack some things?

"That's all taken care of," he said. "I've got a suitcase out in my truck. Let's book."

Madeline could feel her mouth opening in surprise, but she resisted the urge to comment. The man was entirely too sure of himself.

CHAPTER 3

Madeline stood in her driveway watching Kurt as he loaded his SUV with her luggage. Though her garment bag wasn't that heavy, he insisted on handling it himself. Nonetheless, she'd drawn the line at her roll-on overnight bag and had taken it from the house before he had the chance to make her feel like a complete invalid.

She couldn't help noticing the mess in the back of the vehicle, as he moved cartons, bags, and tools to make way for her belongings. How anyone could drive amid such chaos eluded her. For a moment she had an impulse to tidy things. The strong likelihood that he would object, coupled with their time constraint, helped banish the idea from her mind.

"Hop in," he said, once he'd finished.

The step up seemed like more of a climb than a hop, and by the time she'd fastened her seatbelt, her ribs ached. Kurt gave her a look that told her he'd noticed her struggle, but he said nothing. Just as well.

It was after six o'clock before they got underway. Dinnertime by most people's standards, but the thought of food made her uneasy. Now, as Kurt drove north on Randall Road, they passed a number of fast food restaurants. Madeline felt guilty for thinking only of herself. "I'm not hungry, but if you are, I'd be happy to buy some burgers or whatever," she offered.

Kurt looked over at her. "Let's wait till we get some miles behind us." Instead, he pulled into the parking lot of Walgreens.

"Relax. I'll be right back."

She had no idea why he'd gone inside, but she took the opportunity to doze. By the time he returned, he startled her.

"Hey, sorry," he apologized. "Go back to sleep if you're tired."

"Maybe later. That bag you're holding doesn't look big enough to hold a bucket," she joked. "If you're worried about your car, I remembered to tuck a few plastic bags in my purse. Just in case."

He smiled. "Good thinking, but let's hope you won't need them. Here try these," he said, handing her a package labeled, Sea-Bands.

"What are they?"

"Wrist bands to create acupressure. They might help cut your nausea. And no side effects." He started the engine and drove out of the lot. "Give 'em a try."

She took them out of the package and slid one of the tight-fitting bands over her wrist.

"Make sure you read the instructions," he cautioned, heading east on Route Twenty. "They have to be positioned right to work."

"I can't read while the car is moving," she said. "It will only make matters worse."

"Put your middle three fingers on the inside of your wrist and make sure the edge of your third finger is by your wrist crease," he said.

She did as he directed.

"That white button should be right on the spot under the edge of your index finger."

"I think I've got it," she said.

"Good, then do the same thing on the other hand."

"You seem to know an awful lot about being nauseated. Too many wild parties?" she teased.

He took his eyes from the road for a second to give her a

look she couldn't interpret. Somehow she wished she hadn't made the correlation. "Or maybe you come by your knowledge because of all the flying you do—in case your passengers get sick."

"Something like that," he answered.

She had the feeling she wasn't getting the entire story. But with traffic so heavy, she decided to let him concentrate on his driving. There would be time for meaningful conversation later.

All this doting was definitely foreign to her experience. Charles had always been so preoccupied with his own responsibilities that he'd never really been the nurturing type. Not that he hadn't loved her. Why else would he have married her? In truth, that had been his stat answer when she'd occasionally pose the question: "Do you love me, Charles?" *Did you love me? Or was our marriage more of a business arrangement?*

She thought back to the one time when she'd been so sick with the flu, she'd spent a couple of days in bed. It would have been nice if Charles had brought her hot soup. Or candied ginger. Or Sea-Bands. Instead, he'd treated the interruption of their household routine as an inconvenience, and he'd dealt with her almost as if she were an employee instead of his wife.

She glanced at Kurt. Several errant strands of his thick, chestnut hair lay over his forehead. The windblown look was a plus on him. Admittedly, he had a nice profile. Okay, he was hot, especially when he smiled. She'd always been drawn to men with blue eyes, and she couldn't help wondering if the child would take after him. Whatever traits their baby might inherit from each of them, she guessed a thick head of hair would be a given.

Their baby. The concession made her pulse dart, and she took a deep breath to steady herself. Despite that she hadn't planned it, she was, in fact, having a baby with this man. Feelings of resentment and acceptance clashed, until a flood of confusion enveloped her. So she found him appealing in certain ways. It didn't mean she would ever be able to welcome him into her life.

Kurt sensed Madeline's gaze, even though he stayed focused on the road. But at the next red light, he looked her way. Like a child who'd been caught picking the marshmallows out of the cereal box, she turned from him. Still, he caught the trail of red now working its way down her neck. He grinned, fighting an impulsive urge to reach over and touch her face. Damn, she was pretty. For all her feistiness, she hadn't said much since he'd given her those Sea-Bands. She seemed more relaxed, so maybe the bands were helping.

By contrast, he felt agitated. They'd been gone from the house for half an hour, and they were still on Route Twenty. At this rate, they'd be lucky to make it to Canton by three o'clock in the morning. *Lucky* was the operative word. Stop and go traffic wasn't his thing; he needed to keep moving. If only she'd agreed to let him fly her there, it would have been so much faster.

At least her stance toward him seemed to be softening. Maybe he'd won a few points by offering to drive her to Ohio. Another red light. He shifted and adjusted his seatbelt, stealing one more glimpse at her in the process. Yep. Nine hours alone with her could work to his advantage in terms of coming to some agreement concerning the situation they shared. If he played his cards right.

"So, would you like to hear some tunes?" he asked. "I brought a bunch of CDs along."

"Really? What kind of music do you have?"

Was that a note of enthusiasm? The right music could put them both in a better frame of mind. "You name it—Clapton, Aerosmith, Sade, Dave Mathews. If you like jazz, how about John Coltrane or Dave Brubeck? Wait, I know. How about Poi Dog Pondering?"

"Poi Dog who?" Her brows creased as if he were speaking an alien language.

"Grab that carrying case in the back, would you? It should be sitting on the floor. Look for a CD that says Liquid White Light on the side. It's purple," he added, once she had the case in her lap.

Madeline rifled through his collection. "Is this what you want?" she asked, handing him the CD.

"Yeah, this album is one of my favorites, especially the last half." He put the CD in the player and skipped toward the end. At the same time, they reached the eastbound entrance ramp to the Elgin-O'Hare Expressway. Traffic turned surprisingly light as he gathered speed. In fact, there were hardly any other cars in sight. "Mind if I crank it up a little?" he asked.

"Go ahead, I guess."

Her response was tentative, but she'd soon change her mind when she heard this phenomenal sound. *"Breathe deep, fill up with relief, don't go mad, don't go mad."* With an increase in volume, the dynamic cadence began to fill his spirit. He sped past signs, industrial parks and homes, satisfying his need to keep moving, to keep hearing this music.

"Higher and higher, feeling exhilaration."

Again he reached for the volume control button to further amplify the experience. Yes, he was on the *"hydroplane now, feeling so high."* This concert was a perfect expression of the euphoria that had captured him only days earlier when Doctor Kaplan had given him the good news. A colorful blur of trees, ponds, and westbound cars became a maze of white lightning as the 4Runner continued to accelerate—as though some other force were threatening to take charge of the wheel. He felt jubilant and could not be still. The yearning to break the sound barrier collided with his responsibility to maintain a safe speed. It was not an easy battle, but there were other lives to consider.

Animal sounds? The call of the wild? Yes, he was wild—and immortal. He would live. Nothing could hurt him now.

"Slow down!" she shouted.

Her plea jarred him, and he looked over to see Madeline's hands covering her ears and her expression of distress. He checked his speedometer and noted he was ten miles over the limit. Not a dangerous speed, though, clearly he'd upset her. Instantly he took his foot from the gas pedal and paid silent homage to his radar detector.

"Sorry about that," he said, taking the CD out of the player.

"Are you crazy? You scared me!"

Her fear seemed exaggerated, but he could see it was real. He looked in vain for a place to pull off the road to try calming her.

"It won't happen again," he promised. *Not when I'm carrying passengers.*

"You were driving like you were possessed. I'm surprised you're not deaf, listening to music that loud."

"Look, I got carried away. I didn't mean to scare you, but I wasn't really driving that fast. We weren't in any danger. There aren't even many cars around us." Amazing as that was.

"Would you like a gold star?"

He started to answer, then thought better of it. She was mad. But mad was better than scared. The whole reason he'd talked her into letting him drive her to Ohio was so he could protect her and the baby. He'd gotten her to trust him, at least to that extent. Now it looked like he'd have to start from scratch.

"It's not only that you were speeding," she continued, "it's like you were somewhere else on some side trip. Where did you go, Kurt?"

Mad and pushy. "You know, I'm here now. So could we leave it at that? You do want me to concentrate on my driving, don't you?"

"By all means." Madeline folded her arms over her seatbelt

and let out a disgruntled sigh.

The uncomfortable silence that followed lasted for several minutes before Kurt finally spoke. "That doesn't mean we can't talk about something else." Something generic and less likely to cause controversy.

"You know," she said, without missing a beat. "Loud music isn't good for the baby. I want my child exposed to culture. Don't you?"

"What? You mean now? You think the kid can hear—before he's even born?"

"Before he or she is born," Madeline corrected. "I've been researching, and I've learned that music can actually have some impact on the fetus. Sometimes a child will show a preference for certain kinds of music by the way it moves inside the mother's womb. The theory being that if the baby is exposed to the more soothing, classical type of composition, then maybe after that child is born, it will be calmed when it hears that same music again."

Kurt rolled his eyes as he finally reached the ramp to 290 East. Despite his efforts to take her seriously, the premise seemed like a stretch. So he said nothing.

"I think the idea has merit," she said.

"You're telling me you think the baby could hear my Poi Dog CD?"

"I'm telling you I think the entire county could hear it."

"Yeah? If the kid likes it, maybe we have a future musician in our midst," he teased. "Rock stars make lots of money, you know."

Her indignant groan came through above the road noise. "If my baby is going to be a musician, then I'd better be hearing Brahms, Chopin, and Mozart."

"Our baby," he corrected, loud enough to make sure she heard his inflection.

Her silence was enough to tell him he'd made his point. Still, she refused to give him the satisfaction of a verbal acknowledgment.

"I don't see anything wrong with exposing the little one to all kinds of music," he added, more to break the tension than to try and sway her.

"If this baby starts kicking up a Mambo, I'm going to come looking for you."

That was a concept with potential. Still, the playful tone of her threat implied she was lightening up. Then he realized what she'd said. "Can you feel the baby kicking already?" He looked at her for a split second to see her smiling.

"No," she said softly. "It's too early yet. I can hardly wait for it to happen though. It's hard to believe a life is really growing inside of me. I mean intellectually, I know it. But there's something here that goes so far beyond biology. When the baby starts moving, it's like that will be the proof."

Her words were hopeful, expectant, nurturing—definitely directed toward the child she carried and not him. So he couldn't really pinpoint the reason they'd caused such a stirring in his heart. But they had.

"You play piano, don't you?" he asked, switching gears. "Classical, I'm sure."

"Right on both counts," she said. "Music that nourishes the mind and soothes the soul."

"If you look further, you'll see a CD with Beethoven piano sonatas in my case."

She looked surprised when she found it, but soon they were listening to music that offered a more relaxing atmosphere. So soothing that before long, Madeline fell sound asleep. Good. Maybe a little rest would improve her disposition. He wondered what she was like before the pregnancy hormones kicked in and whether she ever did anything impulsive. As far as he was concerned, the woman needed to loosen the elastic on her panties a little.

Now that he could focus solely on the road, he began driving with more purpose. Two hours passed before she even moved. At that, she hadn't opened her eyes. With all this quiet he wanted some coffee, or he'd be falling asleep too. There was an oasis up ahead, and he veered to the right toward the exit ramp.

He parked near the restaurant entrance and shut off the engine. Madeline shifted and turned toward him, continuing to sleep. Despite the darkness, the dim lighting from the lot formed a halo around her tousled curls and face, making her look like an angel. The view fueled his imagination. He felt like a voyeur, fighting the rousing in his groin while trying to figure out whether or not to wake her.

Her stomach had calmed enough to finally let her rest. It didn't seem right to disturb her, especially with the day she'd be facing come morning. On the other hand, she needed food and water. He knew the dangers of becoming dehydrated.

"Madeline," he whispered, without giving into the urge to touch her.

She groaned, but didn't move.

"Madeline." This time he spoke in more of a command as his hand rested lightly on her shoulder.

She struggled for consciousness.

"Sorry to wake you," he said, "but we should get something to eat and walk around a little."

She sat straight up and rubbed her eyes. "Where are we?"

"Indiana. How do you feel?"

"Like I have to use the restroom. Right now," she added.

Kurt smiled. "Good thing I decided to stop. Come on, let's go inside."

Kurt stood waiting for Madeline when she came out of the

ladies' room. "Are you hungry yet?" he asked.

"Kind of. Those wrist bands do seem to be making a difference," she said, checking to make sure they were still in place. "Thank you for thinking of them."

"You're welcome. Let's go see what they have that'll be easy on your digestive system."

His concern for her well being bordered on annoying. Even more perplexing to her, she found it somehow comforting. Aside from the attorneys and her doctor, Kurt was the only one who knew of her pregnancy. A pang of sadness ran through her as she thought about Charles. Though she could only admit it to herself, if he had been alive to share this experience with her, she doubted his attention to her needs would have been nearly as intense.

They walked over to the restaurant area to study the overhead menu. "How about a broiled chicken sandwich?" he suggested. "Or, some soup?"

"The chicken sandwich should work. Plain, no mayo," she said.

"Got it. You go save us a seat. I'll take care of the food."

"Kurt, there are plenty of empty tables. I need to stand a while. Besides, I'd like to pay. It's the least I can do since you're the one doing me a favor."

"I can afford a couple of sandwiches, Madeline. I'm not keeping score in the favor department."

She preferred to maintain her independence, but his look told her she'd probably insulted him. Rather than make a scene, she would think of some other way to repay him. "Fine," she said.

She picked a secluded spot near a corner of the expansive room. The questions about Kurt Williams were mounting, and she had the feeling a little privacy would come in handy should the opportunity present itself to ask some of them.

He stood far enough away that she couldn't hear what he was ordering, but close enough to see he looked as good from the back as from the front. She'd become fixated on his backside when he suddenly turned her way.

She could feel the embarrassment traveling down her face and hoped he wouldn't notice. What was it with all this blushing lately? She'd never been that way before. He grabbed some napkins and headed toward her. Seconds later he set the tray of food on the table.

"You look a little flushed," he said. "You're not getting sick again, are you?"

"No, I just need some water," she answered, running her hands over her face. "I'll be right back." With that, she started to rise.

"Sit, please. I remembered you like herbal tea. So I brought you a cup to go with your sandwich. And a milkshake."

"A milkshake?"

"Yeah. They make 'em with real ice cream here, none of that artificial crap. I thought it might go down easy, in case the sandwich is too dry. But I'll get you some water too."

"Really, Kurt, I'm not helpless!"

Oops. She hadn't meant for that to come out in such a loud, snappy tone, but all this hovering was getting on her nerves. Nonetheless, his expression called for damage control. "I only meant you must be tired yourself," she added, her voice much softer. "The tea is a good idea, so please sit with me and enjoy your meal before it gets cold."

"Sure," he said, grabbing his burger and fries from the tray. He began wolfing his food as though he were afraid someone would steal it.

She took a bite of her chicken sandwich and washed its dry blandness down with the tea. Then she dipped her straw into the thick chocolate treat, sucking the icy sweetness to the back

51

of her throat. He'd been right about the milkshake after all.

She looked over at him, but he refused to make eye contact—a sure sign he was put out with her. She knew she had a tendency to be bossy. Maybe she had gone a little overboard. "Tell me something, Kurt," she said, deliberately adjusting her tone to a more cordial level. "How did you know this milkshake would be the perfect thing for me?"

"Instinct," he answered, without looking up.

Her question had been intended to thaw the atmosphere. His guarded response provoked a more challenging inquiry. "How come you're such an authority on what to do for a queasy stomach? Are you some kind of medical professional?"

He stopped eating and faced her squarely. She had his attention now. "I don't have any type of medical degree, if that's what you're asking. My knowledge comes strictly from personal experience. In truth, I was more of a professional patient."

She took a quick breath. Was he ill? He certainly looked the picture of health.

"*Was* being the operative word," he emphasized. "I'm pretty much fine now."

Pretty much? "Do you want to elaborate on that?" She tried to speak calmly, yet she knew her face betrayed tension as she tried to sort through the possibilities.

"Okay, but it would be easier if you'd wipe the freaked-out look off your face. The baby is in no danger."

That should have been comforting, so why had her stomach tied itself into a knot at the very mention of the possibility? "Please, tell me what you're talking about."

"I had Hodgkin's Disease. I don't have it anymore."

"That's cancer, isn't it?"

"My doctor told me not to even use that word because Hodgkin's is so curable. But it is a form of lymphoma." He reached over the table to touch her hand, and without warning, her senses came alive. "Madeline, were you listening when I told you I don't have it anymore? I've been in remission now for over four years. When I get to the five year point, I'll be considered cured."

"That's wonderful," she said, cognizant that his muscular hand still blanketed hers. Even though his prognosis sounded positive, the thought that he'd been subjected to such a serious disease disturbed her on more than one level. "Were you . . . ? Did you suffer terribly?"

"I was never sick from Hodgkin's. By some miracle, we caught it early, stage one. But six weeks of radiation treatments took their toll. Plus, I had two surgeries, one to remove a malignant lymph node in my neck and the other to remove my spleen."

"They took your spleen?"

"It was part of the staging process. The spleen is kind of like a big lymph node that filters blood. They needed to be sure the Hodgkin's hadn't gone there," he explained, stroking his thumb over her fingers. "Lucky for me it hadn't, or I would have been diagnosed with a much more advanced phase of the disease."

The realization of all he'd been through began sinking in. She wanted more information, but she could not fully concentrate on what he was saying until she could stop concentrating on what he was doing. Gently, and with her eyes still focused on Kurt, she removed her hand from beneath his. Only then could she pose her next question. "Did the radiation make you nauseous?"

"That would be an understatement," he emphasized, leaning his upper body forward.

Now he was in his space and not in hers.

"I had radiation from the waist up to the back of my head, front and back," he continued. "Kind of like bread in a toaster. I puked my guts up for months. That's why I can relate to you and your sickness."

A big stab of guilt poked at her. Whether or not she deserved his empathy, she wished she could be more accepting of it.

"I learned a few tricks about calming a queasy stomach."

"Did the Sea-Bands help you?"

"Sometimes. Plus, I had other medication. Unfortunately I'd reached the point where nothing was very effective. It took weeks for the radiation to work its way out of my system, long after the treatment was over."

"That must have been terrible for you, Kurt. I'm so sorry you had to go through it. But you're well now. You look well," she emphasized, almost as if she were trying to convince herself."

"I feel fine. Truthfully, I feel great. Most of the time."

"You mean you have long term side effects?"

"Mainly, it's the head trips. You know, your milkshake is going to thaw if you don't start drinking it," he added, in a voice that told her that was all the answer she was going to get for the time being. He began to eat again, and she took a few sips of her shake. But her hunger had been replaced by apprehension.

"So, did your sperm donation have anything to do with the Hodgkin's?" she continued to push. It was another personal question, but one she felt she was entitled to ask.

"Yes and no. I did it because of the treatment I faced at the time."

"You donated after you knew you were sick?" she pressed, unable to mask her concerns.

"When I was initially diagnosed, I'd just turned twenty-nine. We weren't exactly sure what treatment options I would have or what their long-term effects would be. Since sterility was a possible outcome, my doctors encouraged me to donate sperm while I knew I could still make babies.

"Madeline, I know you're worried about our child. To tell the truth, I was too. So I called my oncologist and ran a few questions by him. He was very reassuring. In the first place, Hodgkin's Disease isn't hereditary. Doc Kaplan told me that even in the very unlikely event there were Hodgkin's cells in the frozen semen, they wouldn't infect the fetus. It would be virtually impossible for them to survive the freezing process. He said the baby is in no danger."

That should have been soothing, yet she knew her face portrayed anxiety.

"Look, you don't seem very comforted by anything I'm telling you. So, if it'll make you feel better, you can call my doctor yourself and ask him all the questions you want. He's a great guy."

Once again she felt ashamed. Kurt had a wounded look on his face, and she had put it there. Bad enough he'd been so ill, and now she'd been acting as though he had the plague. "I know I must appear to be overly concerned," she said. "I apologize."

"I understand, Madeline. Cancer is scary. Hell, it's the biggest scare I've ever had, and it's natural for you to be worried about the baby."

"It's not that I don't believe what you're telling me. But maybe I feel kind of like you did when you first heard that I'm pregnant with your child. News like this takes time to sink in."

"I can appreciate that. From my perspective, sometimes I look at myself, and I still can't imagine I was ever that sick. I'm trying to put the whole thing behind me and move on with my life."

"Yes, of course. That's what you should do. But my pregnancy is just beginning. My hormones are all jumbled, and my feelings and reactions aren't what they would normally be. I'm anxious about so many things right now, and that's not like me," she confided. "I'm used to being the strong one and taking care of myself."

"I can relate to that," he said. "When I was sick, my whole life was out of control. Everything I did revolved around doctors, hospitals, tests and test results. I used to jump when the phone rang for fear somebody was calling me with more bad news. I couldn't make any plans because each day centered around my illness and treatment for it. I didn't always handle it well."

"Were your friends there to support you?"

"Not all of them. Some people get weird when they hear the 'C' word, and they disappear. Sometimes the person who leaves is the person you're counting on the most."

"Did that happen to you?"

"Yeah," he answered pointedly. "But I don't feel like talking about it. Not now, anyway. So, if you're finished eating, I think we should get back on the road. We've still got a long way to go."

Even though he was talking about the highway ahead, his words had a prophetic ring that made her shiver.

CHAPTER 4

Madeline had fallen asleep again almost the minute they'd left the oasis. Just as well. Kurt knew she was tired, and he needed a break from all the meaningful chitchat. Besides, he wasn't really a sharing kind of guy. Not that he couldn't be—if the right person came along. Then again, he'd once thought that person was Christie Reed. And look where pouring his heart out to her had gotten him.

If anything good had come from his experience with Christie, it was that he'd learned a valuable lesson about human nature and relationships. Ever since she'd taken the hike, he'd been a lot more cautious in picking his friends. Especially his women friends.

He'd watched Madeline's face when he'd told her about the Hodgkin's. She'd thrown him a look that registered her fear. Like when a person has the Ebola Virus. He'd dealt with that reaction before, and he kind of understood it. But that didn't spare him the hurt.

Maybe he wasn't giving her a fair shake on this. After all, she hadn't been mean or even blatant. On the contrary, she'd gone out of her way to apologize. Her sensitivity about his feelings said something about her integrity, and for that he was thankful. It didn't erase the fact that she viewed him as a possible threat. Then again, it was good she'd been honest about her fears. At least that put something on the table for them to deal with.

He couldn't justify criticizing her for being worried about the baby. Admittedly, he'd had some of the same concerns before he'd spoken to Doc Kaplan. Madeline was on information overload. Maybe some time to digest all the specifics would help. Like she'd said.

Now Christie—she'd been mean. And dishonest. And uncaring. And why the hell was he allowing himself to dredge all that up right now? He had enough on his plate getting Madeline to Ohio.

Yawning and glad he'd remembered to buy carryout coffee before they'd left the restaurant, he reached for the huge paper container and guzzled the lukewarm contents. Never mind that it tasted bitter. He needed the caffeine charge. With Madeline out like a light and nothing but "elevator music" to keep him company, it was going to be a long night.

Madeline drifted in and out of sleep, conscious enough to know she'd been dreaming. Images of babies and hospitals played before her as she tried to sort reality from fantasy. Then she remembered what Kurt had told her about being in remission from Hodgkin's Disease. He'd emphasized the word remission. In fact, soon he would be considered cured. Even more significant, Hodgkin's was not hereditary. He'd said so. Her baby would be fine. She had to keep reminding herself of that.

Though she resisted, she forced her eyes to open. She needed to use the restroom. Quickly.

Kurt took his attention from the road for a brief glance her way. "How are you doing?" he asked.

"Umm . . ." Would he be annoyed with her? Charles certainly would have been.

"You're not sick again, are you?"

His tone demonstrated concern, rather than impatience. "I'm sorry, but I need another bathroom break."

"Is that all? For a minute, I thought we had a problem."

"It must have been the tea. I feel bad about making you stop again so soon," she said.

"No big deal."

A shot of panic ran through her as the pressure on her bladder worsened. The speedometer held steady as Kurt continued to drive, and she wished she hadn't delivered that earlier lecture about his speeding. After all, Charles had been going eight-five miles per hour when he'd wrapped his car around the tree. The situation with Kurt had been different.

"How long will it take us to get there?" she asked.

"Twenty minutes or so. If you're not sure you can make it, I'll pull off the road."

No, she couldn't bring herself to consider peeing somewhere in the weeds, while traffic passed and he waited. Still, his accommodating ways were a comfort. By now, she and Charles would have been arguing.

"I think I can hang on. Where are we, anyway?"

"Ohio. We're more than halfway there."

"You must be very tired, Kurt."

"I'm doing all right. I'm sure I'll crash once we get to the hotel."

"I would just like to say how much I appreciate what you're doing for me. I think I would have been in big trouble had I tried to make this drive alone." Where had that come from? She'd meant to thank him, not blunder into an admission of helplessness.

"You're welcome. And I know you would have been in trouble if I'd let you make the trip by yourself," he said. "That's why I insisted on taking you."

Let her? It was just that sort of egoism that activated her defenses, and she made herself suck in a deep breath of air, counting silently before she allowed another word to come out of her mouth.

"That doesn't mean I wouldn't have managed without you," she stressed, with as much control as she could muster. "I only meant it would have been more difficult. For this particular situation. Because I happen to be in early pregnancy. Which won't always be the case. Do you understand?"

"Perfectly."

He stared straight ahead at the road before them. Yet, even in the darkness, his profile could not hide the grin revealing his satisfaction at thinking he'd won this round. Well, it would never do to let him believe she needed a nursemaid for the next eight months, and she certainly had a thing or two to add. But that conversation would have to wait. By some act of mercy, they both saw the sign for the oasis at the same time, and Madeline could only breathe a sigh of relief.

It was nearly three o'clock in the morning by the time Kurt pulled into the parking lot of the Best Suites Hotel.

"Let's leave the luggage till we get checked in," he said. Together they walked into the building. "I'm Madeline Holt," she said to the clerk at the front desk. "You're holding a late reservation for me."

The young woman behind the counter checked her computer monitor. "Oh, yes, Ms. Holt, you're on the third floor. Room three twenty two. No smoking, with a king size bed, as you requested. We were lucky to get that for you on such short notice."

"I'll need a room too," Kurt added.

The clerk looked flustered. "I'm sorry, sir. There is a huge convention in town, and we're completely booked. I don't even have an empty closet, much less an extra room."

Madeline had an uneasy feeling. Until this moment, she hadn't actually considered there might not be room at the inn, so to speak. "That's all right," she blurted. "We'll make do. After all, it is a suite, and I'm sure there's a sofa somewhere."

Kurt's surprised expression was almost worth the angst she felt.

"Oh, yes," the woman said. "It's a sleeper sofa, and I'm sure you'll find it comfortable. The linens and extra pillows are inside the coffee table."

"I'll get our stuff," Kurt said. With that he promptly vanished, no doubt fearful Madeline would change her mind.

In the few minutes it took her to finish checking in, he reappeared. "The elevator is down the hallway," Madeline directed, taking her wheeled suitcase in hand.

Silently, he stepped in alongside her as they made their way down the corridor. Her anxiety level rose as she considered that she was literally going to be sharing a hotel room with a man for the first time in over a year. Of course, that's all she'd be sharing. Nonetheless, she hadn't given it any thought when she'd packed the only thing she'd brought to sleep in—her skimpy silk nightshirt. No bathrobe, of course. That's what she got for packing light. Maybe she would keep her clothes on all night. No, that would be stupid and uncomfortable and . . .

"Here we are," Kurt said, as they stood in front of the elevator doors. They stepped on, and she pressed the third floor button, thinking about her office building elevator back home. The one that never failed to get stuck at the most inopportune times. She hated elevators. Fortunately, this one appeared to be working. The walk to their room was lengthy, which gave her more time to be nervous about how she would react once they got inside.

"I've got the key," she said, once they reached their destination. "Somewhere." She rummaged her purse. Please, don't let it be lost. "Found it." She put her card through the slot. Three times. It figured she couldn't get it to work.

Kurt set one bag down and with his free hand, took the key card from her and slid it into the lock. The door immediately opened. "After you." He made a sweeping motion with his hand, and Madeline entered the room.

Kurt followed her in and set his duffel down on the floor. Then he hung her garment bag on the closet rod. "This is nice," he said, inspecting his surroundings. "I wasn't expecting a kitchenette and a living room area."

"Well, it is a suite. Do you want me to help you set up the sofa bed?"

"No, it's late. Get some rest. Before you know it, your alarm clock will be going off."

What to do next? There must be some sort of etiquette one followed when sharing a room with a man one hardly knew. A man who'd fathered her child, despite that they'd never been intimate. She parked her suitcase alongside of the bed. "I guess I'll use the bathroom first then," she said. "If you don't mind."

"I don't mind." Kurt walked over to the sofa and sat facing her with his legs stretched out before him, his fingers laced behind his head.

His cool blue gaze unnerved her as she remembered the extra key card she'd slipped into her pocket. "Here, I got this for you," she said, putting it on the small dining table in the corner.

"Thanks." He smiled, then flashed her a wink.

Had that been a flirting wink or a gratitude wink? Whether she liked it or not, the man exuded sex appeal. There was power in his presence. And at the moment, she felt vulnerable.

"Um, it's really late, isn't it?" *Duh!* She picked up her suitcase, set in on the bed and began working the combination lock. "We should probably try to get some sleep for what's left of the night." *Double duh!* Could she be any more redundant!

Without responding, he sat watching her fumble in an unsuccessful attempt to open her bag. She grew more agitated by the minute.

Finally he walked over to her. "Looks like there's something about you and locks that don't mesh."

"I don't know why I even bothered to lock it. Force of habit, I guess."

"Would you like some help?"

Maybe if he hadn't been sporting such a smart-aleck grin, she would have taken him up on his offer. "Oh, no, I can get this. Sometimes the numbers stick a little."

Without warning, his hands gently covered her arms. "I think you need to calm down, Madeline. You're as nervous as a student who's about to solo for the first time."

His touch seared her skin, and she immediately pulled away. The last thing she wanted right now was physical contact with him.

"Didn't mean to offend you," he said, throwing his hands up in defeat.

Clearly she was the one who'd offended him. "I . . . um . . . this is very awkward for me," she stammered. "I didn't expect to be rooming with you tonight, and I'm rather uncomfortable about it."

"No kidding! Would you rather I go back out to my 4Runner and sleep there?"

"Of course not."

"I have to say I'm relieved to hear that. Look, Madeline, I'm not Jack the Ripper. And I don't snore. Well, not usually. You can have the bathroom first, and I promise to behave when you come out. You do know you can trust me, don't you?"

Instinctively she did know he wasn't about to do any physical harm to her. Still, she felt nervous. "I guess I'm just anxious to get some sleep before the alarm goes off."

"What time will that be?"

"Seven o'clock. Don't worry; I'll take a taxi to my client's office. It's only ten minutes from here." Once again she tried to unlock her suitcase—and failed.

Kurt shook his head and smiled. "Want to give me your combination?" Thirty seconds after she did, the suitcase lay opened.

Kurt set up the sleeper sofa and then paced back and forth, waiting for his turn in the bathroom. Madeline had gone in first, presumably to change and get ready for bed. Speculation about what she'd be wearing when she emerged caused an unwelcome stirring in his groin, and for lack of anything more distracting to do, he began dimming the lights. At three-thirty in the morning, there was no reason for the place to be lit like a Vegas casino.

Madeline was right. This was damned awkward. He hadn't been expecting they would be sharing a room any more than she had. And his social skills in this situation were a little rusty.

It wasn't like they had a relationship or anything. Yet stamping her with a label of platonic friend didn't seem accurate either. His brain felt too fuzzy to figure out the dynamics of all this right now. He did know he'd been acting like a mother-freakin' hen with this woman, ever since she'd almost fainted in the attorney's office, looking so vulnerable and fragile, despite her considerable height. He couldn't seem to stop himself.

Whether she knew it or not, she needed protecting. And he had the need to protect what was his. Not that she belonged to him. He knew that much, though he couldn't deny his attraction to her. The baby was another story, calling for Kurt to take his role of fatherhood seriously. Even if it had been foisted on him.

He heard the toilet flush, and then the bathroom door opened. Madeline made her way to the bed. Quickly. But not before he saw that she wore a satiny pink little nothing that barely covered her shapely ass. He swallowed hard. Jesus! Was she naked under that thing? The woman was all legs. And no sign of pregnancy to mar her slender figure. Not yet. He wondered what she would look like in a few months, when the baby grew larger. His gut told him she would likely be as beautiful. He caught sight of the tips of her breasts poking their way through the flimsy fabric and realized he'd been staring. Modestly, she folded her arms over her chest. He looked away from her long enough to let her climb into the bed and pull the covers up, while he tried to calm the heavy ache of male hunger. It was going to be an even longer night than he'd thought.

"The bathroom is yours," she said, shyly.

"You know, I think I'll take a quick shower." With that he disappeared from the room.

Madeline tossed and turned while she listened to the sound of running water. The image of Kurt naked and in such close proximity disturbed her in more ways than one. How was she supposed to fall asleep with him in the same room? *You didn't have any problem sleeping next to him in the car all the way to Ohio,* the voice of reason reminded her. An apples and oranges comparison, to be sure. Besides, she'd had all her clothes on then. So had he.

Her skin prickled with nervous anticipation as she considered what he might be wearing when he came out of that bathroom. Or what he might not be wearing! What if she turned all the lights off? Never mind that he would have to find the way to his bed in the dark. Yes, that's what she would do. Then she would pretend to be asleep. Because as tired as she'd been, she was wide awake now.

Madeline's alarm clock rang louder than the bell signaling the opening session at the Board of Trade. Shit! Just when Kurt had finally nodded off. He turned over, aware that his toe still hurt. No small wonder after the way he'd banged it walking from the bathroom to the sofa bed a few hours earlier. He'd run into something downright evil, but had stifled the urge to yell out in pain. Since the room had been pitch black, he couldn't tell whether Madeline had been sleeping through all the commotion. Somehow he suspected not.

Daylight peeked through the drapes, and he forced his eyes to open a crack. He saw Madeline was already up and in the bathroom. Seconds later, he heard evidence that her nausea had come back full force. He groaned, both in sympathy and empathy. And in frustration. No way he'd be able to get back to sleep now.

He threw his jeans on over his briefs and sat inspecting the purple bruised damage to his toe. He could tell he hadn't broken anything, even though it still hurt like a mother. The hungry growl of his stomach came as a surprise. There was no room service, but he knew the hotel offered a complimentary breakfast in the lobby. At the sound of the bathroom shower, he figured it would be a while before Madeline emerged. Impulsively, he threw on a T-shirt and went downstairs to forage for food.

He grabbed a tray and filled his plate with eggs and sausages and juice. For Madeline, he got some tea, dry toast, dry cereal and a plum. The fruit might have been a stretch, but she had to eat something.

He had the feeling they'd both need to be well fortified for whatever surprises the day might hold.

By the time he made it back to the room, Madeline was still in the bathroom. He set the food on the table and turned on the TV set, flicking from station to station until a guy jumping out of an airplane captured his attention. Sans parachute! The hairs at the back of Kurt's neck stood straight. He'd heard about this movie, though he'd never seen it. Seconds later the actor caught up with another guy who'd jumped with a parachute strapped to his back. Now the guy without the parachute clung to the guy with, and they were both free falling through the sky, the ground coming up fast. Drum roll please! The good guy with no chute had a gun and wouldn't let go of it to pull the ripcord. The bad guy seemed to be calling his bluff. Talk about Russian Roulette. Wasn't somebody going to pull the fucking cord?

"Good morning."

Kurt turned away from the television to see Madeline standing, fully clothed, outside the bathroom doorway. Her light gray suit emanated business class, but her milky white face betrayed her.

"I woke you, didn't I? I'm sorry. Maybe you could go back to sleep once I leave."

"Let's just say I know you're not feeling too good."

"That's an understatement. I'll look better though, after I put on some makeup. There's no mirror in the bathroom." Madeline sat at the edge of the bed, rummaging through her purse while Kurt checked on the situation with the skydivers.

Damn! The bad guy and the good guy had somehow landed on the ground, and he'd missed the whole thing. One of them looked like he had an injured knee. Still, both men were alive and talking, which was crucial enough to launch Kurt's adrenaline into first gear. Until Madeline cleared her throat. For the moment, he lowered the volume on the television to focus on her.

"So did the Sea-Bands stop working?"

"I took them off last night when I washed up for bed. I guess it's time to put them back on," she said, pulling them from her purse.

"I got some breakfast for us. It's sitting on the table, waiting to be eaten."

Madeline made a face that indicated her disdain at the mention of food. "That was very nice of you, but I don't think I could handle it right now. You go ahead before it gets cold."

"You have to eat something. An empty stomach will only make you feel worse. Besides, you don't want your blood sugar to get too low."

"You're a veritable encyclopedia of medical information, aren't you?" she said irritably.

No point in throwing a snappy comeback. Not when she was so crabby. Instead, he reached for the phone book and began thumbing through it. Something else had begun to nudge at his thoughts.

Minutes later he sat at the small table and began to eat. "At least keep me company," he beckoned. With that, she joined him, keeping her own food at bay.

"Come on, Maddie. You have to try," he said, in an effort to get her to eat. "If you can't do it for yourself, think of the baby."

She shot him a look full of contempt, and he realized he'd slipped and called her Maddie. Why did that seem to be such an unpardonable sin? Instead of apologizing, he said, "If the smell of eggs and sausage is getting to you, I'll eat over by the sofa."

"You don't have to move," she said, as he started to push away from the table. "I'm sorry I'm so disagreeable. I can't seem to stop myself." With that, she began to cry.

Not again! He'd rather eat worms than deal with a bawling female. Now what was he supposed to do? "Are you crying because I called you Maddie?"

"No! Maybe!" she amended, dabbing at her eyes with a tissue.

Kurt raised his hands in utter confusion.

"My father used to call me Maddie," she explained through her sniffles. "It was his special nickname for me. After he passed away, I wouldn't allow anyone else to call me that. Kind of silly, isn't it? But I was quite young when he died. Sometimes I miss him terribly. I guess this is one of those moments."

"I'm sorry about your dad, Madeline. I didn't mean to be insensitive; it just kind of slipped out. I wouldn't have done it if I'd understood."

"I know. And I don't want you to think I'm a big crybaby, bursting into tears every time the wind changes direction. For the life of me, I can't figure out what's going on here."

"Pregnancy hormones," he interjected.

She shot him a look that made him wish he'd kept his mouth shut.

"It . . . It's only a guess though," he added, sheepishly.

"All the same, I never cry. Well, hardly ever. I feel so stupid about this. Of course, it isn't your fault. You've been very kind. It's just that . . ."

"Go on."

"I'm used to calling my own shots. I'm an independent woman. Or I was until I became pregnant with the aid of your sperm. Suddenly I'm sharing my life with a man I hardly know. This wasn't my plan. We spent the night together, for heaven's sake!"

"Well, how do you think I feel? I'm trying to adjust to all this myself. And by the way, we didn't exactly *spend* the night together. I mean, it's not like we . . ."

"I know, I know," she said. "But you are here. And I'm here. And, oh my gosh!"

"What? What now?"

"I forgot to let the front desk know I need a cab. I have to leave soon."

"Give me twenty minutes, and I'll drive you to your client's office."

"No, you've done enough. You should go back to bed and get some sleep."

"Believe me, I couldn't be more awake." He opened the box of toasted oats and put them in Madeline's empty cereal bowl. Then, in a move that surprised even Kurt, he took her spoon, dipped it into the dry cereal and put the food to her lips. "Come on, try some," he encouraged.

More amazing, Madeline opened her mouth and allowed him to feed her. He watched as she slowly chewed, then painstakingly swallowed. He followed by carefully spooning some of the warm tea to her lips. "We don't want you getting dehydrated," he said in a near whisper. Once again she swallowed and met his gaze. For a few seconds he could swear he saw his reflection in the deepest part of her green eyes, and he became transfixed.

Carefully, she took the spoon from him, breaking the spell. "You're a very caring person, Kurt, and I appreciate your kindness. But I actually do know how to feed myself. If you don't mind though, I will take you up on your offer of a ride to work."

CHAPTER 5

Mason Products was in a total stir, and rightly so. After poring over their books and checking through their computer system, Madeline had discovered that, indeed, someone had been tampering with the company checkbook—an amateur who'd left an obvious trail by creating false invoice numbers to pay vendors who weren't really owed money, and then printed checks on plain paper while making out the real checks to herself. Had the woman been so desperate she hadn't realized how easy it would be to obtain copies of the signed checks, even though she'd hidden the originals?

The details of this scam were familiar, but this was the first time Madeline had seen it for herself. Now it was up to the company heads and their attorneys to decide what to do with the evidence she'd provided. She would need to stick around till the end of the day, especially if they planned to bring in the police. After that, her involvement in the investigation would, most likely, be over.

For the moment, she needed a break. She rose from the desk to stretch her legs. Kurt had insisted she bring the remains of the dry cereal to work since she hadn't eaten much back at the hotel. She hated to admit he'd been right about not allowing her stomach to become empty. After another sick session an hour after her arrival, she'd bought some salt free pretzels from the vending machine in the employee cafeteria. She'd been munching on them most of the morning. Between those, the

Sea-Bands and sips of tea, her stomach had settled some. In fact, considering the lunchtime hour, the idea of ingesting a little protein seemed almost appealing.

On the way back to the cafeteria, her mind drifted to Kurt and the intimate exchange they'd had over breakfast. For a few magical seconds, she'd thought he might kiss her. Logic dictated she would have resisted. Then again, maybe not. Worse yet, a part deep inside her core was disappointed he hadn't even tried.

A couple of days earlier, she'd been determined to exclude this man from her life. Now she was allowing herself to become emotionally unglued over him. She wasn't given to impulse, so it didn't make sense. Was this the result of pregnancy hormones too?

She supposed a child could do worse than to have Kurt Williams for a father. Whether she liked it or not, the man had begun to get under her skin.

So much so, she couldn't help wondering where he'd gone after he'd dropped her off that morning. Common sense demanded he head back to the hotel for some much needed rest. Intuition told her he'd had a different agenda. Back at the hotel, she'd noticed him studying and making notes on a map he'd picked up in the lobby. Plus, he'd been carefully checking road signs once they'd begun the drive to her client's office. None of which had anything to do with the route they'd taken. It was a simple one with only two turns. She knew it by heart and had told him the way even before they'd left the parking lot.

She'd resisted the urge to quiz him. After all, they weren't in a relationship. What he did with his time was none of her business. It certainly wasn't her place to keep tabs on him. Though he had given her the satisfaction of saying he would see her back at the hotel that evening.

Okay, well that was fine. Surely they weren't going to be driving home until the following morning, even if she did finish up with her client that afternoon. Therefore, she had no justifiable reason to obsess over Kurt's whereabouts. Why then, couldn't she seem to stop herself?

The drop zone was about twenty miles east of Canton, and Kurt had made the decision to head out there right after he'd driven Madeline to her client's office. He'd been thinking about skydiving for some time, but hadn't really made any serious plans for it until he'd caught the jump scene in the movie earlier that morning. Now he was psyched for it and couldn't let go of the idea.

Apparently weekdays were slow at the Center. The Tandem Class consisted of Kurt and another guy who'd wandered in on a last minute whim, plus a female reporter who was researching a story idea. Petite, attractive, and perky, the brunette looked familiar, and Kurt kept trying to figure out where he'd seen her. She took her seat alongside him in the first row of desks and began to write. If Kurt were a betting man, her name was Tammy.

"Hi Mindy," said a kid who barely looked old enough to vote. He walked over to shake her hand. "My name is Glenn, and I'm the instructor for this Tandem class. Is there anything you need before we get started?"

Mindy, Tammy—most especially, Christie. They all brought to mind that cheerleader/break-your-heart persona, and it would be interesting to see if his perception went any deeper than mere sour grapes.

"Not at the moment," she answered. "You go right ahead and teach the class the way you always do. I'll take notes, then later it would be great if I could interview your students for my show."

Mindy Sanders. Sure! Kurt had seen her weekly cable show in the Chicago area. He had to admit it was respectable programming. *So maybe you should save the character assassination for someone who really deserves it.* Nonetheless, Ohio seemed like a long way to travel for a local television program, and he wondered what had brought her to this particular drop zone?

"That sounds like a plan," Glenn said, heading to the front of the room. "Let's get the unpleasant stuff out of the way first. It's my job to inform all of you that parachuting is a dangerous sport. All activities related to skydiving, including the flight in the plane, can result in serious injury and even death."

No kidding. Even if the instructor wasn't exactly a kid, all decked out in board shorts and a Hawaiian print shirt, he came across as more apt to be surfing the beaches of Maui than proclaiming a lesson on mortality. All the same, Kurt listened with a keen smugness as Glenn continued.

"There is no perfect parachute."

There is no perfect disease. Though, if you have to get cancer, Hodgkin's is the kind to have.

"There is no perfect airplane."

Ah, but was there a perfect treatment? Would it result in a permanent cure?

"There are no perfect pilots, instructors or students," Glenn warned.

Did that apply to doctors? "Let me take care of you Kurt," Doc Kaplan had said. "There's every reason to expect that you and I will grow old together."

"Everyone and everything connected to this activity is subject to human error or malfunction."

How about the model patient? The one who is doing everything crucial to good health. Would he malfunction again?

"Before you make your first jump today, you'll be required to sign a waiver. Please read it carefully. Understand, your signature means you will be giving up all of your legal rights to sue anyone who is associated with the activities in which you participate in this facility—even if your claim is based on negligence. It means you're willing to accept the possibility of serious injury or even death in exchange for the thrill of jumping."

If Kurt could cheat the Grim Reaper with a five-minute fall from eleven thousand feet, then wasn't it reasonable to assume he'd make it to the five-year point of cure with Hodgkin's disease? *I'll sign your forms, kid. I didn't come this far to get nailed diving out of an airplane.*

Glenn spoke for the next hour, teaching and demonstrating the fine points of tandem jumping down to the last detail. At the end of the session, he checked to see if there were questions.

"Do I pull the ripcord when the altimeter reads fifty-five hundred feet?" the guy off the street asked.

"You and the jumpmaster hooked up to you," Glenn stressed. "I'm not sure who that will be yet. We don't require you to pull the cord by yourself till your second jump. We do expect you to signal that you know when it's time. You do it by flashing the five-five sign with your hands. That's why you keep checking that altimeter every five seconds. Any more questions?"

Kurt kept quiet, though he hated feeling so overwhelmed by everything he needed to remember. Not to mention jumping out of a well functioning airplane was contrary to common sense and everything he'd learned as a pilot. Still, he was determined to do it.

"It's a lot of information. Your jumpmaster will go over everything with you again before you board the plane and also during your flight," Glenn assured them. "Once you leave this classroom, you'll have a chance to read and sign those release forms. Then you'll be given a jumpsuit and the chance to practice body positions and maneuvers while you're on the ground."

Glenn turned toward Mindy. "How about it? Have you caught the fever yet? I'd love to take you up there myself," he offered.

Mindy laughed. "Oh, no. I didn't come here to make a jump. I came here to interview those who do."

"Why not experience some first-hand research?" Glenn asked. "Think how much better your story will be."

"I really can't. I'd be terrified."

Boy, there was a lot of that going around. Kurt's thoughts drifted to Madeline, wondering how she was doing with her client and whether she still felt nauseous. *Stay focused. You don't want to miss anything important.*

"You could always ride up in the plane with us and watch us jump," Glenn persisted.

Mindy brightened. "You'd let me do that?"

"Yeah, I can set it up. The Cessna holds five people, including the pilot. He's the only one who gets an upholstered seat, but you can sit right behind him on the floor. You'll be strapped into a seat belt, and you'll be able to look out the windows."

"That would be awesome!" she said. "I can't wait."

Glenn looked puzzled. "You'll fly, but you're afraid to jump?"

"I'd say there's a big difference in the thrill factor," she countered.

The young instructor hooked his thumbs over the waistband of his shorts. "Babe, at eleven thousand feet there's only two ways to get back down on the ground. Personally, I think you'd be better off with me strapped to your back. 'Course, it's your call."

Good one, Glenn! Cocky, but good. Was she going to bite?

Mindy seemed to be thinking it over. "Are you saying you don't trust the pilot?"

"I wouldn't be getting on the plane if that were the case. Just know you'll be coming down a whole lot faster than the flight up. The pilot has a reputation for his aerobatic touch. Given your fear of heights and all . . ."

For a minute she looked uncertain. Then she smiled. "I'll be sure to bring my videocam so I can film your jump."

Nice try, Glenn, but score one for the pilot. Kurt decided it was a good omen.

Kurt sat in the lounge area reading through eight pages of release forms and signing his name in the appropriate places. Each section pertained to a different issue. Essentially, they all meant the same thing. If you bounced, you couldn't sue, no matter who was to blame. Anxious, he shifted in the chair while past memories of signing medical forms clashed with the moment. By the time he set the pen down his hands were clammy.

He'd met his instructor earlier. If Kurt had to entrust his life to a virtual stranger, Mike seemed like a competent enough guy: personable, knowledgeable and older than twenty. How ironic Kurt's choice of oncologists had been so much more calculated. In truth, it made no sense.

Still, the urge to skydive was relentless. Maybe some voodoo mind magic that guaranteed a lifetime of health, if only he survived the experience. He couldn't afford to analyze it right now. He did realize the choice carried power. And, for a change, he had control.

He checked his watch. Mike had gone off on some errand, though he promised to be back soon to help fit Kurt with a jumpsuit and go over the maneuvers. In the meantime, Kurt stood and began to pace as overhead video footage played on a large screen, declaring proof of dozens of satisfied customers. Tandem jumps, free falls, cliff jumps, multiples, you name it. The divers all wore shit-eatin' grins. Just one, big happy family. Where the fuck was that jumpmaster?

Twenty long minutes later, Kurt and Mike stood in the

hanger recapping the procedures while other jumpers suited up. "Oh, they're letting you back so soon?" one of them called out to Mike. "I didn't even think you were out of the hospital yet."

Kurt knew by the look on Mike's face, the guy had been yanking his chain. In spite of it, the remark set him on edge. *Asshole.*

"Don't pay any attention," Mike said. "He's just kidding around."

"I figured."

"You all right?" Mike pressed. "You look a little pale."

"Fine," Kurt lied.

"Good. The plane's ready, so let's head out to the runway."

"Right there with you," Kurt said, as they set out on the marathon walk to the Cessna 182. The other guy who'd been in the tandem class followed with his instructor, and before long they'd boarded the aircraft. A fuselage with no seats was foreign to Kurt's comfort zone, even assuming the pilot's competence.

From the window he noticed Mindy standing over by the hanger with Glenn, waiting to catch the next flight out. Again an image of Madeline flashed before him. Quickly, he tried to banish it. Stay centered. He checked the altimeter secured to his wrist. Moments later they were airborne.

As the noisy plane climbed, Kurt did a mental recap of the procedures he would soon be carrying out. That he felt light-headed could only be explained by his apprehension, an unwelcome sensation that was all too familiar. But he would not let it best him.

Finally Mike passed him the frappe hat, and Kurt fastened it to his head. Next came the goggles. Then, time to hook up the gear. As the instructor synched the upper and lower left and right quadrants of their harnesses, it became more and more difficult for Kurt to breath and relax—so connected he could feel the heartbeat of the jumpmaster against his back.

A slight jerk of the plane told him the pilot had slowed to make it easier for them to jump out. Beads of sweat trickled down Kurt's neck, though the temperature was at least twenty degrees cooler at this altitude than on the ground. *You don't have to do this. You've got nothing to prove.* But he had everything to prove, if only to himself.

Strapped together, the first tandem jumpers made way to exit, and the instructor opened the door. With arms crossed over his chest, the novice knelt with his back to the jumpmaster as they rocked back and forth. At the count of three, they were gone.

Kurt's heart took up residence at the back of his throat, pounding out a staccato of dread. *Tell him you've changed your mind!* His instructor motioned, and they started the duck walk toward the open door. Backing out was for cowards, and Kurt was no coward.

He positioned his feet at the edge of the plane and clung to the ledge with both hands. The ground below looked far more ominous than from the cockpit he normally occupied. "Cross your arms in front of your chest!" the instructor yelled. Kurt complied, then felt a tap on his thighs. He understood Mike meant for him to kneel. Instead, a compulsion greater than his fear propelled him forward and out of the plane with the jump-master on his back. Before Mike had given the okay.

"Damn!" Mike shouted.

Kurt knew he'd screwed up, and he went rigid with terror as they began to spin. Screwed up bad. He thought he would choke on the rush of air filling his sinuses. The jumpmaster forced Kurt's head up, reminding him that arching his body was paramount. In an effort to cooperate, he formed an X with his arms and legs outstretched. Ultimately, they stabilized. Awash with emotion and a sense of relief, he realized he was flying. Flying and falling fast!

"Altimeter!" he heard the instructor shout over all the noise. Kurt checked their altitude, noting that in a matter of seconds it would be time to deploy the main chute. With Mike guiding his hands, together they reached for the security of the ripcord.

Abruptly Kurt felt the impact of the opening chute, and the horizontal descent of their bodies went vertical. He desperately wanted to hold onto something, then remembered he dared not, for fear of pulling the toggles down and causing further problems. They had been freefalling for about the first fifty seconds, but now the ride had slowed considerably.

The scenery was breathtaking, and that included his colorful parachute. The noise had lessened enough for him to hear the instructor's voice, and together they made a turn that enabled them to head toward the airport. Though the huge letters identifying the drop zone still appeared small, Kurt could recognize them, and he relaxed measurably.

They continued to glide, with the ride taking longer than Kurt had expected. But as they neared the ground, he had another rush of insecurity. "Remember to keep your legs out in front of you when we land," Mike warned. "I'll tell you when to get ready."

Mike held the toggles high until they were about twelve feet off the ground. "Flare!" he shouted, lowering the toggles to his torso, then all the way down. Kurt followed the landing instructions. The ground that came up under him was soft and non-jarring. All at once he understood why all those jumpers in the video had seemed so euphoric. He was alive. He was unhurt. And he'd cheated death!

"Good landing," Mike said, once they were unhooked and face to face.

"Thanks, man," Kurt said, shaking the instructor's hand. "Sorry about the premature jump."

"Yeah, I was about to get to that. We could have had a really bad scene up there."

Could have doesn't count. Nevertheless, Kurt knew it would take some time for him to shake the guilt plaguing him.

"I almost hit my head because you weren't positioned right, and I was totally out of sync for a while. That's why I didn't get the drogue shoot out when I should have. What were you trying to prove?"

That I'm invincible. "Nothing. I got anxious and screwed up. Again, I apologize."

"Apology accepted. But if you plan on making any more jumps, I'd like to see you spend more time practicing the correct way of exiting the plane."

"I'll do that," Kurt promised. Because the only decision concerning whether or not he would jump again was when it would happen.

CHAPTER 6

The Vice-President of Mason Products had driven Madeline back to the hotel, grateful for the thorough job she'd done in uncovering their embezzlement situation. He'd wanted to take her to dinner at a four-star restaurant to show his appreciation. Ordinarily, she would have welcomed the invitation. Instead, she'd begged off, saying she feared a touch of the flu coming on. That hadn't been a total lie, she rationalized. Her nausea had persisted throughout the day. Thankfully, it hadn't been constant.

And there was something else to consider. Rather some*one* else. She decided if she should be dining with anyone, she certainly owed Kurt the courtesy of a meal. After all, she had no idea how he'd spent his day, but there was a good chance he'd be hungry by now.

As she headed down the long hotel corridor, she thought about seeing him with anticipation that was a tad more eager than she would like to admit. She'd seen Kurt's 4Runner in the parking lot, so she knew he was around somewhere. Presumably waiting for her in the room they shared. Unless he'd gone for a swim in the pool, or for a drink in the bar, or even to the nearby shopping mall.

In truth, she found herself impatient to tell him the details of her day. Anxious to see whether he would share the particulars of his day with her. Even if he'd spent the whole time sleeping. Which she doubted. She'd gotten so accustomed to coming home to an empty house. This had the potential of being a welcome change.

Standing outside the door of her room with key card in hand, she listened for any clue that Kurt might be inside. There were no telltale voices from the TV set. No music coming from the radio. Should she knock first or simply walk in? If he happened to be sleeping, she didn't want to risk waking him. Not after all the rest he'd sacrificed for her. What if he slept naked? *Wishful thinking?*

Still, she couldn't erase the image from her mind, and she covered her mouth to stifle a nervous laugh. Such adolescent behavior was not only out of character for her, it was completely out of her comfort zone. She made herself draw in a deep breath to regain some measure of composure. If she stayed in the hallway much longer, especially with her ear pressed to the door, someone would probably call Security.

"The soldiers have the net!"

What? Who said that?

"Grab the safety net!"

The directive came from inside her room. It sounded like Kurt's voice. That settled it.

"Kurt," she called out, unlocking the door. Cautiously she entered the room and immediately saw him lying in the sofa bed. Now what? And to whom had he been talking?

"Hi," she said timidly.

"Heads up!" he shouted.

Of all the responses he could have given her, that one hadn't been in the running.

"Can't breathe!" His declaration was followed by a series of wheezing and choking noises, so desperate sounding she raced to his side. He was bare-chested and covered in pools of sweat. His face contorted with pain as he fought with his pillow and thrashed beneath the sheet.

She wondered if he was having an asthma attack, and she reached for the phone to call for help.

"I see the drop zone!" he yelled.

Whatever he was talking about, this time he hadn't said it like a man struggling for air. Madeline put the handset down to take a more scrutinizing look at him. His eyes were closed, but his face had relaxed, and he was breathing more evenly. No sooner had the relief set in at the realization that he was dreaming, he started to flail again.

Without any thought to propriety, she placed her hand firmly over his shoulder. "Kurt, wake up," she said.

He groaned, but lay still.

"Wake up," she demanded a second time.

His eyes opened, and he took a few seconds to orient himself. "Madeline."

"I'm sorry for disturbing you, but you were having some sort of nightmare."

He sat up in the bed, shivering.

"You're soaking wet. Stay right there," she said, hurrying toward the bathroom.

Seconds later she returned with two clean towels. She draped the first one over his back, then sat at the edge of the sofa bed, drying his brawny chest and arms with the other. She worked intently, unaware of time, until sensing his penetrating gaze. If she allowed herself to lock eyes with him, she would have to acknowledge she'd invaded his personal space. That maybe she'd overstepped her bounds. That quite possibly he would look as uncomfortable as she now felt. Instead, she kept moving the towel over his body at a hearty pace. Until he took hold of her hand.

"I appreciate what you're doing, Madeline. But if you keep this up, you're going to take a couple layers off my skin."

Oops! Embarrassed, she let go of the towel and looked away.

Gently, he tilted her chin, forcing her to face him and that captivating grin of his. His eyes sparked with amusement. "I, uh, think I'm dry enough now."

His eyes had seduction written all over them, and his hand still clung to hers. Though it was contrary to everything she'd thought she wanted, she longed for him to scoop her into his arms. Instinct told her if she offered him even the smallest hint of encouragement, he would do exactly that.

Time froze while she realized how selfish it would be to let Kurt think he could occupy that sort of place in her life. Not when she knew her emotions were without substance, especially allowing for the short time she'd known him.

Granted, she was hormonal and needy—due to the pregnancy. She had to remember it was temporary. Maybe because Charles was no longer there, she'd begun to lean on Kurt as a substitute. No matter, it wasn't fair to him.

"I'm sorry," she finally said, rising in an effort to move away.

He continued to hold tight. "Please don't go."

His appeal was polite and composed, but his expression implored her to stay at his side. What if he needed her in a way that went beyond testosterone overload? How could she refuse him such a small request? She sat back down.

"You were yelling about a safety net. Do you have any idea why?" she asked.

"Guess I was talking in my sleep again. I do that sometimes. I was dreaming about the radiation," he said, releasing her hand. "Partly, anyway. I know this is going to sound weird, especially if you haven't been through it. But when I was sick and going for treatments, I decided in order to get well, I would visualize my healing process. I thought if I envisioned all of my white blood cells—those are the infection fighting cells—forming a net, they could capture all the cancer cells and flush them out of my body while I was under the machine."

"That doesn't sound weird," Madeline said. "But you had me worried with the way you were struggling to breathe. I'm sorry the dream caused you so much pain."

Suddenly his expression took on a strange aura of excitement. "It wasn't painful, Madeline. I just remembered something else in the dream. It had to do with how I spent my day."

"Tell me. If you don't mind."

"I'd planned to. In fact, I've been waiting for you to get back here so we could talk about it."

Her curiosity heightened. There was satisfaction in knowing he felt the same way as she. At the same time, it was all the more reason to be on guard.

"I jumped out of an airplane today."

"What?" She stared at him.

He smiled with a magnitude that revealed so much fervor, it made her uneasy about what he might say next.

"Yeah, I did. The breathing part of the dream probably had to do with the force of air shooting through me when I first started to fall."

"Kurt, I don't understand. Did you fly today? Did something go wrong with the plane that you had to jump out of it?"

"No. And definitely, no. I jumped because I wanted to sky-dive. I did a tandem, so I was hooked up to an experienced instructor. If I was yelling about a safety net, it probably had something to do with the parachute. I suppose somehow my subconscious linked the parachute with the safety net of the white blood cells and the radiation. Anyway, it's all connected to surviving and beating death."

Madeline leapt to her feet. "I don't get it. I don't get this at all. You go through all the rigors of fighting a life-threatening illness, and then you're willing to possibly toss your victory out the window by jumping from a perfectly good airplane. Now *that* sounds weird."

"*Possibly* is the key word." He swung his feet over the side of the sofa bed. "I never had any intention of endangering my life. Lots of people skydive, and I took a class beforehand. Don't you see? I lived."

As animated as he was, none of this made sense to her. "Isn't it a bit like playing Russian Roulette?"

"Well . . . not really. Anyway, I won."

He threw back the sheet and got up, only to reveal that he slept in navy blue briefs that matched his eyes. With a start, she turned her back to him. How was she supposed to follow this ludicrous conversation with him standing there half-naked? Yet she couldn't stop herself from stealing a glance at him via the dresser mirror. His legs were as stocky and muscular as the upper half of his body. Then her eyes traveled to the bulge between his thighs. A noteworthy bulge, to be sure. She swallowed hard, and for a few erotic seconds that had nothing to do with the matter at hand, she pictured him without those briefs.

Loudly, he cleared his throat, making her jump and face him. He studied her for a nanosecond before throwing on his jeans and a T-shirt. She knew she'd been caught, and she wondered if he could hear the pounding of her heart over the uncomfortable silence.

"Every time I ace one of these battles," he continued, as though nothing had transpired between them, "I'm that much closer to winning the entire war. I figured if I could survive jumping out of an airplane, then something like Hodgkin's isn't going to keep me down. It's like when I leave the doctor's office knowing I'm still in remission. Each episode brings me closer to the day I reach that five-year marker, and I'm cured. It makes me feel like listening to music that's loud enough to break the sound barrier. It makes me feel like speed dancing. It makes me feel immortal."

"So is that what was happening with the deafening music

during the drive up here?" she asked, trying her utmost to empathize. "Were you reliving the victory of one of your medical battles?"

"Exactly." He wore a triumphant expression.

"Well, I can understand wanting to celebrate and shout your good news. But I can't equate jumping out of a plane with some sort of medical conquest. It's a mindset you've established for yourself. If such and such happens, so and so will follow. That doesn't compute with me, Kurt."

His smile faded. Instantly she felt culpable. She hadn't meant to suck the wind from his sails when he'd been so happy.

"Of course," she added, "you have to remember I'm an accountant. When I add two and two, I always come up with four. Having said that, when it comes to certain situations, I can appreciate the existence of the gray area." *It's just that my own life is so distinctly black and white.*

He shot her an optimistic raise of his brows.

"Was it fun?" she asked tentatively. "I mean, I can't imagine jumping out of a plane. I'd be so scared. What did it feel like?"

"Pure euphoria."

There was no mistaking the passion in his answer.

"I had power, Madeline. I decided whether or not I wanted to take the journey. For a change, I was in control rather than some disease dictating my every move. I flew through the sky— without a plane to shield me. I didn't get hurt, and I lived to tell about it. Skydiving literally took my breath away. It was amazing!"

"You're amazing," she said, caught up in his spirited account.

Both of his eyebrows rose a fraction. "In what way?"

He stood, fixated on her, waiting for an answer, while she tried to decide why she'd allowed that remark to come spilling out. What was she going to tell him? That he was brave? Maybe too brave for his own good. Should she tell him she was intrigued by his passion for life, maybe even a bit envious of his spontaneity?

God knows, she'd never had the luxury of such impetuosity growing up. She hadn't even had the option of being a child. Her role had been that of a grownup in a ten-year-old body. She'd learned to be the responsible one from early on. Should she let him know she found him dangerously appealing?

The jarring ring of the telephone was a welcome intrusion, and she rushed to answer it. "This is Mindy Sanders," the caller announced. "If Kurt is there, may I speak to him please?"

"Could you hold the line a moment while I see if he's available?" *Wasn't that a territorial response?*

"Someone named Mindy Sanders," she said, covering the mouthpiece. "Do you want to take this call?"

Kurt practically knocked over a chair getting to the phone. Up to this point Madeline had naively assumed he had no current love interest. What if this Mindy person was his girlfriend? Or his fiancée. No, surely if he were engaged, he would have said something.

"Mindy, how are you doing?" Kurt said, with more enthusiasm than Madeline would have wished for.

She walked over to the other side of the room and picked up a magazine to give the appearance of disinterest in his conversation. It wouldn't do to have him think she was purposely eavesdropping.

"Uh-huh. Mmm-hmm," he drawled. "Now, there's an idea that's rife with possibilities."

Was that innuendo she'd heard in his tone? Madeline set her eyes on the pages of the magazine and stridently began turning them.

"Yeah, lunch sounds like a plan. We should go somewhere quiet."

Okay, so it wouldn't hurt to turn the pages a bit more softly.

"I thought it was pretty unforgettable. How about for you?" he continued. There was a pause, and then Kurt chuckled. "Next time maybe we can persuade you to go the whole nine yards."

Madeline stopped breathing and turning pages at the same time. Eyes that had been pretending to read flared upward. "Sunday it is. Right. I'll call you to confirm the time when I get back into town. Me too," he added.

He put the handset back in the cradle. Madeline forced her attention to the open magazine before her, refusing to look at him. She was surprised at the crestfallen knot that had formed at the back of her throat.

"So, you were telling me I'm amazing," Kurt had the audacity to say. "I'd still like to know why you think so."

Amazing was an understatement, she decided. Particularly since Kurt could stand there fishing for compliments right after having such an intimate exchange with this Mindy person.

She supposed it was the cold splash of water she needed. After all, it made sense that a man like Kurt would have a woman in his life. Well, good. Now she could stop having these mindless fantasies about him that were going absolutely nowhere and get on with the life she'd planned for herself and her unborn child. One that would exclude Kurt, as much as possible, starting the minute they got back to St. Charles. Which couldn't happen soon enough for her.

In the meantime, he just stood there with his arms folded in front of his chest, wearing that expectant smile, as if she intended to further feed his ego. "You know, I'm getting really sleepy," she said, completely ignoring his question. To emphasize her point, she gave an exaggerated yawn.

"It's only seven o'clock. 'Course, it stands to reason you'd be tired," he added with concern. "Have you eaten anything? You need to eat, Madeline. Then you can turn in for the night.

Restaurant or take out? I can run and get something. You know, I didn't even ask how your day went. Did you solve your client's problem?"

Back to his annoying, doting mode. "Do you think you could throw out one question at a time?" Her tone was deliberately caustic, and she didn't even care. "Yes, I was able to eat a little lunch. Takeout food would be fine. And my day went well. Thank you for asking. In fact, I'm finished with the job, and we can leave tomorrow morning. Not that you were under any obligation to stay here with me. If I had to, I could always rent a car to get back home.

His features twisted to an expression of irritation, and his eyes became two balls of granite. "What's biting your backside all of a sudden?"

"My backside is just fine."

He ran his thumb and forefinger along his chin, as if he were assessing her statement. "Let me put it another way. You and I were having a warm and fuzzy chat before the telephone rang. The minute I hung up, an arctic breeze blew through here. So, excuse me while I try to guess what I'm supposed to do next."

"Try putting on a sweater." Before he could respond, she added, "Doesn't your girlfriend mind you sharing a hotel room with another woman?"

"My what?"

The man had the nerve to look puzzled. "Not that it's any of my business. Though if you'd warned me she might be calling, I would have let you pick up the phone."

The corners of his mouth coiled into a grating look of delight as he straightened his shoulders. He was enjoying himself!

"So that's what this is about," he said. "I don't have a girlfriend. Or a wife. Or a fiancée. At least, not at the moment. I apologize if I didn't make that clear. Somehow, I thought you knew."

"My attorney told me you were single. I didn't feel the need to pry for any further details about your personal . . . relationships."

"Oh, but you would like to know why I was talking to Mindy Sanders, wouldn't you?"

"You're certainly entitled to your privacy, and frankly, I couldn't care less about your caller. Although judging by your suggestive remarks to the woman, one would surmise you're at least trying to cultivate a romance."

Kurt threw back his head as he rocked with laughter. "There was nothing suggestive about that conversation. You'd understand that if you had been able to eavesdrop on both sides of it."

"I was not eavesdropping." Her face began to heat, betraying both her lie and her humiliation.

"Admit it, you were listening. Not that you could help yourself."

"How dare you insinuate—"

"That this room is small," he interrupted, stepping directly into her space, locking eyes with her. "That's all I'm saying. That you'd have to be deaf not to have overheard. Mindy Sanders has a weekly cable show that's based in the Chicago area. Haven't you ever seen it?"

Her memory jogged. "Maybe I have. So, that was the Mindy Sanders you were talking to?" She wouldn't stoop to asking him why.

"Yep. She happens to be in Ohio visiting her brother who, coincidentally, did a tandem jump the day before she got into town. When he told her about it, she came up with an idea for her cable show. She was at the Skydiving Center today, doing some preliminary research that she plans to continue once she gets back home."

"I gather she wants to interview you?"

"Looks like it. After my jump, she came over to ask me some questions. When I told her it was my first time and that I'm also a pilot, she thought it was an interesting angle. The fact that I live in the Chicagoland area makes it that much easier for her to track my progress."

Progress? What did that mean? "Really." She made herself smile.

"Yeah, really. What you heard was us setting up a lunch date so she could ask me some questions. She went up in one of the planes today, but the instructor couldn't convince her to jump. Maybe next time."

"Next time?" She could already feel her body tensing. "Are you planning to do this again?"

"I might."

His words were tentative, but his expression was explicit, and she had no doubt he already knew he would. *Save the lecture, Madeline. You're not his girlfriend.*

"It's not something I have to decide this second. For now, I'd just like to get back to where we were before the damned phone rang. Because I happen to think this is more important," he added, sliding his hands over her shoulders.

Gulp! She'd taken her shoes off, and without them she and Kurt stood at nearly equal heights. Yet, at this moment he seemed larger than life. His gaze trailed over her, causing a tingling in the pit of her stomach that had nothing to do with pregnancy. As unsettling as it was, she made no move to back away.

"You want to know what else I think?" His voice had gone to a disturbingly low octave.

No! "Possibly," she answered.

"I think the chemistry in this room is about as thick as that milkshake you had last night."

The same chemistry that would account for the sudden weakness she felt in her knees? "I have no idea what you're talking about."

"Don't you? The reason you got so hot and bothered about that phone call was because you thought I was involved with another woman."

"That's ridiculous. I have no claims on you. We hardly know each other."

He leaned in even closer and smoothed her hair away from her face, exposing her ears. "That could be remedied," he said, his whisper husky with innuendo.

His blue eyes were intoxicating as they darkened to midnight. Everything about him beckoned her, and she locked her arms around his waist, giving him the only signal he needed. His warm lips pressed against hers, sampling, exploring and persuading. Zealously, she gave in to her need, hungrily tracing the recesses of his mouth with her tongue while he groaned with approval. Then he was on fire, capturing her mouth with skillful force and urgency.

Wet with yearning, she leaned into him, wrapping her leg around his thigh in search for further gratification. Kurt was a quick study, moving one hand down the small of her back while his other hand found the swell of her breast. His thumb circled the tip until it rose hard through her bra and even through the silk sweater she wore. She let out a whimper of pleasure, then gasped as he lifted her top and reached for the clasp of her bra. The front opening did not deter him, and in no time he'd snapped it open.

"Oh, Madeline."

He'd made her name sound like poetry, and her pulse raced under the heat of his gaze. He cupped both of her naked breasts in his hands, and she closed her eyes in rapture. He circled one nipple with his tongue, then suckled her until she thought she would burst.

"Kurt!" she cried out with longing, her fingers curling over his muscular forearms. He drew her yet closer, and in that intimacy she could feel the rigid power of his shaft. But it was the harsh, uneven rhythm of his breathing that brought her out from under his magnetic spell, back to her common sense. And in that sobering moment, she could only wonder what she'd done?

"No," she said, struggling to get free from his hold.

Instantly he released her, though with a shaken look, he continued to stare. She felt naked and vulnerable, and she rushed to cover herself. "I'm sorry, Kurt. This should never have happened. It's my fault for sending you mixed signals, and I hope you can forgive me." Without another word, she hurried for the seclusion of the bathroom, closing the door behind her.

CHAPTER 7

Son of a bitch! Kurt paced the room, trying to think. Trying not to overreact. Trying to figure a way to get Madeline not to overreact.

Fully aroused, he needed to calm down. He poured a glass of ice water and sat in the chair next to the table. No telling how long she would hide out in the bathroom. Or what she would say once she emerged. Though she'd been partially right. Things shouldn't have gone as far as they had. Not that the chemistry wasn't there or that he hadn't enjoyed every hot-blooded moment of their encounter. Clearly she had too. But the timing was all wrong. He knew she wasn't the kind of woman who would let chemistry rule over protocol. Not indefinitely, anyway.

He should have been the one controlling the pace. Should have given her a little taste, and she'd have been aching for more. Eventually. Instead he'd scared the bejeezus out of her—out of both of them. He couldn't remember the last time he'd felt such intensity for a woman. Maybe he never had. He doubted lust alone would account for it, but this wasn't the time to start an in-depth analysis.

The problem was what to do now? He chugged a healthy swig of water and checked his watch. They needed to eat, especially Madeline. At this point the restaurant next door seemed more neutralizing than eating in the room, and he hoped she would go along with him when he suggested it.

He moved from the chair and stood outside the bathroom

door, listening for some sort of sign. It didn't sound like she was sick or running water. Or, God forbid, crying again. "Hey, are you okay in there?" he called out.

"I'm fine," she answered, in a tone that indicated the direct opposite.

Even so, it would be easier to operate under the assumption she'd told him the truth and move on from there.

"I'm guessing a little change in atmosphere would be good. What do you say to dinner in the restaurant? I could use some food."

A lengthy silence passed before she finally opened the door. "All right," she said. "I'm getting hungry too."

After several minutes studying the menu, Madeline elected to order liver and onions, despite the disapproving look she got from Kurt. The liver because of some inexplicable craving even she couldn't comprehend since she'd hardly been able to tolerate it before she'd gotten pregnant. And the onions—well, possibly they were part of a subconscious plot to deter any further intimacy between the two of them. At least for the remainder of the night. She hoped the meal wouldn't play havoc with her digestive tract.

After the waitress had taken their menus, Madeline was compelled to turn her attention to the man sitting across from her. *The incredibly attractive, sexy man, who'd nearly brought her to the summit only moments into the climb.* No wonder she'd allowed herself to lose control.

Images of what he'd done to her with his hands and mouth came flooding back, and if she weren't careful, she'd be encouraging a repeat performance. All things considered, her principles wouldn't justify such behavior. Embarrassed, she pretended to examine the pictures on the walls, the other patrons—anything to avoid facing him directly.

She had no room in her life for a man like Kurt Williams. He was doting, controlling, and she had no doubt once the baby arrived, he would want a say in everything involving the child. Furthermore, his career, his hobbies and his philosophies gravitated toward danger. She'd picked up on that in a very short time.

Unlike her own upbringing, she had every intention of providing her child with guidance and stability, not another chapter of *living-on-the-edge*. She resented Kurt, big time. Especially now, because she was drawn to him regardless of her resolve to the contrary.

"So, when do you want to head out in the morning?" he asked, casually.

"You're the one who's disrupted your schedule for me. I can be ready whenever you say."

"Tomorrow's Friday. I've got nothing pressing till that interview with Mindy on Sunday. I don't have to be back at work till Monday. So why don't we see what time we wake up and take it from there?"

"That sounds reasonable," she agreed, as the waitress set their meals in front of them. The revolting smell of onions went wafting up her nose. Whatever had possessed her to order them? Kurt gave her a *See, I told you so* look. That alone was enough incentive to begin eating. "Mmm, good," she lied, forcing herself to smile.

He said nothing, but his derisive grin indicated she wasn't fooling him.

If she scraped the onions to the side of the plate, there was a chance she could at least get through enough of the liver to claim she was full.

"Have you given any more thought to what you want to do in terms of a possible lawsuit with the lab or that technician?" he asked. "I checked my phone messages earlier, and my attorney is waiting for me to call her back."

Did Kurt truly want to discuss litigation, or was he just trying to avoid talking about the intimacy they'd shared? He didn't strike her as the type of man to run from anything, let alone conversation about a matter he'd basically initiated. *Basically.* Not that she wanted to talk about it or even knew what she would say. But waiting for the issue to surface was like walking through a minefield. In the meantime, another disquieting thought emerged. It was one thing for *her* to wish it hadn't happened. Somehow it would be far worse if she knew Kurt felt the same way.

"Madeline, did you hear me?"

His question nudged her into locking eyes with him, and even then she couldn't read his expression. Okay, if he wanted to pretend nothing between them had taken place, she could play that game too.

"You know, I had the opportunity to talk with the lab technician the week before my procedure, and I can identify with her. In fact, I like her. I put myself in her place, and if I had been held up at gunpoint, I would have been a basket case. Yet she showed up to perform her job because she knew how important that morning was for me, and she wanted to do the right thing."

"Yeah, but under the circumstances, maybe what she did was irresponsible."

"Her intentions were honorable," Madeline countered. "I happen to know she's a single mom who's raising a toddler. I have no control over whether or not she loses her job because of this, though I just can't bring myself to initiate a lawsuit against her or the fertility clinic. I suppose that makes me a bleeding heart. Or worse, stupid, in light of the severity of the situation. But that's who I am, and I doubt I'll change my mind. Obviously I don't expect you to feel the same way about the situation."

Kurt looked irritated. "I don't see that it's so obvious. Actually, I'm not sure where I stand. I need more time to think this through. I'm not out to hurt anyone or destroy someone's career, but it seems like somebody ought to be accountable. After all, this is a life changing event for both of us, and it's not going away."

"No, it certainly isn't. At least, I would hope not."

"You've already accepted this baby, haven't you Madeline? Even though your husband isn't the father. How did you do that so easily?"

Easily? Kurt's involvement was an intrusion in her life, and she had no idea how to cope-—now or in the future. "My deceased husband," she reminded him. "Don't assume it's easy. But this life I'm carrying is already a part of me, with some of my genes and my attributes."

"And mine," he added, a bit too emphatically for her comfort zone.

He cut into his steak, and she wished she'd had the good sense to order one as well. Instead she took another bite of liver and washed it down with some tea. "I have this philosophy, Kurt. I feel we should all decide what we want from our lives, tangible or otherwise. Once we know, we should do everything we can to attain our goals. Being a realist, I also understand we don't always have control over what happens to us or to those around us."

"No kidding."

"So when I take an action and my plans are thwarted, I presume it's for a reason—even if that reason is a mystery. You may not agree, but I regard it as divine intervention. If a power greater than myself is calling the shots, then I believe it's my role to submit to the alternate plan as best I can."

His eyes sparked. "So, you think I should have just accepted the verdict of Hodgkin's without fighting it? 'Cause it certainly wasn't on my agenda."

"That's ridiculous, and not at all what I meant. You had a life-threatening illness. You did everything within your means to fight it, and you won."

"I hope I won. I believe I've won," he corrected.

"I'm sure you have," she said softly. "Time will prove that. The point is you were forced to engage in a battle you never expected. So you accepted what you couldn't change and dealt with it from the standpoint of what you could control. Like picking the best doctors and researching your treatment options, and then going through with the therapy to cure yourself."

He looked at her, and she realized how she must have sounded. Next she'd be doing *Sermon on the Mount*. "Sorry, sometimes I can be a real Pollyanna."

"Tell me something," he said, with a flicker of his brows. "What if your plan starts out flawed? Can you change course midstream, or do you figure you have to live with your mistake till a higher power comes along to alter it?"

She had a feeling she knew where this was going but said nothing. Instead she let out a suspicious smile.

"For instance, I'm thinking liver and onions might qualify as a good example. Do you plan on cleaning your plate just to show me I was wrong to suggest you order something more palatable? Because I see you gagging every time you swallow that stuff."

"I'll have you know liver is a very nutritionally sound food and good for the baby," she said, in the most convincing voice she could muster. But her insides had already begun to protest.

"Whatever you say."

She took a sip of tea, hoping it would help calm her queasiness. It didn't. "All the same, I think my eyes were bigger than my stomach, and I'm feeling rather full. Should we ask for the check?"

"Uh, do you mind if I finish eating first?"

She needed to get to a restroom. Quickly. She pulled some money from her purse and set it in front of him. "The least I can do is pay for our dinner," she said, rising from her chair. "Please forgive me, but suddenly I'm very tired. I need to get back to the room."

He gave her a look of concern, but before he could say anything, she put her hand out to stop him. "Don't' worry, I'm fine," she said. "I'll see you later." With that, she went running.

Kurt took the money Madeline had given him and counted it out for the check. Beside the fact that she'd been too generous, even including the tip, it made him uncomfortable letting a woman pay for a meal. He supposed that attitude was out of step with the times, especially since they weren't even on an official date. But that's how he felt.

He didn't have to wonder how *she* was feeling. He'd seen that *green* shade on enough people know what it meant. He just hoped she'd made it back to the room in time. He fought an urge to go check on her, figuring she might want some privacy. Instead, he left the restaurant. The mall was a little hike, but he needed the exercise.

For all he'd been through the last couple of days, he should have been tired enough to sleep for a week. Instead, his mind and body had slipped into overdrive, and nothing would shut down. Especially his thoughts. *Madeline, impending fatherhood, skydiving, Hodgkin's, attorneys, lawsuits, sex, Madeline, lovemaking. Madeline.* All this clutter wasn't good, and he quickened his stride, looking for a way to focus.

Skydiving. Maybe he should concentrate more on conquering his fear of flying through the sky—sans a plane. A solo jump? If he did that, all those other concerns could seem like a walk in the park.

The stores were still open, and what better place than a bookstore to find more information on skydiving? At least that had been his intent when he'd first walked in. Instead, he'd somehow gravitated to the aisle with all the volumes on PREGNANCY and PARENTHOOD.

The first book he picked up outlined it well. Nausea, fatigue, frequent bathroom visits. That was Madeline. Even weird food cravings. Which might explain the liver. His eyes were riveted as he scanned the table of contents. Jeez! There were enough topics for a semester of school. And then some. Stuff he'd never thought about. What the hell was membrane rupture? Stuff he wished he could stop thinking about. What kind of father was he going to be? What if he never got the opportunity to find out?

The weight of the demon bore heavily on his shoulder, turning his mouth to cotton, knotting his insides with the whisper of dread, and clouding his vision of a bright future with the reality of uncertainty. What if his worst fears were realized and the Hodgkin's returned?

Then his child would have to grow up like Kurt had grown up—never experiencing the love and attention a real father was supposed to lavish on his offspring. Memories flashed of grade school plays with no father in the audience to clap for his performances, father-son nights that were never attended because there was no point in showing up alone, high school basketball games with no parents to cheer him on—because his mother was always too busy earning the money to keep a roof over their heads.

He knew there were plenty of single parents who had raised, and were currently raising, their children. Admirably. His mother was at the top of the list. But as far as he was personally concerned, he could write his own chapter on why it was so important for him to be a father to his child.

First he had to breathe. And banish the demons. He'd gone into a full-body sweat now, as anxiety began to flood his veins. Losing control was not an option. He'd learned that much from his piloting skills. The advantage of experience was on his side, and he knew he could win this battle with patience.

No one ever died from a little sweat. *Diversion tactics. Keep breathing—don't forget to exhale!* A nearby drinking fountain provided the water that began to cool his body and settle his mind.

"Your probability of a complete cure is ninety-eight percent," Doc Kaplan had told him. The odds couldn't get much better than that, and Kurt would do well to keep them in mind. "You have a greater chance getting hurt bungee jumping than for the Hodgkin's to come back. So don't do it," he'd joked. Kurt gave a wry smile, wondering what Doc Kaplan would be saying about his skydiving adventure.

His breathing steadied, and he knew he would be okay, at least for now. But whether he felt tired or not, his body needed rest and sleep. He would buy the books on pregnancy and study them later. It was time to get back to the hotel and check on Madeline.

Kurt knocked softly from the hallway outside their room. He owed Madeline some warning—in case she happened to be running around naked. *No harm in fantasizing.* On the other hand, if she had managed to fall asleep, the last thing he wanted was to wake her. No response. Which could also mean she was in the bathroom and out of earshot.

He slid the key card in the lock and slowly opened the door. The room was dark, except for the soft light coming from the corner of the room where a lamp had been left on.

"Madeline," he whispered, giving her one last chance to answer. When she didn't, he entered and quietly shut the door.

He found her prone under the covers, her thick curls spilling in disarray around her face. Her breathing convinced him she was sound asleep.

The sight of her triggered primitive yearnings as he relived the kiss they'd shared earlier that night. The kiss and much more. He stood, unable to move, though his conscience protested. Was it voyeurism to stare at this exquisitely beautiful woman? After all, she carried his child. And didn't he have the right, in fact, the obligation, to watch over what was his?

He remembered Madeline's theory about divine intervention. He wasn't too thick to admit that a higher power had played a role in his ongoing recovery. How many times had he pleaded for his life—and been heard? Okay, maybe it was a stretch to consider the possibility that Madeline and the baby had been sent to save him. To force him to live so he could care for them in turn. Then again, what if the idea wasn't so far-fetched? Shit happened. Sometimes for reasons people might never understand.

He was tired. Way overtired to be playing all these mind games. *Unglue your feet from the floor, and haul your weary ass to your own bed,* common sense dictated. Somehow his body obeyed. He turned off the light, threw his clothes onto the nearby chair and tumbled onto the sleeper sofa. If he got lucky, he'd nod off the way she had—instead of spending the remainder of the night fighting off primitive yearnings for the woman mere feet from him.

Madeline stood, letting the warm water from the showerhead glide over her back and shoulders, soothing her tired muscles and calming her rattled nerves. It was after nine o'clock before loud hallway chatter had served as her morning wakeup call. But she didn't have the heart to wake Kurt as well. He slept so soundly that he hadn't even stirred when she'd opened the package of pretzels she'd gotten out of the vending machine the night before, quiet as she'd tried to be. Poor guy, he had to be exhausted.

Checkout time wasn't until noon. There was no reason she shouldn't let him rest a while longer. Besides, the pretzels had quelled her stomach enough to let her move around and function. Maybe she would be up for some real food before they hit the road for the long drive home.

In the meantime, the shower felt heavenly, and she was in no hurry to leave its comfort. She turned forward, uncapped the shampoo bottle, and poured a small amount of the contents over her hair. Some of the lather trickled onto her breasts, and she let her fingers glide over them, realizing they were tender. Funny she hadn't noticed it the night before when Kurt had suckled them.

Was she imagining it, or had they become larger? She saw the pigment around the nipples seemed darker than usual. Her adrenaline spiked at the memory of the way Kurt had touched her, and she wondered if he'd found her attractive. Instinct told her he had, and her flesh came alive with an unexpected tremor of arousal. Suddenly she was lost in the fantasy of what had transpired between the two of them. Only it hadn't been a fantasy. It had really happened.

Her feelings for this man, this unwelcome intruder who'd invaded her life and her space in a way that could now never be erased, were beginning to frighten her. Lust was one thing, but their differences were quite another. Anyone could see how completely ill-suited they were to one another. Yet she was drawn to him.

She forced her hands to her head and vigorously rubbed the shampoo into her scalp, as if the action would shut down her thoughts. It would take three washings before her hair would truly be clean. There was so much of it. Who knew when Kurt might wake up and want to use the bathroom? Best she hurry so she would be showered and ready whenever he wanted to leave. It wouldn't do to keep him waiting.

By the time she'd finished, the bathroom was so steamy the walls were dripping. She wrapped a towel around herself and opened the door a crack to let some air in and to find out whether Kurt was still asleep. She could see him lying face up on the sofa bed, his chest rising and falling with even breaths, and his throat hissing like a teakettle just coming to a boil.

She couldn't help smiling——or staring at this man who looked almost boyish. Yet the flush, hot feelings he stirred in her were unquestionably adult. The piercing ring of the telephone made her jump, and she quickly stepped back into the bathroom.

The phone rang three more times before it stopped. She heard Kurt's voice as he struggled to orient himself and communicate with the caller. Hopefully, there wasn't another problem at Mason Products. The only other person who'd be trying to reach her at the hotel would be Elsie Carlisle, and she generally called Madeline's cell phone. The very last thing she needed was to be required to come up with an explanation to Elsie for why some man was answering her hotel room phone. *Please let the call be for Kurt,* she willed.

"No, you have the right number," Kurt grumbled through early morning congestion. "She just can't come to the phone right now."

Madeline poked her head out from behind the bathroom door. "Is that for me?"

"Excuse me," he said to the caller, without bothering to cover up the mouthpiece. "Yeah, it's Elsie Carlisle."

Wonderful! "Please ask her if she can hold on for a couple of minutes," Madeline whispered, scrambling for something to wear.

"Can you wait while she finds some clothes to put on?" Madeline heard him say. "She's getting out of the shower right now."

Madeline stared at him with her mouth wide open, while Kurt had the audacity to flicker his brows and smile.

Did he think he was amusing? Madeline wondered, rushing to throw a baggy sweater over her soaking wet head. No time for her bra, not with Elsie waiting on the phone to quiz her. Kurt Williams needed a lecture on discretion, which she would deliver once she finished with this dreaded phone conversation. How could she have been so careless as to have left her slacks draped over the chair at the far end of the room? She grabbed her panties and quickly stepped into them. Backwards!

"Madeline, the lady says it's important," Kurt called from the bedroom. "Should I tell her you'll call her back?"

"No," she shouted. Clearly something was going on that she needed to know about. "I'll be right there."

Kurt could think whatever he would think. Modesty aside, she yanked the sweater down as far as it would go, hoping her undies would compensate, and went stomping out into the room.

"Elsie," she said, after snatching the phone away from Kurt. He shook his hand and made a face, as if she'd done him bodily injury. But she knew full well it was all theatrics. Besides, he didn't know from bodily injury.

"What's happening?" Madeline said.

"I might ask you the same thing," Elsie responded.

Might? "Kurt mentioned there was something important going on. Do we have a problem at the office?"

"Kurt. Now would that be the man who was chatting with me while you were scrambling to put on your clothes? He sounded a bit groggy, like he'd just gotten out of bed."

Actually he was still lying in bed, bare-chested and perched on his elbow, eyeing Madeline with as much subtlety as a laser pinpointing its target. The phone cord wasn't long enough for her to reach her slacks without bending over. Not that Kurt would be gentleman enough to hand them to her. Obviously he was aware of her predicament.

"Madeline, are you still there?" Elsie demanded impatiently.

Madeline reached for her slacks in one rapid motion. Seconds later she had them on and zipped. The situation with Elsie called for some sort of detour around the information superhighway. Time to pull rank.

"Elsie," she said in a tone that would have been a lot more difficult to muster if she'd been standing toe to toe with the older woman. "I appreciate your interest, but that's a conversation that's going to have to wait. I really need to know why you called."

Elsie's response came in the form of a loud huff, which meant she was either frustrated or angry. Or both. Madeline braced herself.

"The Martin account is facing an audit, and Jake is quite upset. He has some questions that need to be addressed right away. Julie can take care of that, but not without their file. It seems to have disappeared off the face of the earth. I can't imagine *I* misfiled it," Elsie said, with enough emphasis on the *I* to let Madeline know she was angry. Definitely angry and most likely, hurt. "Of course, it is possible," she added.

"Aw, oh. I'm sorry, Elsie. I locked the folder in my desk just before I left the office on Wednesday. And I have the key here with me." She reached for the notepad and pen on the nightstand. "Give me the phone number, and I'll contact him myself."

Elsie recited the number and Madeline politely begged off, promising to touch base when she returned. She knew calling Jake Martin without his file folder handy was a bad idea, but she would do her best to placate him. She also knew Elsie's nose was out of joint. She would have that problem to fix as well.

In the meantime, there was Kurt. With one hand on her hip, she turned to face him.

CHAPTER 8

"What?" Kurt played innocent with an annoying grin.

"What? You as much as told my assistant I was standing in front of you naked."

"I didn't exactly say that," he countered. "But now that you mention it, you were almost . . ."

"Never mind," she interrupted. "You could have been more judicious with your word choices."

"Sorry," he grumbled. "I was half asleep and just getting my early morning bearings." But his tone was hardly contrite.

"Now I'm in the position of having to come up with an explanation for her as to why I happen to be sharing my hotel room with a man she's never even heard of."

"The fact that I answered the phone, period, put you in that position."

Let's not cloud the issue with facts.

"Though personally, I don't see why," he added, sitting up. He started to throw off the covers, and her heart skipped a beat in nervous anticipation. But then he switched gears, instead leaning up against the head of the sofa bed, his muscular chest heaving in and out as he breathed. "You're a grownup, Madeline. This woman works for you. Why do you feel you have to justify anything to her, particularly when the situation has nothing to do with your business or her?"

"You don't know the nature of my association with Elsie. She's far more than an employee. She's my dear friend; she's been like a second mother to me. That means a lot since my own mother lives out of state. Sometimes the boundaries between our business relationship and our personal connection are hard to define, particularly since I'm her boss. The last thing I want to do is hurt her. I haven't even told her I'm pregnant yet, much less the entire convoluted story."

"Why not? If you're that close, it sounds like she'd be a good person for you to talk to."

"I am planning to confide in her. But everything has been happening so quickly, the right time hasn't presented itself yet."

Kurt looked at his watch. "Speaking of time, it's getting late, and I have to shower. The sooner we hit the road, the sooner we'll get home. Do me a favor and hand me my jeans, please. They're over there on the chair."

So now he was shy? Yesterday he hadn't been one bit timid about climbing out of bed in his navy briefs—briefs so alluring, they'd rendered his eyes the color of cobalt. She handed him his jeans, all the while cognizant of her wet, tangled hair, that her bra was still in the bathroom, and that he'd undoubtedly seen a good portion of her bare rear only moments earlier. He took the jeans from her and actually put them on under the privacy of the covers.

"Hmm, it would have been nice if you'd done the same for me, instead of ogling me while I was struggling to reach my pants."

"I would have if you'd asked," he countered. "You're always going on about how you like to do things for yourself and how you don't want me waiting on you. I'm not a mind reader, you know."

She was beginning to wonder about that. He always seemed to be one step ahead of her moves. In any case, he'd made his point, and she was fresh out of arguments.

He got up and walked into the bathroom. Seconds later he

came out holding her towel and bra. "I'll leave these things with you," he said, setting both items on the bed. "I won't be too long, in case you need to get back in."

"No problem. The sink and mirror are out here anyway. Take your time."

"Oh, and one more thing," he added with a wink. "I promise I'll be in there long enough for you to finish getting dressed and rearrange your undies. Sexy as they are, I think you'll be a lot more comfortable on the long ride home if you're not wearing them backwards."

It was almost nine o'clock at night when Kurt pulled into his driveway. The garage was cluttered with crap he'd been meaning to sort and toss, but he made a path through the rubble, through the laundry room doorway, and into the kitchen. First things first. He dropped his duffel bag in the middle of the floor and grabbed a beer from the refrigerator. One pop of the top, and it was straight to his favorite chair. A black leather recliner that doubled as a makeshift bed on nights when sleep wouldn't come, and the TV acted as his faithful companion. He pulled the lever back and stretched out to contemplate.

The trip home had been exhausting to the point where he'd even let Madeline drive for a couple of hours so he could catch a few zees. In truth, he probably shouldn't have. She was still plenty sick, but putting up a good show, insisting she wanted to do her part. Despite the wrist bands, they'd had to stop a number of times so she could run to the can. She hadn't said, but he knew she'd tossed her lunch. She'd barely eaten any dinner, though he'd strongly encouraged her to drink fluids.

Just before they'd reached her townhouse, they'd stopped at the ice cream place and he'd bought her a milkshake. He'd been adamant about her sipping it in the car and making her promise to finish it after he'd dropped her off. If he kept this up much longer, they'd be inducting him into the Mother-Hen-Hall-of-Fame.

He stared up at the ceiling rehashing the past few days. Life-changing events were hardly a new concept, allowing for all he'd been through. He knew full well how things could turn at the snap of a finger. But damned if he was prepared for the assault that had torpedoed him lately. No question he'd boarded the train for the journey, though maybe it was time to slow the engines so he could study the landscape better.

Take Madeline. Surprisingly, he felt like she'd been in his life for years. In truth, he barely knew who she was—this woman who carried his unborn child. So how come he already had feelings for her? Not that he'd been having the kind of vibes that would propel him to the altar. Hell, he had no clear indication what he felt. Except for the lust part. That was elementary. What red-blooded guy wouldn't yearn for the likes of her?

Which was why he'd decided to change his strategy. No more kissy-face. At least not for a while. Hey, it was what she'd claimed to want, anyway. No parading around in his underwear in front of her, hoping she'd enjoy the scenery. And no more innuendoes. Maybe he'd have to rethink that one. She was fun to tease, and he really couldn't have stopped himself from making that crack about her underpants.

He'd seen legs like hers in the movies, but not on any woman he'd actually known personally. It made him stiff just thinking about what it would feel like to be wrapped up in them, like some kind of present begging to be untied.

But again, that was lust. Slowing down the train meant he needed to find out whether this involvement he felt was based on anything more substantial.

The ring of the phone made him jump. *Shit!* He was in no condition to fly an airplane, and he just hoped Cromwell's bigwigs hadn't had a last minute change in plans. He let his answering machine pick it up.

"Hi, Kurt, I thought you would be home by now." He swallowed hard when he heard the silky smooth tone in Madeline's voice. "In case you're already asleep, I hope this call doesn't wake you. I just wanted to tell you how much I appreciate that you gave up so much of your time to get me to Ohio and back in one piece. And it was nice traveling with you."

Was it? That last admission was a stretch for her, and every fiber in his body beckoned him to leap off the sofa and pick up that phone. But he didn't.

"Um . . . I guess we'll talk again soon. Bye now."

She guessed. Yeah, that was good. Keep her guessing, even though she was right. Maybe the new game plan would have her aching for him so bad, the next time he reached for her he wouldn't get shot down. That way, even it was just lust, at least it would be mutual.

"Good gracious." It was the third time Elsie had said it in response to Madeline's shocking tale. Once more, and Madeline was going to heave. Again. In fact, she was probably going to do that anyway because she'd been foolish enough to go into work Saturday morning without first eating so much as a cracker. She'd been so worried about oversleeping, she hadn't taken any time to think about the ramifications of trying to function on an empty stomach. She wished she'd thought to wear those wrist-bands, even though they only seemed to work sporadically.

"Oh, Elsie," she wailed. "What am I going to do?" For the first time since she'd learned she was carrying Kurt's baby instead of Charles's child, she allowed herself to really break down. All of those other uncharacteristic crying spells had been mini events compared to the sobs that came pouring out of her now, and she reached for the box of tissues.

115

"The first thing you're going to do is sit down before you fall down," Elsie ordered, gently guiding Madeline to the sofa at the far end of her office. "You're as pale as copy paper. Have you had anything to eat?"

She was beginning to hate that question, bearing in mind the number of times Kurt had posed it this past week. The harder she cried, the worse she felt, and without answering Elsie, she simply buried her head in her hands.

"Child," the older woman soothed, cradling her with both arms. "It's all right. Let it all out."

Something about receiving permission to cry made the whole display seem almost ludicrous—and useless. Suddenly Madeline was finished, and she sat upright. Since she'd been pregnant, her moods had become more erratic than the Chicago wind. "I don't know what's happening to me," she said. "I never used to cry about anything."

"Hormones, darling. And by the looks of it, low blood sugar. Sit still a minute."

Elsie left the room, and Madeline grabbed a handful of tissues to mop her tears. By the time she'd finished, Elsie had come back with a cup of peppermint tea and some crackers. And some of her favorite cheese. Bless her heart. Madeline began to eat and sip.

"Now tell me the options you're considering," Elsie said.

"In terms of what?"

"Madeline, you just asked me what you're going to do. Does that mean you're thinking about not going through with the pregnancy?"

"Of course not. I have every intention of carrying this baby to term."

Elsie looked relieved, but she didn't say as much. "Then are you contemplating putting the baby up for adoption once it's born?"

"What kind of question is that? Give up my own flesh and blood?"

"Then it seems to me you know exactly what you're going to do. You've already made the choice to prepare yourself for motherhood."

"And what do I do about Kurt? He's made it clear he intends to be a part of my child's life. I'd never planned on that."

"Hmm, would it be so terrible? After all, he is the baby's biological father. From what you've told me, he does have some rather appealing traits."

"Did I also mention the man is a loose cannon? He decided to jump out of an airplane while we were in Ohio."

"Oh, my," Elsie said. "That was daring. Though I'm not sure it qualifies him as a loose cannon. Assuming he was strapped to a parachute at the time."

"Actually, he was strapped to his instructor. And yes, they had a parachute, which is beside the point. Why would any reasonable person jump out of a perfectly functioning airplane?"

"Did you ask him?"

"He has the crazy idea it's the equivalent of some sort of medical conquest."

Elsie furrowed her brows. "I'm afraid you've lost me on that one."

Madeline turned to face Elsie. Up until the present, she'd been successful at pushing the reference of Kurt's brush with a life-threatening illness on the back burner. But now it was at the forefront of her thoughts, screaming for attention. Her throat felt tight with trepidation.

"There's one more thing I haven't told you," she said, taking a deep breath. "On top of all the other complications of this whole situation, Kurt had Hodgkin's disease awhile back. That's the reason he donated his sperm, on the chance the radiation treatments rendered him sterile. He's in remission now, but I'm a little worried about what effect this might have on the baby."

Elsie looked uneasy. "My heavens. It's no mystery why you're upset. There are more subplots to this story than in a soap opera."

"Tell me about it."

Elsie stood and paced the room. "I happen to know a little about Hodgkin's disease. A good friend of mine had it nearly thirty-five years ago. Keep in mind that medical technology is far more advanced today. Anyway, she recovered nicely. In fact, she went on to marry her high school sweetheart and have two children with him. Everyone in their family is healthy. I understand the prognosis for Hodgkin's is usually quite good, especially if it's caught early. How long has your young man been in remission?"

Her "young man?" Madeline ignored the remark and recalled Kurt's reassuring words. "Actually, he's been healthy for about four years. He said that at the five-year point, he would be considered cured. He also told me his doctor said the disease couldn't be transmitted through Kurt's sperm."

"That all sounds like good news to me. Don't you believe Kurt?"

"It's not that. Although I might rest easier if I could speak with his doctor myself. I don't want to hurt Kurt by making him feel like he's a health threat to anyone, but I'm worried about my baby, Elsie. If that makes me a bad person, an insensitive person, then I'm guilty."

"You're not a bad person, Madeline. I do think your fears might be exaggerated, though I can't say I wouldn't feel the same way if I were in your shoes. If you're that anxious, I'm certain you could find some diplomatic approach in discussing it with Kurt."

Madeline took another swallow of the hot tea, grateful her stomach had begun to calm. "The fact is, he's already told me I could talk to his doctor. Then again, he hasn't offered me the phone number, and so far I haven't been comfortable trying to press the matter. Kurt realizes I'm worried, that this is a lot for me to digest in such a short time. I imagine he'll give me the number soon."

"Have you stopped to think how he must feel? It's a lot on his plate, too. How is he handling it?"

"When he's alone, I'm not sure. Logically, it would make sense that he'd be harboring some serious resentment, but to his credit, he's not taking it out on me. Other than the fact that he's downright maddening," Madeline said. "He's like an annoying draft, always in my face, wanting to feed me, chauffeur me, check up on me, and curtail my activities. If he's acting this way now, what's he going to be like when the baby is born? I'm an independent woman. I don't need a keeper."

"Hmm," Elsie said again.

That exasperating "hmm" usually spilled out when Elsie was mulling over something. Even so, it could be weeks or even months before anyone would find out what it was.

Kurt had slept in then spent a good portion of Saturday afternoon reading the books he'd picked up in Ohio. He'd definitely entered the pregnancy zone. Not that he didn't have reservations about impending fatherhood. One minute he'd be high on the prospect. Seconds later he'd find himself hating that all this had been foisted on him without his prior consent. His emotional perspective was kind of like flying through bad turbulence.

The fact that Madeline had given him an out should have eased his pressure. In reality, she wasn't demanding a damned thing from him. On the contrary, she'd probably love it if he would just disappear. Or maybe not. No matter, it wasn't going to happen. He'd already made up his mind he was in this for the long haul. He had an obligation to his child. Whether or not he would ultimately welcome the idea of parenthood remained to be seen.

His brain was on the way to becoming an informational guidebook for the journey he and Madeline were about to share. Not that she'd quite accepted the concept of the sharing part yet. But that would change. It had to, because whether or not the two of them were drawn to each other, they had another life to figure in. From everything he'd been reading about pregnancy and fatherhood, his participation and support were paramount.

He checked his watch. At five o'clock in the afternoon he hoped she'd be home because it was about time he returned her phone call from the night before. He counted seven rings before she finally picked up. Bad sign, especially if she'd been asleep.

"Hey there," he said, keeping his tone deliberately innocent and cheerful.

"Hi, Kurt," she said softly. Not enough of a clue to know whether she was glad to hear from him, but at least she recognized his voice.

"I got your phone message from last night. Sorry, I'd already crashed." He felt a twinge of guilt, though it wasn't a total lie. "I hope you got some sleep too."

"I did," she said. "In fact, I overslept and got into work late this morning."

"You've had a rough week. Since it's Saturday, I thought you might take the day off."

"I wish I could have. I needed to get caught up after being away."

"Well, you're home now, and I'm wondering if you have any plans for tonight? I thought maybe we could go out for a bite to eat."

"Um . . ."

Her hesitation told him she was about to say no. "I'm flying out of town on Monday. There's a good chance I'll be gone for several days, so it would be nice to see you before I leave."

She let out a tiny groan. "I've already changed into my sweats, and there's nothing on my face but moisturizing cream. In general, I look pretty grungy. Plus I'm kind of tired, Kurt."

"Okay, forget about going out. I'll lay odds you haven't eaten. How 'bout if I come by with some Chinese carry-out and a rented movie? What would you like to see?"

Silence.

"Remember, I already know what you look like with your hair down." *Like a supermodel.* "If it'll make you feel better, I'll wear my sweats too."

"Wear whatever makes you comfortable. Actually there is something I'd like to discuss with you. Does seven o'clock seem okay? That would give me the chance to take a little nap before you get here."

"You got it."

"Oh, Kurt. You don't need to rent a movie. There's a special later tonight on cable television about the origin of classical music. I thought we might watch—if it's all right with you."

"Trying to get me to soak up a little culture, are you?"

"Not you as much as the baby. Actually—"

"I know, I know," he cut her off, "the musical impact on the fetus. You want our baby to be exposed to it and soothed by it from early on."

"Oh, I'm surprised you remembered."

And impressed. He could tell he'd impressed her. He wasn't about to admit the books he'd been reading supported her theory. "Hey, I just hope the kid isn't going to jump at the first sound of an electric guitar."

"We'll have lots of time to talk about that," she said. "I'll see you at seven."

Kurt rang the doorbell exactly on time. Though nothing stood in the way of her greeting him promptly, Madeline decided to make him wait at least thirty more seconds. It wouldn't do to seem too eager.

Somehow she'd never gotten around to that nap. Instead, she'd taken a nice, soothing bath. Who would put on scruffy old sweats after getting all cleaned up? Not Madeline. It made far more sense to wear her beautiful lime green, silk sweater and her black, somewhat form-fitting Capris, while she could still fit into them. Her black, high heel sandals with the green straps were a perfect match, even though she knew they would make her feet hurt. She could always kick them off later. And didn't such lovely clothes demand her to throw on a touch of makeup? She couldn't see any crime in wanting to look nice. Heaven only knew what she'd be like once she started bulging out.

The doorbell rang again, and she took a few seconds to get centered. Even though she told herself this was only an informal get-together for the purpose of tactfully obtaining Doctor Kaplan's telephone number, it felt strangely like a date.

Kurt held two large bags of piping hot food. The smell of garlic went wafting up her nostrils, and she choked down a gag, praying nausea wouldn't rear its ugly head. "Just set everything on the counter," she instructed, as he followed her into the kitchen.

Once his hands were free, she noticed he'd worn sweatpants—and a T-shirt that emphasized his broad shoulders and muscular arms.

In turn, he gave her a head to toe once-over that made her skin tingle. "You're not exactly dressed to go slumming, Madeline. In fact, for a person who described herself as looking 'grungy,' you clean up pretty good. You gave me the impression we were going to be casual tonight, so I dressed accordingly."

"I said to dress comfortably, and you did. You look fine, Kurt. So relax."

"I look like I'm about to mow the lawn. You, on the other hand, look like you've been primping for the past two hours. It wasn't necessary, but I'm flattered."

"I have not been primping," she lied.

"Did you have a nice nap?"

"Not exactly."

"I rest my case. And for the record," he added with a brash grin, "I'm very relaxed. So let's eat."

Once again, he'd bested her. All the same, he'd given her the satisfaction of letting her know her efforts to look good had not gone unnoticed. She turned her back to him and with new-found I-am-woman attitude, strolled over to the kitchen cabinets to get some dishes. She could feel his eyes boring into her. That probably meant he was checking out her butt which, in her view, had already begun the pregnancy spread. Still, she couldn't remember the last time she'd been so conscious of her feminin-ity. Maybe sexuality was the word that more accurately described it.

"What can I do to help?"

"You've already provided the food," she pointed out, with the most charming smile she could muster. "We can either eat in the dining room or right here in the kitchen. Wherever you'd like."

"If we were at my place, we'd be eating on snack trays in the family room, watching the tube."

"I nearly forget about the cable show. Fortunately, it's not on for another half hour," she said. "I don't have a family room. But I do have snack trays, which are next to the bookcase in the living room. Why don't you set them up in front of the sofa while I transfer the food to some serving dishes."

"If we were at my place, we'd be transferring the food from

the cartons directly to our plates," he said.

Something she would have been tempted to do, had she not owned a working dishwasher. Charles would have hated that. Most of their rituals, particularly eating rituals, had been terribly civilized. Furthermore this wasn't Kurt's place. It was hers. "The snack trays," she reminded him, completely ignoring his comment.

"Right." But before heading to the living room, he reached into his wallet and handed her a business card. "This is Doctor Kaplan's phone number. I think you should contact him next week while I'm away. It's important for you to get all your questions on the table, and he's great about explaining everything."

He'd caught her off guard, and their eyes met in awkward silence until she could find her voice. "What about patient confidentiality?"

"Not a problem. He already has my written and verbal permission to be as candid with you about my condition as he feels is necessary, in order to address your concerns."

"Oh. Thank you."

"You're welcome," he said, on his way to the living room.

It was that simple. Here she'd gone and worked herself into a froth over picking the right words to broach the subject. She'd even rehearsed what she might say to lessen the discomfort. Instead, he'd handled the matter before she'd had the chance to botch it up. What a guy. She wondered if getting through the rest of the evening would be as uncomplicated.

She hurried to spoon the food into the dishes before it turned cold, but he was at her side before she'd finished. "All systems are go," he said.

"You brought enough food for a week, Kurt. Literally."

"I wasn't sure how your taste buds would react to Beef with Peanuts and Hot Pepper Sauce. I got enough for both of us, in case I'm wrong, but I figure you're more the Moo Goo Gai Pan type. Don't worry about MSG. The restaurant doesn't use it."

Score another one for the mind reader. "That accounts for two of these containers. Pray tell, what's in the other eight?"

"We got some Steamed Chicken with Vegetables, in case you're up for bland but nutritious, some Egg Rolls, lots of rice, some Hot and Sour Soup, and a few other dishes."

"Kurt, this is very sweet of you, but who's going to eat all of this?"

"You are," he said, looking quite pleased with himself. "I'll be gone till the end of next week, and this way you'll have enough food in the house, and you won't have to cook. You can put some of it in the freezer. It's important that you eat balanced meals, even though you don't always feel like it."

Think before you speak, Madeline.

"You'll notice all the main courses have lots of protein and vegetables. I kept the fat content low, but you can get some carbs from the rice."

She couldn't stop the upward motion of her eyeballs. "What, no chocolate covered strawberries? Think of all the antioxidants and vitamin potential there."

"Vitamins! Good thing you reminded me. I'll be right back."

To her astonishment, he went running out the front door, leaving her to speculate on whether or not he'd been completely oblivious to her condescending response. *Inhale . . . Exhale.* She only hoped she could resist the urge to emit nasty comments about whatever it was he'd gone out to fetch. After all, the man meant well. *Air.* She was starting to feel smothered, and she threw open the kitchen window as wide as it would open.

"Here we go, Madeline," Kurt said, reappearing with a bottle of vitamin pills. "I talked to the nutritionist at my local health food store, and she said these were the best for your particular condition."

"My condition?" The pin on the hand grenade was situated

precariously between his fingers. And he didn't even realize it.

"Pregnant, nauseated, and hormonal. Especially the hormonal part. Did you know mood swings are very common during the first trimester? That's probably why you find yourself crying so much. Actually, chocolate covered strawberries might only aggravate your problem. Once you're teetering on the edge, sugar, chocolate, caffeine—all that stuff can make you go even lower."

The explosion rocked her senses. "Hormonal! You think I'm hormonal? I was in a great mood before you came in here and started treating me like I'm a candidate for the psych ward.

"Did it ever occur to you that I have my own doctor, with his own set of instructions? I don't need you discussing my 'condition' with some nutritional wizard who thinks she can control my disposition with a vitamin pill. Guess what else? I actually know how to cook. Not that I have much interest in eating these days." Her voice had taken on a surprisingly high decibel level. She knew she'd been ranting. Furthermore, she felt energized.

Kurt stood there staring at her, with his arms folded in front of his chest. Wisely, he said nothing.

Madeline stomped over to the pantry and flung open the door. "Look, Kurt," she heard herself screech, as she pulled out a box of unopened chocolates and tore into the cellophane wrapping. "If I want to eat chocolate, I'll damned well eat it." To illustrate her point, she opened the box and popped one of the candies into her mouth. Before she'd even finished chewing it, she took a bite of another. And then a third.

Kurt's eyes widened as he threw up his hands. "Fine! Enjoy your chocolate. If you want to eat cow manure, that's fine too. Whatever makes you happy. And if you want me to treat you like yesterday's flotsam, rather than the woman who is carrying our child, I can do that. Hey, I can act like a jackass. I've certainly had enough practice over the years."

Flotsam? Is that what he'd said? Kurt seemed to be having some sort of conniption. Maybe this hormonal stuff was contagious. In any case, it seemed like a good opening for a time-out. "Um . . . uh . . . it's quite possible I overreacted. A bit."

"Ya think?"

His retort was as sharp as uncut glass, and she shot him a glare to indicate she was far too raw for him to push it. She certainly had no intention of apologizing. After all, she had her limits, and he'd been the one to invite himself over, despite her initial objections. Nonetheless, she was equally certain he hadn't come there for the express purpose of aggravating her—as he had. Admittedly, she'd been on the edgy side.

Suddenly she started to giggle. Kurt stared at her as though she were an alien. Maybe it was the sugar charge, but the more befuddled he looked, the more her laughter rippled through the air. "No, I certainly wouldn't want you treating me like yesterday's flotsam," she managed to say.

Was that a glimmer of amusement he was trying so hard to suppress?

"Does that mean we're still on for dinner? 'Cause I'm getting pretty hungry here."

"Absolutely," she said, handing him a plate. "I'm not really sure how much nutrition I'll be able to get down." Or how much would stay down after she'd indulged in that foolish candy binge on an empty stomach. "But I'll give it my best shot."

That brought a satisfied smile to his face. Moments later the atmosphere had calmed as they sat together in the living room.

"So, before we turn on the television, tell me about your flight on Monday. Where will you be going?"

Kurt brightened. "I'll be flying Mike Jensen and some Cromwell people out to Houghton, Michigan. He's going to be filming a commercial for Cromwell, and hopefully, I'll get to hang around and watch. I'm a real fan of his, and a few days on the Pro Rally course sounds like fun to me."

"Mike Jensen? The race car driver?"

Kurt responded with a look of surprise. "You've heard of him," he said.

"The name sounds familiar. I was at the Indy Five Hundred once, and I'm pretty sure I saw him drive."

"No doubt. Primarily he's part of an open-wheel team. But Cromwell thought the commercial would carry more weight if people could see how well their transmissions hold up under the pressure of unexpected potholes, and muddy, rocky trails that make the Pro Rally circuit so treacherous. What an opportunity, huh?"

Madeline felt a jolt in the pit of her stomach, and it wasn't the kind she'd been experiencing from her pregnancy. Too afraid to quiz him, she could only wonder what type of opportunity Kurt had in mind.

CHAPTER 9

It was Monday afternoon by the time Kurt pulled his rental car into the motel parking lot in Houghton. He couldn't help noticing the For Sale sign on the red, Mazda 323 parked in a spot next to the front entrance. A closer look told him the car was a GTX, and he gave way to the temptation to peer inside. Save for the front seats and the roll cage, the interior was stripped nearly bare.

He supposed the owner would be asking five or six grand for a car that was in such good shape. Being so close to the rally course, somebody was bound to come along and bond with the high-powered econo-box. In the meantime, he was anxious to get to that course himself. Twenty minutes later, after checking in, dumping his luggage and wolfing down a bag of cashew nuts, Kurt was back on the road, mentally replaying the events of the day.

Jasper Cortland, Vice-President of Cromwell, had introduced Kurt to Mike Jensen as soon as they'd boarded the plane earlier that morning. The May weather had cooperated, and the flight in the luxurious Falcon 2000 had been smooth. Because they'd been transporting a celebrity, they'd had the luxury of an attendant on board to serve the passengers. Kurt had taken advantage of the situation to make sure he'd had a few quality moments to interact with Mike Jensen while the co-pilot flew the plane. Mike was around the same age as Kurt, unquestionably drawn to adventure, and couldn't wait to get behind the wheel of the rally car they'd reserved for him. Kurt had liked him right off.

It had taken some time to park the plane and secure it, so Mike and the Cromwell people had gone directly to the motel, then on to the rally course. Kurt's co-pilot had gone off to vacation with friends and would meet up with everyone later in the week. But not Kurt. The scent of thrill had crept into his system, and once he got to that stage, he planned to stick around. With any luck, maybe he'd get the chance to do some driving too.

He thought about the interview he'd had with Mindy Sanders the day before. She'd quizzed him about his motives for his first skydive and whether or not he intended to make another jump. Just talking about it had made him restless for want of another chance, and he planned to go as soon as time and circumstances permitted.

He slowed the car for a yellow light, suddenly realizing he missed Madeline. No reason to wonder how she'd seeped into his testosterone-charged fantasies. She was the epitome of exciting, all by her lonesome. Take the tantrum she'd thrown Saturday night—just because he'd made a few suggestions about her health. It wouldn't hurt her to be a little more open-minded.

Logically, he could understand why she placed so much emphasis on her independence. He still remembered how he'd felt when illness had robbed him that freedom. Yet logic wasn't stopping the part of his brain that turned to mush when it came to Madeline and his unborn child, both of whom he'd begun to think of as his family. This overwhelming urge to protect them seemed natural.

And yes, there was a fine line between protecting and controlling. One he was trying not to cross. Even though it fed his ego to think he could sweep in and take care of everything, he could see Madeline was a capable woman who was used to running her own show. Which was all the more reason to get his own life under control—as soon as he could figure out how.

By the time Kurt made it to the course, it was nearly four o'clock. He was surprised to see so many people hanging around since he'd been told this was a practice day and the film crew wasn't supposed to arrive till morning. There stood Mike, all suited up and standing next to the blue Celica All-Trac, signing autographs and posing for pictures. Apparently news of his arrival had leaked out to his fans.

Kurt spotted Jasper and went over to say hello.

"If this keeps up," Jasper said, "we're going to have to get someone to run interference. Mike's been talking to these people for over two hours, and he's too nice to turn anyone away."

"I could do that," Kurt volunteered. *I'm getting good at pissing people off.*

"Chet, the guy who brought the rally car here, said there were at least four stages he wanted to show Mike. One of them is on a mountain road, and all of them are five miles or longer," Jasper said. "Maybe I should get him to handle these people."

Before Kurt could protest, Chet appeared. "Hey, we gotta get this show on the road," he said, pointing to his watch. "Before you blink, it's gonna be dark."

"Precisely my thinking," Jasper agreed. "Chet, this is Kurt Williams, our corporate pilot. He flew us up here in the company jet."

Kurt and Chet shook hands and then Chet said, "So, why don't you two walk over there with me while I bust up the party. Maybe you guys could do crowd control while Mike and I jump into the rally car and take off."

Chet had it backwards. What Kurt had in mind was busting up the crowd so he could jump into the rally car with Mike. "Actually, from what I know about Pro Rally racing, Mike's going to need a navigator. I got an 'A' in map reading, so why don't I go along with him for the stage tour?"

Chet furrowed his brows. "You ever done any rally racing?"

"Not exactly, but . . ."

"You ever been on any of these roads, especially Eagle Bluff?"

"No, but . . ."

"In that case, I'll have to ask you to stick to navigating the sky. This ain't about a real race. It's about a commercial and the dollars spent making it. Time is money, and so are damaged cars. There are more switchbacks on these roads than hairs on my ass. And I happen to know where all of 'em are. See my point?"

"I see your point." *Jackass.*

Reluctantly Kurt followed Jasper and Chet over to the crowd. Chet immediately jumped into the passenger side of the All-Trac. "Get in," he said to Mike.

The surrounding crowd protested as Mike tried to get in the car. "Come on people," Kurt ordered. "Let's give them some room. Otherwise we'll have to close the set and send everybody packing."

With that, people grumbled but backed away. Mike and Chet took off. "Nice job," Jasper said. "Good thing you showed up. There's no telling what the situation will be like by tomorrow morning."

No, there wasn't, Kurt agreed. But a picture was already beginning to form in his head.

Monday at the office had been non-stop turmoil, and Madeline hadn't gotten home until nearly eight o'clock that evening. She was exhausted, and by some miracle, ravenous. She took hot, Chinese food from the microwave into the living room, kicked off her shoes and turned on the stereo to relax and eat. Admittedly, it was a relief not to have to think about what to cook or how long it would take.

For that, she owed Kurt. The same Kurt who hadn't called her in two days now since she'd chastised him for his thoughtfulness. Chastised him? That was an understatement. She'd been a raving shrew. It's a wonder he hadn't up and left, and taken all of his food with him. She had to give the man credit for his tolerance.

In truth, she'd been glad he'd stayed. Once she'd calmed, they'd actually had a fantastic evening. He could be witty and quite entertaining, when he wanted to be. He'd made her laugh out loud more than once, evoking the kind of guttural response from her that could only be lodged at the depth of one's soul. In fact, she hadn't permitted herself that kind of abandon in so long, she was almost startled by it.

Plus, he hadn't said, "I told you so" when she'd run to the bathroom to toss the chocolate she'd gorged on. Instead, he'd made her a cup of peppermint tea. He'd scored a lot of points for that.

Despite the attention he'd lavished on her, she'd sensed he'd been holding back. How could she blame him for distancing himself after the way she'd been treating him? Especially since he'd kissed her. She'd told him it shouldn't have happened. Not that it should have. She just hadn't figured he'd take her at her word so quickly.

It was almost dark, and in Michigan it was an hour later. She wondered if Kurt had gone to dinner or if he might even be sleeping by now. He'd given her his pager number, his cell number, his home phone and the number of the motel where he was staying.

Just in case she needed to reach him.

For any reason.

Of course, she had no pressing reason to phone him. She'd just seen him two days earlier. Again, they didn't have . . . a relationship. So, she shouldn't be missing him. *But you do miss him, don't you?* She missed double tall lattes too, but it didn't mean all that caffeine had ever been good for her.

Besides, if Kurt wanted to hear from her, he'd have called. And he hadn't.

So he didn't—want to hear from her.

Kurt didn't want to hear from her. Ouch.

Well, she wouldn't stoop to calling him. Not tonight, anyway. Instead, she would finish her meal, and then phone her mother and her sister in Tucson. It was about time they learned of her pregnancy. After she got through the ordeal of trying to explain her situation, and after they got over their initial shock, she needed to ask them some questions about their own pregnancies. Maybe their answers would give her some indication of what she should expect down the road.

It was nearly ten o'clock by the time Kurt got back to his motel room. He threw his jacket on the bed and tore into the fast food bag containing his supper. Two burgers, an order of fries, and an apple he'd picked up at the front desk.

What a day it had been. What a week. He reached for the phone and dialed Madeline's number from memory, hoping he wasn't about to wake her out of a sound sleep. She answered on the first ring.

"What's happening?" he said, without bothering to identify himself.

"Kurt?"

"Yeah, I would have called sooner, but this was the first chance I had. How are you feeling?"

"Tired, a little queasy, certainly not hungry. I've been eating all the delicious food you brought me. I want you to know how much I really appreciate your thoughtfulness," she added.

Now she was thanking him? "My pleasure." He resisted the urge to throw in any comments about it being his responsibility to see to it that the mother of his child didn't become malnourished. Instead he popped a couple of fries into his mouth and tried to chew discreetly.

"Tell me about your trip," she said. "Have you gotten behind the wheel of any race cars yet?"

Not, how was your flight? Or, what's Mike Jensen like? Kurt could feel a pulsing knot in his throat. She'd sure zeroed in on the highlight of his day.

Quickly he washed down the fries with a swallow of mineral water. Though he'd rather have a beer, technically he was working.

"Funny you should ask. I did, but I didn't go very far. Or very fast." Test driving his GTX down Highway 41 in the dark wasn't comparable to high-speed racing.

He heard Madeline sigh and wondered if that meant she was relieved. "So, did Mike let you try out his racing car?"

"Actually, that car belongs to my company. And no, I never really got the chance to ask if I could drive it. Mike was pretty tied up with his fans and the people who are doing the commercial." *You're hedging.*

"Oh. Somehow I had the idea that you and he would be driving around together," she said.

Coincidentally, so did I.

"Then, did you borrow someone else's car and take it for a drive?"

What the hell? It wasn't like he'd been obliged to clear it with her first, so why didn't he just tell her about his purchase? "You know, the neatest thing happened today. I can hardly believe it."

"Try telling me, and let's see if I have that same reaction," she coaxed, in a tone that was a bit too controlled for his comfort level.

"I bought a rally car today."

Glaring silence.

135

"Uh, did you hear me?"

"That's a surprise," she finally said.

"Amazing as it sounds, the car was parked in the motel lot when I drove in. 'Course I wasn't interested in buying it right then." *Not till Chet dissed me in front of my boss and made me look like a buffoon.*

"What changed your mind?" she asked, after another long pause.

"It turns out the only way I'll be able to do any driving is if I supply my own wheels. I wouldn't chance taking a rental on those rough roads. It could get damaged."

"Damaged? How? You're not planning to enter a race, are you?"

"Definitely not." Entering a race and driving fast were two different things. "I'd just like to take a joy ride through some of the courses."

"Not that it's any of my business, but that seems like a big expense for a joy ride."

She was right, it wasn't her business. So why did he feel the need to justify himself? "See, that's the good part. The car belonged to one of the maintenance men at the motel. His son used to own it." *Before he died of carbon monoxide poisoning, running the car in a closed garage in the middle of winter, with no outside hose.* "Before he passed away in a tragic accident."

"His son died driving that car in a race?"

"No, no. It wasn't a driving accident. He wasn't even in the car when he died." He'd been under the hood of the car, adjusting the idle so he could take it for a spin, just before he passed out. "Still, the father is devastated over the loss of his son. The car is kind of an in-your-face reminder of the boy and how much he loved racing. So, he sold it to me dirt cheap." *One thousand dollars in American Express Traveler's Checks. Never leave home without them.*

"Dirt cheap. Why would he do that?"

Because it's a small town, and everyone who knew the story felt like the car had bad Karma. "On the one hand, I guess the father would like to see the car get driven because that's what his son would have wanted. On the other hand, I think having the car around was like rubbing salt in his wounds. The poor guy just wants to get on with his life."

"I see."

Judging by her caustic tone, he wouldn't be surprised if she did.

"And how will you get the car back here? Don't you have to fly the plane home?"

It wasn't like he hadn't asked himself the same question after the owner had signed over the title. "I'll figure something out, but I have several options. By the way, have you called Doctor Kaplan?" That's it. Change the damned subject before she asks how the kid really died.

"Um. I thought about doing that today, but things were chaotic at the office. I didn't even get home till an hour ago."

"Madeline, it's late."

"Don't forget it's an hour earlier here."

"Doesn't matter. You need rest. How much sleep are you getting?"

"Not enough. I think if I slept ten hours a night, it wouldn't be sufficient. I'm always tired lately."

Kurt looked at his watch and felt guilty for staying on the phone with her this long. "You know, you might not be able to keep up this pace indefinitely. The sooner you start delegating, the more time people will have to get used to taking on more responsibility. And, in the long run, the more control you'll have over your business."

"You're probably right. I'm just so used to handling things."

"When I put my plane on auto pilot, I'm still handling it. It's just that it makes it easier to do other things I might need to do at the same time I'm up in the air. Know what I mean?"

"Yes, I think I do," she said, with a laugh.

"Why don't you go to bed, and I'll check in with you tomorrow."

"I'll take that advice. Oh, and Kurt, please don't do anything reckless."

One "goodnight" later, she'd hung up the phone.

"He bought a race car," Madeline said to Elsie, as they sat in her office having tea. "I'm beginning to wonder if Kurt Williams has a death wish."

"Oh, honey, don't you think that's overreacting a bit?"

Madeline stood and paced the room in her stocking feet, having given up her high-heeled shoes the minute her last client for the day walked out the door. "I don't know what to think, Elsie. Honestly I don't. I called his doctor this afternoon, and we had a very interesting conversation."

"Are you talking about his oncologist?"

"Yes, Doctor Kaplan. He was very reassuring about the Hodgkin's not being any health threat to the baby."

"And what about Kurt's health?"

"Well, that's the interesting part. Doctor Kaplan feels Kurt has the potential to live a long and healthy life."

"The potential?"

"In other words, if he dies young, Doctor Kaplan doubts it will be from Hodgkin's disease. But he doesn't think Kurt is convinced of that. Not deep down inside."

Elsie stood, and now they were both pacing: "Did you tell him about the skydiving incident?"

"Yes, and about the racing car. He didn't seem surprised. He's known Kurt for almost five years now, and from the start he could see Kurt is a risk-taker who loves a challenge. I suppose you would need that kind of personality to be a pilot. But there's a difference in taking a responsible risk and being reckless. Apparently this *you-only-go-around-once* behavior is something that started after Kurt went into remission."

"But again, Madeline, it's not like he jumped without a chute. So is that being reckless?"

"I don't know. I'm not sure Doctor Kaplan does either. It's just an underlying uneasiness I have, based on some of the things Kurt has told me."

"You don't think he's trying to kill himself?"

"Not consciously. On the contrary, I think he's terrified of getting sick again. I told Doctor Kaplan I wondered if Kurt is trying to prove he's invincible. You know, by being brave and confrontational in the face of lethal danger, he can survive anything."

"Maybe that isn't necessarily a bad thing, Madeline. People do have different coping mechanisms."

"That's one way of looking at it. But if Kurt's motivations for taking part in all of these activities are skewed, he'll be more apt to take chances he shouldn't and make mistakes. What if the outcome is unhealthy? Or worse, maybe even deadly?"

"I understand your concerns, dear. If I were in your shoes, I might be thinking the same way. Then again, we're all going to die someday. There are simply no guarantees about how much time any of us has on this earth."

Madeline felt a headache coming on and rubbed her forehead. "I realize nobody gets out of here alive. But sometimes it's hard enough to play the hand you're dealt, without deliberately looking for trouble. If Kurt keeps pushing the envelope, I'm afraid he may leave this world prematurely. The last thing I want is to become emotionally involved with someone who isn't going to be in it for the long haul. I've done that twice now, and it's way too painful."

The early morning darkness was dominant when Kurt drove the Mazda out of the motel parking lot. He gave careful attention to engine and gearbox noise, gauges, and the feel of the car. As he approached the mountain road, a hint of the sun rose above the towering peak in the distance. He preferred to think of that as a good omen, counteracting the "bad Karma" he'd been warned about the day before.

It didn't scare him that Robert Parker's son, Jack, had died working on the car he now drove. In fact, it fueled him to know that his only competitors were nature, the car—and himself. He knew he could best them all. The poor kid had made a mistake in judgment, thinking it wasn't dangerous running an engine in a closed up space. If only just for a minute. Kurt was much smarter than that.

Still, he hadn't mentioned buying the car to Jasper or to Mike. Not after the way he'd been excluded from all the fun yesterday. Oh sure, he'd been issued a pass for the closed set filming. Did they think he wanted to hang around to do more "crowd control?" Well, he wasn't being paid to do that. Nor had he promised anyone he would. His obligations to Cromwell on this trip were to stay sober, wear his pager and carry his cell phone, so he could be on call to fly the company plane at a moment's notice. He was good on all three counts.

He'd managed to secure some maps of the stages they planned to use for the filming, and he knew the mountain drive was scheduled to be last. That meant he would be first. After listening to Mike talk about the thrill of Eagle Bluff, he wasn't about to be left out of the equation.

Robert Parker had been nice enough to throw in his son's helmet and fire suit. The kid must have been a head taller than

Kurt, but no matter. He made do with the fit.

He'd gone about six miles from the turn-off on M26 when he saw the road leading to the mountain base. Two bouncer-type guys stood guard over the saw horses forming the street barricade. Kurt stopped the car while one of them came over to deliver his spiel.

"Sorry, this road is closed to the public today," he said. "They're doing some rally racing on the Bluff, and you can't get in without a special pass."

"Will this do?" Kurt said, pulling out the document he'd been given.

"Yes, sir," said the guard, examining the pass. "You one of the racers?"

"In a manner of speaking," Kurt answered. "Can I go on through now?"

"With that, the two men moved the barricade, and Kurt drove a couple of blocks to the starting line. He fastened his helmet, then dropped the clutch to spin the tires. Not that it would get him to the top any faster, but the noise helped to mask the thundering of his heart.

He tried to swallow, but there was no spit. Compliments of the radiation he'd had or his adrenaline kicking in. Or both. What did it matter? It was time. He took a breath, then trounced the gas pedal. Up the hill for a short distance, then a sharp left. Straight for a few seconds more, then a 180-degree right, followed by a left. Higher still and gaining speed.

The road was filled with asphalt patches that made the surface rough and the ride brutal. Somehow the needle on the speedometer touched eighty. When he came to the blind crest, the scream of the engine sent him airborne. It was a far less secure airborne than the Piper offered. He came down like a rocket, the pavement beneath him unforgiving, his bladder threatening to burst. But unlike the demons in his head, the mountain was tangible—an accessible enemy. And he would not let it win.

Was that water on the windshield? Freaking drizzle? Another curve, shifting into third, then fourth and then a right-hander. Off the throttle, tap, tap, pound on the brakes. "Shit!" He wasn't going to make it. The sound of grinding gears competed with a course that was now slick with fresh-fallen rain.

The Mazda veered off the road, slinging mud in all directions and squeezing through trees toward the gully ahead. All at once, time stood still. The car stopped moving and Kurt dared not breathe. The driver's side of the hood was nose down in the ditch, held secure only by the muddy leaves and tree branches in its path. The passenger side of the car dangled over the mountain ledge, threatening to plunge forward at the slightest provocation.

Icy fear knotted Kurt's throat, and he whispered a prayer. Years of flight training had paid off while he fought not to act in panic. One wrong move had the potential to send him flying over the edge. This time with no parachute or tandem master to guide him. His cell phone was deep in his pocket, but the digging motion could be his last.

With the engine still running, he considered his options. Throwing the car in reverse to back up the hill was next to impossible. But the balance was in his favor. If he kept to the left and managed to open his door, he might be able to slide out of the car. Climbing back up the hill to the road was another matter.

It could be hours, if at all, before anyone would come to his rescue. In the meantime, the rain continued to fall, making the ground beneath him all the more unstable. Maybe the Mazda had bad karma after all.

Wouldn't it be ironic if his story ended before he ever had the chance to find out if he would have made it to the five-year mark? The notion of leaving this world before he would ever lay eyes on his unborn child wasn't one he cared to foster. Add to that the idea he might never have the chance to love Madeline— that he might never get the opportunity to share his life with her. Those were his catalysts to action.

Slowly, he turned off the engine. With calculated caution, he began to pry open his door, praying the frame wasn't bent. The wind picked up, and beads of sweat formed on his brow as the car swayed. His fear intensified when a gust of wind held the door closed. The car began to turn, sliding farther to the right.

It was now or not. Kurt pushed with all his strength, creating an opening large enough for him to escape from the vehicle. He grabbed for a nearby branch as he started to fall downward, then forced his legs apart, hoping he would latch onto something that would save him. His right foot caught on a solid mass, holding him steady while the car continued to plunge toward the ledge.

"Please, God!" he said aloud, making himself focus on the terrain above. As if an angel had come and loaned him wings, Kurt found another branch with which to pull himself up, and a rock to climb higher still. Then another branch and another ledge. And by some miracle, he made it to the road.

He sat on the wet pavement to catch his breath and whisper thanks, then dared to look at his car, dangling by a seeming thread. The rain had stopped, and once again the sun put in an appearance. Yet, the Mazda seemed doomed to go crashing to the ground.

He reached for his cell phone but as he began to dial, he heard the sound of car engines. The Park Ranger? The County Road Commission? Quickly he stood. The film crew. It was the film crew, followed by the Celica All-Trac that Mike Jensen was driving. The whole fucking caravan had slowed to witness his predicament.

Chet was the first one off the truck. "Holy shit!" he said, his eyes focused on the skid marks leading to the GTX, now swinging in the breeze. "What the hell did you do?"

Mike left his car and came running over. "Are you okay, Kurt?"

"I'm fine," he said. *Definitely humiliated, though.* "A little shook up is all."

"I was wondering where you were this morning," Mike said.

"Well, now you know." And judging by the film crew pointing their cameras, there was definite potential for lots of other people to know too. "I don't suppose anybody has an idea about how we might stop my car from falling through those trees?"

"I've got a winch on my pick-up," Chet said. "But it'll be damned tricky getting it hooked up. Time consuming too," he added, with emphasis.

"Yeah, I know. Time is money," Kurt said, not even trying to keep the frustration out of his voice. "Just send me your bill."

CHAPTER 10

"What were you thinking?" Mike said to Kurt, once the two men were alone in the restaurant.

It had taken all day for the smoke to clear, and Kurt was tired of fielding questions from everyone. All he really wanted now was some down time and a shower. And to call Madeline. But he'd agreed to have dinner with Mike, especially since Jasper was tied up in some meeting.

"Actually, I was thinking it was a great day to go for a ride."

Mike raised a brow.

"A fast ride," Kurt amended.

"You're not trained. If you wanted to race, you should have taken a co-pilot with you. At least someone to navigate. Hell, why didn't you ask me?"

"You were busy. I thought it would have been an imposition."

"I would have worked something out."

"I appreciate that." He did. He liked Mike. "In fact it would have been the highlight of my trip. Sadly, my company isn't paying you to go joyriding with me."

Mike threw up his hands in exasperation.

"Hey," Kurt continued defensively, "I was on my own time, in my own car, on a road that was designated for racing. I had clearance to be there, and I didn't endanger anyone else's life. So what's the problem? It's not like I broke any laws."

"How about the law of averages?" Mike asked. "The one that dictates if you don't learn to recognize the limits before you

145

challenge them, some day your luck might run out. Don't tell me you planned to finish your little excursion with your car hanging off that mountain ledge."

No, that had never been part of the plan. Kurt felt his jaw tighten. On the other hand, here he stood, all in one piece, talking about the whole fiasco.

"That's not exactly how things ended. Fortunately, they were able to save the Mazda. Granted, the back axle got pulled from the frame, but the rest of it can be used for parts. Chet was happier than a pig in slop to take the car in trade for the rescue mission."

Mike let out a sigh and shook his head. "You know, looking at you is like looking at my clone ten years ago. Before I woke up. You'd better figure out what's driving you, man. Next time you might not be so fortunate."

Yeah, but Kurt would worry about next time when and if it came. Because now was all the time he had for sure. And for now, he'd won another round with the Grim Reaper.

"Kurt, Sunday is Mother's Day," Madeline said, over the phone. "You should be spending it with your own mother instead of making plans with me."

"Mom's with her sister in Michigan. She's helping out while my aunt is recovering from a broken leg. Lucky for me they're less than an hour from Houghton, so I had the chance to take both of them to dinner last Thursday. We had a great visit."

"Aren't you the model son?" she said, thinking it was probably true.

"So, here's the plan," he said. "I'll pick you up at ten-thirty tomorrow morning. Brunch is at eleven. The weatherman is predicting sunshine and temperatures in the seventies. After we've eaten, we'll walk along the river for a while and then head over to my place."

"You're pretty sure of yourself. What if I say I can't make it?"

"I promise to be charming."

Of that, she had little doubt. His offer was tempting, but the more time she spent with him, the harder it was going to be for her to get on with her life the way she'd planned it. Just her and the baby—and no one else to interfere. No one else to disappear and break her heart. This was war, even if it was her own internal discord.

"I know your mother lives in Tucson," he persisted. "Unless she flew into town. Did she?"

"No, I had to settle for sending her roses. Of course, I'll call her tomorrow and spend some time catching up. After that I need to get over to my office. Truthfully I'm on overload, and I was planning to get some work done while it's quiet and no one can disturb me."

"Hmm," he grumbled with irritation. "I thought we agreed you were going to start delegating."

"Yes, though there are some things no one else can do. It is my company, you know."

"I also know if you keep pushing yourself like this, there's bound to be a breaking point."

Talk about the pot calling the kettle black. On the other hand, she did have to eat. Plus, a walk along the river after brunch was an appealing idea. If she gave in, it wouldn't be like she was throwing the entire war up for grabs. It was brunch, for heaven's sake.

"How about if you change the reservation to two o'clock and pick me up at my office around one-thirty? We'll still have time for the park. I can't promise I'll have energy for anything beyond that."

She was drawing the line at going to his house. By leaving her car at work, he would have to take her back to pick it up. She could beg off then.

"You drive a hard bargain, Madeline. It was tough enough getting last-minute reservations for Mother's Day. I don't suppose it's going to be too easy to change them now. But I'll figure something out."

"Where are we going, by the way?"

"Mill Race Inn."

"Oh! Their food is fantastic, and the river view is so soothing. I love that place."

"Enough to stick to the original plan?"

"I'll see you at one-thirty, Kurt."

At quarter after one on Sunday, Madeline walked down the office hallway to the restroom. As long as Kurt was going to all the trouble of taking her to brunch, she wanted to at least run a comb through her hair and refresh her makeup. She'd opted to wear her new, loose-fitting, print dress and cushy sandals. Comfortable, yet stylish was becoming her new mantra.

Fifteen minutes later she checked her watch and realized Kurt had no way of getting into the building. She took the stairs down to the lobby, figuring it would be quicker than waiting for the elevator. There he stood, hands behind his back, right outside the entrance door, grinning like a kid who'd just gotten a new toy. Was he hiding something? Her pulse quickened at his good looks, and it disturbed her to realize the more she resolved to put distance between them, the more she was drawn to him.

"Hi," she said, after opening the door. "I hope you haven't been waiting long. I seem to be the only one in the building today, and I completely forgot about the lobby being locked until now."

"That's okay, I just got here."

"I'm ready, but we have to run back to my office to get my briefcase. Once I lock up and set the alarm, I don't want to have to do it again."

"Yeah, sure, let's go back to your office."

A delicious scent went wafting up her nose. Definitely, he was hiding something behind his back. She noticed part of a basket swinging out from beyond his thigh. Was he carrying food? They stepped into the elevator, and she hit the third floor button while Kurt continued to beam the entire ride up.

"All right, what's going on?" she finally insisted, as they walked into her reception area.

"Bad news first," he said, not looking all that disturbed. "I wasn't able to change the reservations. Here's the good news." With that he produced a picnic basket from behind his back and set it on top of the front desk.

"What's all this?" she asked, feeling an eager sense of expectation.

"This would be the brunch I promised. It turns out by the time the restaurant would be able to accommodate us, the sun would be setting. I saw no point in wasting the chance to enjoy this beautiful day. So, after we eat, we can head out to the park."

"My goodness, something smells wonderful."

"It's always a good sign when the aroma of food appeals to you."

"I'm learning to take it a minute at a time. For now, I'm fine."

"In that case, go over and sit on your office chair and turn toward the wall."

"What?" she said, with a guarded smile.

"Please," he added. "Try meditating or something till I can get everything ready."

She was too taken aback to offer any resistance. In truth, she couldn't remember the last time anyone had gone to the trouble of arranging a surprise of any sort for her. Not even Charles. The feeling of hopeful anticipation clashed with her uneasiness, and she fought to stay quiet, trying to regain some modicum of inner composure. Maybe Kurt was on to something by suggesting she meditate.

After what seemed like an eternity, he turned her chair to face him. He had cut the overhead fluorescent lights, and now four burning candles illuminated the room. A small tape recorder had been placed on top of the nearby end table, and Kurt hit the play button. Soft, classical music served as background for the sumptuous feast sitting on the blanket he'd spread out on the floor in front of them.

"Oh wow!" she exclaimed. There were warm chicken breasts and pasta salad with artichoke hearts and Kalamata olives. An assortment of cheese slices and liver pâté decorated a tray, along with her favorite hazelnut crackers. He'd brought a selection of herbal teas, bottled juices, and even grape juice champagne, which he proceeded to open and pour into real crystal flutes. Then she spotted the chocolate covered strawberries.

This was a very elaborate picnic he'd put together, and she bit her lip to keep from tearing up. Then, to her dismay, she began to tremble.

"You're shivering," he said. "Are you cold? I'll get my jacket to put over your shoulders."

"I'm not cold."

"Is your blood sugar getting low? I knew we should have eaten earlier."

"No," she said, turning to face him. "I'm just feeling overwhelmed. I've never had anyone make such a fuss over me before."

"I can't believe that," Madeline. "A woman like you—your husband must have been falling all over himself trying to—"

"Believe it," she said, deliberately cutting him off. She didn't want to think about Charles right now, or about the lack of passion in their marriage. She didn't want to think at all. She just wanted to feel. Right now she felt like a queen. In a palace. With her king.

She turned away from him to focus on the brunch, and moved from the chair to the carpeted floor. "How did you put all of this together? Candles! Music! Crystal?"

"Well," he admitted sheepishly. "That part of the surprise was an afterthought from a friend who has a great carryout business. She'd thought it would be a nice touch."

"She was right."

"*But*—I did coat the strawberries myself. I actually bought the darkest chocolate I could find so you would have the full benefit of all the antioxidants."

Madeline smiled. "You remembered how much I love chocolate covered strawberries. What a special gift that you made these just for me." With that, she reached for the platter.

He caught her hand. "They're supposed to be for dessert." All the same, he looked pleased. "I promise they're worth the wait."

"And how would you know that?" she insisted, her hand still midair, touching his.

"Uh, I did a taste test. You know, to be sure I wasn't going to poison you or anything."

With that, he picked up one of the berries by the stem and put it to her lips. She took a bite of the luscious fruit, letting the chocolate melt over her tongue. The creamy, sweet taste made her spine tingle, and she closed her eyes to savor the experience.

"These are heavenly," she finally said. "You must have some."

His blues eyes darkened, remaining fixed on her, though he didn't move. "I think it's more fun watching you eat them," he said.

For a few seconds she forgot to breathe. "Nonsense." She picked up a berry, and as he'd done for her, she put it to his lips. But, instead of taking a bite, he began to lick the chocolate. Her pulse skittered. No question he'd mastered Tongue Skills 101. Suddenly she was flooded with feminine longing, and her thoughts turned to the fact that it had been such a very long time since . . . *Hello! Do you really want to lose your heart to someone who lives on the edge of a cliff?*

"My mother always taught me not to play with my food," Madeline said, looking away from him, trying to free herself from his spell.

"Maybe your mother missed the boat on that one. Parents don't know everything."

On the other hand, Dad had always told her to keep her options open.

"So, does that mean you'll teach our child to play with food?"

"Children don't need to be taught those things," he said, popping the entire strawberry into his mouth and practically swallowing it whole. "It's instinctual. It's when we become adults and turn all mature that we forget how to play. You should learn to loosen up a little, Madeline. Broaden your horizons."

With that, he spread pâté on some crackers and placed them on a real china dish. Then he handed one of the treats to her. "See, I remembered your passion for liver, too."

"You're bad," she said, taking a bite.

"Lady, you have no idea how bad I can be."

Maybe not, but she was getting a pretty clear picture. Where could she go after that? She did her best to maintain some emotional distance while they finished eating, asking Kurt about his trip, his car, and making generic conversation. She was surprised when he told her he'd sold his Mazda to someone in Michigan. Surprised, yet relieved, that he seemed to have gotten rally racing out of his system so quickly.

She went to the ladies room, and by the time she returned to the office, he'd already repacked the picnic basket and cleaned up the entire mess.

"I would have helped," she said. "Why are you catering to me like this?"

"Because it's Mother's Day, and you're carrying our child. Regardless of how it happened, it means something to me. I want to convey that."

She stared at him for a moment, trying to think how she should respond. "It means something to me too, Kurt. But my emotions are so jumbled over the situation I don't have a handle on them yet. I do know this is the nicest, most memorable brunch I've ever had. And I appreciate all the trouble you've taken to pull it off. Though I'm not sure I deserve this much attention, considering the way I've treated you."

Kurt smiled at her. "The day's not over. How 'bout we head to the park and get a little exercise?"

"Fresh air sounds good right now," she agreed, grabbing her briefcase and purse, while Kurt took the basket. Madeline set the office alarm, and they walked to the elevator and stepped in. She pressed the ground floor button to start their descent. A descent that lasted approximately three seconds. Before the journey came to a thudding halt.

"Oh no," she said, setting her belongings on the elevator floor. She tried not to panic. "People have been getting stuck on this elevator for the past several weeks, but I thought the problem had finally been fixed. Usually, if you wait a while and then start pressing buttons, the computer will reset itself."

"Usually? What happens if the computer doesn't reset itself?"

He would have to bring up that possibility. "Then we hit the alarm signal, and someone comes to help."

"Hmm." His voice remained amazingly calm. "I was under the impression we're the only ones in the building."

Her skin started to itch, and those luscious chocolate covered berries were giving her heartburn. "You do raise a valid point.

Which is why we have this," she said, opening the little door that was supposed to house the emergency phone. "It's gone, Kurt! Somebody took the damned telephone out of here."

That was the first time he'd heard her swear. Why couldn't he have waited to see if the elevator would start to work on its own before asking all the questions? One look at her fearful expression told him she was claustrophobic. All he needed now was for her to go ballistic.

"I left my cell phone in the car," she said. "I realized it when I got inside the building this morning, but since my office phones work, I didn't even think to go back out to get it. Of all days."

"Chill. I have mine." No need to mention the likelihood of getting an outside signal in such a confined space was slim.

"Oh, good," she said, though the relief in her tone was marginal. "Maybe we should dial nine-one-one."

"Sure. We can always do that." Not that he was anxious to put it to the test. "If you want to deal with people busting the front doors to get in the building. Then we'll have to contact a security company to replace the broken glass or, at the least, fix the locks. Don't forget this is a holiday, so it could be a long time before somebody shows up."

She fell silent, and he saw she was considering what he'd said.

"Well, I suppose it would make more sense to wait a bit and see if the problem corrects itself."

"Exactly," he said, hoping the strategy would work.

She sank to the floor, and he sat down beside her. "Look at it this way. We have plenty of leftover food and all kinds of stuff to drink. We even have a blanket."

"How long do you think we're going to be stuck here?" she asked, with an anxious tone.

"Hard to tell. I'm not sure what's wrong with this elevator, but we'll be fine. Trust me to take care of you, Madeline."

She turned to face him and in that instant, she knew she was safe. No matter what, he wouldn't let anything bad happen to her. Even so, she was confined to a space the size of a walk-in closet. With no windows and no way to know what was going on around her. She hated that, and once again she began to shiver.

"Scoot forward," he said. When she did, he sat behind her, enveloping her with his arms and legs. "Just lean into me and relax."

She did that too. If he'd been taller, the back of her head might have fallen just below his chin. But because they were close in height, her cheek brushed against his. He smoothed her hair behind her ear, and she felt his breath warming her face.

"Are you comfortable?" he asked, as if nothing were wrong. As if they weren't trapped like two animals in a cage.

"Not exactly. But I'm getting there," she answered, realizing it was true.

He stroked her arms and pulled her closer, up against the wide expanse of his chest. "At least you're not shivering any-more."

No, she wasn't. In fact, her blood seemed to be heating with rapid speed. She actually felt the beat of his heart against her back. And she could feel pulsing in a lower part of his anatomy, as well.

Her body had been void of intimacy for so very long—aching for this kind of touch. There was a high voltage current in that elevator that could ignite a blazing fire—with the right catalyst. But Kurt sat subdued, his movements constrained to warming her arms. Instinct told her he would not activate a connection that might be threatening to her. She would have to first offer a sign. *Decide, Madeline. Decide what you want.*

"Are you still hungry?" he asked.

Oh, yes, she had a hunger that permeated her very core. "Starved," she answered.

He stopped rubbing her arms. "Really? I'll open the picnic basket."

"No, Kurt."

The rhythm of his breathing changed to deeper swells.

A knot rose in her throat when his eyes met with hers. "What I'm craving isn't inside that basket."

"Be more specific," he said.

She hesitated, then turned and gently traced the outline of his lips with her little finger. "Is that precise enough?" she whispered.

"I don't think so." With that he took her little finger into his mouth and sucked on the tip.

With newfound daring, she drew back her hand and lightly touched her lips to his. Then she kissed the hollow of his throat. "How about that? Does that give you any more indication of what I'm craving?"

His breathing grew labored, and he steadied her cheek with his hand. The kiss that followed was urgent, as he captured her lips. His tongue met with the corners of her mouth, coaxing her to open and taste him further. When she did, the sweet sensation made her feel heady. The man had lit a brushfire, then doused the flames by ending the kiss far too abruptly.

"I know what you're hungry for, Madeline," he said, with seductive emphasis. "I just need to understand whether you're looking for an appetizer or the whole enchilada. This is serious, and we're in a place where neither of us can leave right now. I don't want you getting spooked, in case I've got my signals crossed. Know what I mean?"

His caution made her trust him all the more. Still, she owed it to both of them to take a moment to reconsider. Certainly, Charles would never have gone along with anything so audacious. Charles had been methodical and in charge of his emotions. He'd been civilized. There was a time and place for everything, and he would have been adamant about this being neither the time nor the place. But Charles was gone.

Kurt was here. With her. Call it pregnancy hormones; call it lust. Or maybe she felt something deeper. She wanted him in the most personal way. "Right now, my appetite is voracious," she said. "Know what *I* mean?"

"Oh, that's sexy," he said, in a voice gone husky with desire. "I don't have to be told twice." He moved her legs over his until she'd turned, directly facing him. His fingers worked quickly to undo the front buttons of her dress, and he slid the top portion down over her shoulders. She was glad she'd worn her new yellow bra with the front opening and matching panties—and that her tummy wasn't bulging out of them yet. Still, her breasts were tender, and swollen enough to give her some much needed cleavage.

His gaze traveled from her eyes to her chest. Then he ran his thumbs over the sheer satin until her nipples were taut and begging for release. Without undressing her, he flicked his tongue along the crevice that separated them. Already, she was wet. She let a whimper of pleasure escape as he opened the clasp, allowing her breasts to spill out into his hands.

Self-conscious about the darkened color her nipples had taken on since the pregnancy, she looked away. But he tilted her chin, forcing her to look at him. "Everything about you is beautiful," he said. "Everything."

Despite the air of sophisticated experience she was trying to portray, she felt herself blushing to the roots of her hair. "Maybe you should reserve judgment until you've seen for yourself."

"I already know I'm right, but if that's an invitation, I'm on it," he said, slipping his hands inside her dress and sliding it off her body with accomplished ease.

No, that hadn't been an invitation. It had simply been the timid ramblings of a woman who had little experience in giving of herself with wanton abandon.

She and Charles had begun dating in high school. Up to this point, he had been her first and only lover. This was so unlike anything she'd ever shared with him.

She held her breath as Kurt drank in the sight of her near naked body, save for the scant cover the lingerie provided. From somewhere, he produced the blanket and threw it down on the elevator floor. "You'll be more comfortable with a little padding underneath you," he said.

It wasn't like she didn't want to let herself go. Undeniably, she did. "Maybe you should be my padding, Kurt. After we get these clothes off of you." With quivering hands, she started to unbutton his shirt. Had she really said that to him?

He shook his head and grinned. "Not that I wouldn't enjoy being the waves beneath your sails, but you sure are full of surprises today."

That was an understatement. She wasn't used to asking for what she wanted, not when it came to intimacy. Moreover, she wasn't used to getting it, and she hoped she wasn't jumping in over her head.

Nonetheless, she continued to rid him of his clothes. One pulse-pounding tug on his zipper told her he was as aroused as she. He didn't wait for her to remove his pants. Or his shoes and socks. Now they were both nearly naked.

This time he wore burgundy briefs, the hot color only accentuating the proof of his readiness. He was so handsome, so virile looking, so—intimidating. She froze, unable to do anything but stare.

"Hey, come here." His voice was gentle, as he knelt before her with his arms outstretched. Shyly, she fell into his embrace. He held her close and smoothed her hair. "One word from you, and this doesn't have to go any further," he said. "If you're not sure . . ."

"I'm sure, Kurt. I'm just nervous. It's been a long time for me."

"Me too. On both counts."

She pulled away enough to study his face. "But I thought . . ."

"What? What did you think?"

"I mean, you're single, you're good-looking, you're a pilot . . ."

Kurt grinned, that sexy smile that made her go all weak inside.

"I don't know about good-looking, but it's nice of you to say it."

Good-looking didn't cover it. The man was breathtaking.

"I'm thirty-four years old, Madeline. I'm not a virgin. But contrary to what you might have heard about male pilots, most of us don't have women waiting at every stop."

"I didn't mean to imply you're promiscuous," she said.

"Good. Because I'm not into meaningless sex. Unless it's with myself," he qualified.

She coughed at his implication, but he didn't flinch.

"Well, it's the truth, and these days people ought to behave responsibly. Don't you think?"

"Yes, I do," she answered. "Charles has been gone for over a year now, and there hasn't been anyone since."

With that, he grabbed his pants and pulled a condom from his wallet. Then he took her hand and placed it directly on his arousal. "As you can see, I haven't lost focus."

Before she could respond, he put his hands inside her panties and slipped them down over her hips, onto the floor, rendering her naked. He laid her on the blanket and took her breast into his mouth, devouring her like the chocolate on that strawberry she'd watched him eat. At the same time he slipped his finger into her most intimate spot, slowly at first, then with deeper rhythmic penetration, as she cried out with pleasure.

He added another finger and more pulsating movement, until she thought she would burst. "Oh, Kurt!"

"Are you okay? I don't want to hurt you or the baby."

"I'm fine. I want to make you feel this good."

"Trust me, you are," he said, sitting her up like she was a featherweight. Then he took off his briefs. "Believe me now?"

Obviously he was comfortable with his nudity. She was not nearly so at ease. Yet, she couldn't help looking to see that he was large and swollen—and magnificent. There was no fumbling when he fastened the condom. Then he swooped her onto his body so she lay facing him with his back on the floor. "Let me be your mattress," he said. "It's what you wanted."

She bonded to his chest and felt his arousal between her legs. "Would it be all right if you just held me this way for awhile?" she asked.

"It would be more than all right."

She felt his hands stroking her hair, her back, the curve of her spine, and then lower. Until his fingers became feathers caressing her bottom. The sensation was stimulating. Extremely stimulating.

Her need for gratification had surpassed her fear, and suddenly it became paramount. She squirmed in an effort to position herself so he could fill her.

Kurt was a quick study, and with skillful maneuver, they were one. She gasped at the thrill of his entry.

"Are you sure you're okay?" he asked again.

"Definitely," she said, feeling the gate to her femininity open still wider, to accommodate him. His initial thrust sent a wave of adrenaline shooting up her spine, and she tensed her bottom, thinking she might peak right then.

"Let it happen. Let yourself go," he said.

One more thrust, and she would be powerless to resist. But

she did not want to reach the crest without him. Dropping a knee to each side of his hips, she sat up and began to move up and down.

"Oh!" he groaned loudly. Still very much inside of her, he held onto her arms and scooted upward, so they sat facing each other.

Together they rocked back and forth. Then a deep plunge, another thrust, and one more pulsating move. He called out her name at the same instant she shattered. "Kurt!" she cried, realizing this was the first time she'd ever experienced this kind of bliss.

He laid his chin on her shoulder and continued to hold her tight. "That was mind-blowing," he whispered.

With that, the elevator lurched.

CHAPTER 11

"I might have accidentally leaned into one of the control buttons," Kurt said, as the elevator began to move. He scrambled for their clothes and handed Madeline her dress. "We're on our way down. Throw this on quick, in case somebody's waiting for us when we stop."

Frantically, Madeline put on the dress and shoved her bra and panties into her purse. By the time the doors slid open, she was still barefoot and disheveled, and Kurt had only managed to get his pants on. There, in front of them, stood Elsie Carlisle.

"Goodness gracious, you scared me!" Elsie said. "I really wasn't expecting anyone to be on the elevator."

They scared her? Madeline was mortified. How was she going to explain this? "What brings you here?" she managed to ask the older woman.

"I was just on my way home from spending the day with my son and daughter-in-law. I saw your car in the parking lot, and I was concerned that you were spending the holiday all by yourself, working. Besides, I wanted to thank you for the beautiful flowers you sent me."

"Oh, you're very welcome. Happy Mother's Day to you, Elsie."

"Uh, why don't we continue this conversation in the lobby?" Kurt suggested, motioning Madeline to exit the elevator while he followed. With shirt and shoes in hand, he flashed Elsie that disarming smile of his. "Lucky you came along," he said. We've

Fly Me to Paradise

been stuck in that elevator a long time, and it sure was hot in there. I thought Madeline was going to faint, so I made her take off her shoes."

Madeline couldn't quite make that connection, and she wasn't sure Elsie would either. Nonetheless, Kurt threw on his shirt while Elsie watched, quietly taking in his story.

"I was beginning to think we were going to suffocate in there," he continued, without missing a beat.

"Elsie Carlisle, this is Kurt Williams," Madeline interjected. "Elsie is my office manager and dear friend."

Elsie's face lit up. "It's nice to meet you, Kurt," she said, extending her hand to his.

"And you must be the lovely lady Madeline has told me so much about. She's always singing your praises and telling me she doesn't know what she would do without you."

Elsie actually blushed, and she definitely looked pleased. The man was good; she'd give him that.

"Heavens! What a horrible way to spend the afternoon. Are the two of you all right?" she quizzed. "Is there anything I can do?"

"We'll be fine now that you've rescued us," Madeline answered. "Wait till tomorrow morning though. I'll have a few choice words for the maintenance people who assured me the elevator had been repaired. In the meantime, I think we'd better put up a sign telling everyone to take the stairs." She reached into her briefcase, pulled out some paper from her legal pad and jotted off a note to the affect. "Now all I need is some tape."

"I don't have any tape, but I have gum," Kurt said, reaching into his pocket and accidentally pulling out the empty condom wrapper.

Help me, Jesus! Madeline prayed, while Elsie's eyes widened to saucer size.

"Whoops, wrong pocket," Kurt announced, swiftly pulling the gum out and stuffing the wrapper back inside, as though nothing out of the ordinary had occurred. Before long he'd chewed enough to fasten the paper to the wall. "It may not be hygienic, but it works."

"Indeed it does," Elsie said, with a smile. "Well, now that I can see you're both all right, I'll be on my way home."

"Yes, we'll be leaving too, just as soon as I make a quick stop in the restroom to freshen up." *And to put on my underwear.*

"You drive safely now," Kurt said, "and enjoy the rest of your evening."

"The same to both of you," Elsie called on her way out of the building.

Madeline let out a sigh of relief at Elsie's departure, even though she knew the older woman would be seeking further details at the first available opportunity.

Madeline drove her car out of the parking lot, trailing Kurt onto the street. So much had happened that she no longer had the energy for a walk along the river. All the same, she and Kurt needed to talk, which was why she'd agreed to follow him to his house. Things between them had changed. Considerably.

She'd never planned on letting her guard down, though now that she'd had sex with the man, she supposed it was reasonable for them to have some discussion about new parameters. *Not sex, Madeline. Admit it; the two of you made love.* Every fiber of her being glowed with the memory of their encounter. Just thinking about the feel of his kiss, his hands—his body joined with hers, stirred her to the core.

Suddenly she slammed on the brakes, realizing he'd stopped for a red light. And she almost hadn't. Adrenaline went streaming through her veins with such force, it cleared her sinuses.

Kurt looked into his rear-view mirror, spreading his hands

apart to signal his concern that she'd avoided rear-ending his vehicle by about six inches.

She mouthed, "I'm sorry." Still, the minute the light turned green, he pulled off the main road onto a side street. She drove right behind him, stopped her car, and braced herself for a lecture.

"I'm really sorry," she said again, as he ran to her side window.

"You okay? What happened?" he asked.

"I made a stupid mistake. I'm a good driver. Usually. I guess I got distracted."

"Oh yeah," he said, with a sly look. "Too many things to think about, huh?"

"Maybe." She couldn't help smiling at the inference.

"Think you can manage to concentrate on the road for another five minutes or so? We're almost at my place. Once we get there, you can let your thoughts run wild."

"If you're concerned about it, I could go home instead," she said, baiting him.

"Not unless you want me to follow you there."

"Just drive, Kurt. I promise not to slam into you."

He flashed her a satisfied grin and got back into his car, heading west on Route 38, then north on Route 25. She thought about his reaction. If that had been Charles, she wouldn't have gotten off with teasing banter. He would have been furious and yelling. How strange that Charles had been so zealous about his anger, yet when it came to intimacy he'd been so programmed and reserved. Whereas Kurt . . . well, he was full of surprises. And raw passion.

It wasn't long before they pulled into his driveway. The cedar-sided ranch looked like it had been renovated, and it was beautiful. "You didn't tell me you live on the river," she said, getting out of her car as he came toward her.

"I have to say I love it here. You should see the sunsets from my deck. Come on, I'll give you the nickel tour by way of the backyard first."

She didn't resist when his muscular hand blanketed hers, and he guided her down the sloping sidewalk to the large, grassy area behind the house.

"You have a canoe," she said, spotting it in the grass near the shoreline.

"I'd take you out on it, but it's getting a little chilly for a trip along the river tonight. I don't want you catching a cold. We'll have plenty of time for rides later on in the summer when it warms up."

Rides. In the plural sense. She wanted to hate that he was making long-term plans for them, since it was so contrary to the vision she'd had for them merely a day earlier. In truth, the only thing she could conjure hatred for was the fact that the more time she spent with Kurt, the more irresistible he became to her.

"Oh, look at the mama duck with her babies over there," she said. "I count six of them."

"We have geese and swans and even a couple of herons that live around here too."

The sound of water splashing against the stone wall edging his yard was tranquilizing. "It's so peaceful here, Kurt. What must it be like to wake up in the morning to such beautiful surroundings?"

"You could find out," he said, suggestively.

"I didn't mean . . . I wasn't hinting."

"Neither was I. Hinting. I was stating fact."

"Um, you were right when you said it's starting to get cold out here," she said, trying to skirt the subject.

He pointed toward the brick patio in front of the basement entrance and unlocked the French doors. They stepped inside the huge, walkout recreation room, complete with pool table, bar and entertainment center.

"Kurt, this is incredible! Was the basement like this when you bought the house?"

"Nope. It's all the result of hard work and sweat. Mine. And lots of all-nighters. I wasn't sleeping much then anyway," he added. "It helped pass the time."

"You did this while you were sick?"

"Pretty much after I finished the radiation treatments," he said. "I told you I've had some bad head trips. I suppose all this activity was therapeutic for me."

"You've done a remarkable job. I'll bet you've had some great parties in this house."

"Not too many, actually. Mostly just my buddies who come over to hang out and play pool."

His eyes glazed over, and she could tell he was remembering something. Or somebody. It was obvious someone had broken his heart. He'd alluded to it that night at the oasis, on their way to Ohio. Though he'd been clear in letting her know he didn't want to talk about it. Still, she wondered. Now, more so, because she seemed to be fighting an odd pang of jealousy. *You have no right,* she told herself.

"If you need to use the bathroom, there's one around the corner," he said. "Otherwise, we can head upstairs."

"For a change, I don't. Brunch even stayed down, despite that I had a couple of anxious moments in the elevator."

"Heck, I did my best to divert your attention."

"I would have to say your efforts were successful. Including the way you handled Elsie. She was putty in your hands."

"I do aim to please."

Oh, his aim was definitely pleasing.

"Ladies first," he said, pointing the way to the stairs.

The climb ended in the kitchen, which immediately impressed her, in a different way than the basement area had. The room was spacious, though the cabinets were the old-fashioned metal type, and things were strewn all over the counters. Not dirty, just messy. He studied her face, obviously waiting for her comments. "So, this is the kitchen," she finally said.

Kurt began to laugh. "That was diplomatic. I know the place isn't as tidy as your house, but I'm a bachelor. I'm not home that much, and when I am, I'm not too neurotic about cleaning."

"Are you saying I am?"

"Not exactly."

"Well, the room does have potential—with the right flooring, countertops, and cabinets. If you ever decide to renovate, I'll bet we could . . ." What was she saying?

He stood there with his arms folded in front of his chest and a gleam in his eyes as she fell silent.

"Go on. Continue. We could what?" he pressed.

"I just meant that I love to redecorate. So if you ever need any help, maybe I could make some suggestions."

"I'll bet. Fact is, I was thinking about redoing part of the house. Don't be surprised if I take you up on that offer at some point."

They made their way through the family room off the kitchen, down the hallway, glancing at two bedrooms and the main bathroom, which also needed work, as far as she was concerned. Then they reached his bedroom. He stepped into the spacious area first, walked over to the window, then looked back at her standing in the doorway. For some reason, it seemed dangerous to be in that room with him.

"I won't bite," he said.

Was she that transparent?

"Come take a look at my river view."

Timidly, she stepped in and walked over to stand beside him. Any reservations she had quickly took a back seat to the sight of the brilliant orange sun, as it began to sink beyond the trees at the other side of the river. The purple-gray and gold-red hues of the sky formed a spectacular display. "It's mesmerizing," she said. "I could stay here all night, looking out this window."

"Yes, you could. Stay here all night."

While she hadn't meant that as another innuendo, his eyes met hers as he waited for her reaction. Some sort of magnetic impulse drove her to his arms, and then to his lips, until she felt the searing heat of his kiss.

Euphoria.

It was the only word to identify the sensation that had overtaken her, making her cling to him.

Until uncertainty made her pull away. This wasn't supposed to be happening. His labored breathing was palpable through the awkward silence that passed between them, telling her he'd been just as affected.

"This room was the deal maker for me when I bought the house six years ago," he finally said. "I was only twenty-eight then, but I already recognized the significance of harmony with nature. I knew I had to have this place."

Harmony in a relationship was even more imperative, as far as she was concerned. How could she ever have that with Kurt when they were so completely opposite? As much as she'd sometimes resented the orderly, methodical way in which her life had been with Charles, she could see merit to the system. Meals were on time, the house stayed clean, work and recreation schedules were maintained. Sure, there hadn't been much spontaneity. Then again, there hadn't been much clutter either. There was nothing wrong in raising a child who respected order, discipline and culture. How much of that would their baby get from Kurt?

Come on, Madeline. How trivial is clutter? Children need parents who are going to stick around for them. They're entitled.

She'd been entitled. Just like wives needed their husbands. She'd lost out on both counts, and wasn't that the real issue? "We should talk," she said.

"I was thinking that too. You'd probably be more comfortable in the family room." He led the way, muttering what sounded like, " 'Course I have no objection to staying in the bedroom."

Madeline pretended not to hear him.

"My leather recliner is the most comfortable seat in the house," he offered, with a sweeping motion.

"I appreciate the sacrifice. But if I get in that chair, I'll have a hard time getting out of it. Especially now because I'm tired. You take it, Kurt."

"If you insist."

She smiled at the forced reluctance in his tone and positioned herself on the sofa directly across from him. She watched while he settled in, sliding so far back the recliner almost became a bed.

Just then the phone rang, and he let out a sigh. "Murphy's Law."

"I'll get that for you," she offered.

"No, relax. The answering machine is in the kitchen, and I've got the volume turned up. If somebody wants to get my attention, they'll leave a message."

"Hey, Kurt. This is Mike Jensen," the caller said. "Just checking to see how you're doing after your race car fiasco."

Kurt's eyebrows furrowed, and he struggled to hurry out of the chair. Meanwhile, Mike continued to speak. "I'm sending you a copy of the video they shot of your car hanging off the edge of that mountain. Next time you get the urge to do something insane, you might want to take a look at what almost happened. It's a pretty scary reminder. Call me when you can, buddy. I'd like to hear from you."

Kurt reached the phone in time for the hang-up click. He

swore under his breath, and Madeline could see he was upset. He really *was* living his life on the edge of a cliff. Why hadn't she paid attention to the logic that had been screaming at her ever since she'd laid eyes on this man? No, instead she'd let hormones dictate her moves. And her heart.

She rose, grateful that her car was in the driveway. She wanted to leave. Then he caught her gaze.

Had to leave.

"It's been a long day, Kurt. I'm tired."

"No!" he exploded. "No," he said again, his tone more controlled. "I can see you're far from tired. You're pumped up over what you just heard. At least let me explain."

"What? That your new Mazda fell off the side of a mountain? You told me you sold your car while you were in Michigan. Was that just something you said to placate me so I wouldn't ask too many questions about your trip?"

"Please, Madeline, give me a chance to tell you what happened."

She stood, rubbing her forehead, battling with her emotions. "You need to give me a chance to tell you what happened! To Charles. My husband was perfection personified. He wasn't reckless, he never tempted fate, he didn't break laws, and he never sped. Until one day when he did—trying not to be late for a meeting with a new client. That's all it took, really. Just that one time. Whatever possessed him to go eighty-five miles an hour when the limit was fifty, I'll never know. It wasn't part of his psychological make-up. But it doesn't matter because he wrapped his car around a tree. And now he's dead."

"I'm sorry. I didn't know," he said quietly.

"Would it have made any difference? You are who you are. You like to take chances with your life, and I . . ."

"Madeline!" he interrupted. "Hear me out."

Wordlessly, she sat back down on the sofa.

"Thank you," he said, facing her squarely. "First off, the Mazda didn't fall off the mountain, and neither did I. I took the car up there for a tour the morning they started filming the commercial. It's not like I was doing a hundred miles an hour. I sure wasn't racing anyone. In fact, I was the only one in the area at the time."

He paused and began pacing back and forth. "It started to rain, and the road got a little slick. The climb wasn't a straight shot, so you couldn't really see that far ahead. When I went around a corner, I landed in a gully."

Madeline took a nervous breath. "Go on."

"Unfortunately, the gully wasn't far from the ledge, and the car started to slip further down. I got out okay. You can see I'm here and in one piece."

She had to admit he didn't look or act any worse for the wear. "So you left your car dangling at the edge?"

"In a manner of speaking. It wasn't exactly hanging by a thread. Before I knew it, Mike came along with the film crew, and they were able to pull the car back onto the road. At which point, one of the guys really did take it off my hands. I traded the car in exchange for his help."

"And that's all there was to it?" she pressed. "Mike drives race cars for a living, so I would think he wouldn't be prone to exaggerating danger. He made it sound like . . ."

"Like a scene from a movie," Kurt interrupted. "Mike is used to the limelight. It's a lot of theatrics with these guys. In reality, the worst of the situation was that I drove the car like a rank amateur, and the pros will never let me live it down. I'm supposed to be a pilot."

"You are a pilot. Considering your job status, you must be a very good one. I don't see what one thing has to do with the other."

"Can we drop this subject now, Madeline?"

His abruptness jolted her. "Yes, I guess we can." She got up from the sofa and slung her purse strap over her shoulder. "I should be leaving anyway."

"That's not what I meant. I was hoping we could move on to other topics. Considering the day we've had, I think we have more significant matters to talk about."

"Maybe we should discuss your lifestyle versus my lifestyle and my expectations," she said.

"Fair enough. I'm all ears."

She laid her purse on the sofa and stood toe to toe with him, knowing full well she was on overload. And that she was likely to say something she might regret later. "I don't want to sound presumptuous, and maybe I'm getting way ahead of myself. Still, you are the baby's biological father."

"Madeline, dancing around your concerns isn't going to solve any problems, so please say what's on your mind, and we'll work it out."

"That's just it. I don't know if we can work it out. I don't feel I have the right to tell you how to run your life. Worse yet, if you knuckle to my edicts only because I ask you to, it won't be long before you start resenting me, maybe even hating me. That would be very detrimental to our child's development."

"Not to mention whatever's developing between us. Good thing I got an F in Knuckling 101."

"Kurt, I'm being serious."

"And mysterious. I'm still not sure what we're talking about."

"I'm talking about this need you have to prove something. That you can beat death. At least I think that's what you're trying to do. It's an intriguing goal, if the irony weren't that you keep putting yourself in situations that could wind up killing you."

"You think I have a death wish?"

"I don't know. If you do, I doubt it's on a conscious level."

"It's not on any level. I have everything to live for. Especially now."

She wanted him to elaborate, but dared not ask. Instead she took a deep breath. "I know you grew up without a father, Kurt. My father had a heart attack and died when I was only ten. I loved him so much, and there was such a void in my life when he left. For years I felt completely abandoned. When my husband died in that car accident, the cycle started all over again. Nobody could have predicted either of those events. But you—you're like a tragedy waiting to materialize."

"No, Madeline. I fought hard to hang onto my life. I'm still fighting."

"Well, I don't understand this battleground you've chosen. I do understand heartbreak, and I don't need any more of it. I might be reading too much into what happened today. All the same, it meant something to me. Which seems like a really good reason to take a step back and do some serious thinking."

"It meant something to me too. You have to believe that."

She took a breath, trying to keep from crying. "Kurt, I can't talk about this anymore tonight. I'm tired. I need some rest and some time alone."

"Sure you do. I was just being selfish. Why don't you let me take you home?"

"No. That would be silly since I have my car. And we'd have a dilemma come tomorrow morning when both of us need to get to work. I'm all right."

"Then I'll walk you to your car."

His tone said there was no point in arguing, so together they went outside. Night had erased the majesty of the sunset and with it, the purity of what they'd shared earlier that afternoon. Doubts and worry now marred the sanctity of her memories.

He stepped in front of the car door so she couldn't open it, then placed his hands over her shoulders. "Don't let that phone call spoil what we've begun to cultivate."

The moon provided just enough light for her to see his pleading expression, but she could not respond. Not with words. Gently, he kissed her forehead, and her heart went soaring. If she didn't get out of there, she was going to fall apart. Then he opened her car door.

"Will you call me when you get home?" he asked.

She slid in and started the engine. "I'll be fine, Kurt," she managed to choke out, before fastening her seatbelt and locking the doors. She turned away from him so that he couldn't see the tears spilling down her cheeks, and she just hoped she could see well enough to back out of his driveway.

CHAPTER 12

Month Four

"We should go shopping," Elsie insisted. "All the stores are having sales and before you know it, you'll need maternity clothes."

Madeline patted her expanding abdomen. "The fact of the matter is I need them now. But it's the middle of the afternoon on a workday. Why the sudden interest in shopping?"

"I wouldn't call it sudden. The malls are like my second home, especially since I lost my Edward. Even if I don't buy anything, the walking is good exercise. And I enjoy getting out and talking to people."

What people? Strangers? Madeline had been so preoccupied with her own troubles as of late; she hadn't given much thought to Elsie's personal life. It sounded like she might be lonely and looking for company.

"Well, it has been a while since I've treated myself to new clothes of any sort. You're tempting me, Elsie."

"You surely don't have to feel guilty. For a change, we're actually caught up around here."

"You're caught up," Madeline corrected. "I still have a few hours' worth of work I could put in. Though I suppose it's nothing that can't wait."

"Does that mean we can go to the mall?"

Elsie's voice had taken on an "oh, goody" quality. It was a side of her Madeline rarely saw, and it gave her pause. "Why not," she relented. "It sounds like a fun idea."

"I was hoping you would say that. Maybe we can have an early dinner too? You do need a diversion."

"Yes, absolutely on the dinner. Now, what is it that I need a diversion from?"

"Madeline, you've been out of sorts ever since that day I caught you and Kurt in the midst of your elevator love-in."

"Love-in?" She pretended to be shocked, when in reality she'd expected Elsie to broach the subject long before now.

"For heaven's sake! I'm sixty-seven years old. I know when two people have been caught 'in the act,' so to speak. At any rate, it's nothing to be ashamed of. I'm rather envious that you had such an escapade."

Madeline raised her brows at Elsie's admission. Now she was shocked.

"At least I was until I saw the aftermath. What is going on between you and that darling young man?"

"When did you upgrade him to 'darling' status?"

"Right around the time he started making random pilgrimages to the office with plates of cheese and fruit for you. And flowers for me, no less. He's so thoughtful—and so concerned about your welfare. What I don't understand is your lack of enthusiasm when he comes to visit. Did you two have a falling out?"

"Elsie, it's not like we're a couple, you know."

"All right, dear, if you don't want to confide in me . . ."

"I kind of do want to talk about Kurt. It's just that I'm so confused about my feelings for him. It's like riding a seesaw. By the time I tell you one thing, I'm already starting to go in another direction."

"All this vacillation could have something to do with the state of your hormones."

Madeline pursed her lips into an angry curl. "You know, if

one more person suggests that to me . . ."

"I didn't mean it as a criticism, Madeline. Forgive me. I don't seem to be much comfort to you these days."

This was the woman who'd mothered her as an adult during the many times when her own mother had been painfully inadequate and absent. This was the woman who'd encouraged and supported her during the startup of her accounting business—the one who'd worked many late nights right along with her. This was the woman who'd insisted on staying with her the night of Charles's death—the person who'd nurtured her through his wake and funeral and had even helped her plan the arrangements. One glance at her downtrodden face, and Madeline felt consumed with guilt.

Immediately she went to her with outstretched arms. "Oh, Elsie, I didn't mean to snap at you. I'm the one who needs forgiveness. I guess I am hormonal."

Elsie returned the hug affectionately. "I was only trying to point out that pregnancy can sometimes alter the way a woman reasons. It's been forty years since I gave birth to my son. I still remember my tolerance level being at an all time low the entire time I was carrying him."

"Yes, but my situation—" Madeline stopped cold, realizing her feelings were so muddled, she had no idea how to put them all into words.

"Your situation is compounded by the fact that you never intended the father of this baby to be Kurt," Elsie finished for her. "Under other circumstances, I think Kurt Williams is a man you would be terribly drawn to."

Not exactly. In truth, Madeline was drawn to Kurt despite the circumstances. And that was a big part of the problem, seeing as how she didn't want to be attracted to a man who had the potential to cause his own premature death. All of this lack of enthusiasm she'd been displaying for him was simply show.

In order to make him realize what she already knew. The two of them together amounted to a bad mix—like putting chocolate sauce on eggs.

"You know, it goes much further than the issue of resentment over the lab mistake." Madeline took a deep, cleansing breath. "How does Woodfield sound?"

"Like you're changing the subject. But Woodfield Mall is my favorite, and I haven't been there in a while."

"Tell you what. Get your things together and let's book before we get caught in rush hour traffic."

"Book?"

Madeline sighed. "I guess I picked that up from Kurt. He says it when he's in a hurry. Anyway, I'll be happy to drive. We'll do some power shopping, and then we can continue this discussion over dinner."

"I'll hold you to that, Madeline."

"So, how's this for business professional," Madeline said to Elsie, glancing at her reflection in the dressing room's three-way mirror.

"I think the colors are stunning on you, dear. All three pieces are washable. That's certainly a plus. The entire outfit should travel well. It's a far cry from the maternity clothes that were available in my day."

Madeline smiled. "You should be a fashion consultant. No, I take that back because then you wouldn't be my office manager, and that would definitely be a loss for me."

"Don't worry. I'm not planning to go anywhere."

"Still, you've talked me into three pairs of slacks, two jackets and four interchangeable tops. Not counting this outfit. I'm through shopping for myself. Your turn."

"I want to talk with you about that," Elsie said, as Madeline got dressed and gathered her bargains. "I need a couple of new outfits."

"Any special occasion?"

"Actually, I have a dinner date on Saturday night, and I want to be sporting a certain look."

"A dinner date. You mean, with a man?"

"Well . . . yes."

"How exciting!" Elsie had been widowed for ten years and since Madeline had known her, she'd never even spoken of the desire to date anyone. "Who's the lucky guy?"

"His name is Henry Burbank. He's taking me to a supper club, and we're going dancing." They made their way to the cashier so Madeline could pay for all of her finds. Then Elsie steered them toward the evening dresses.

"I'm afraid I'm into a plus size now" she said, regretfully. "I was hoping you could help me pick something that's not too matronly."

"How dressy are we talking?"

"Henry did say it's a very nice restaurant. I'm sure he'll wear a suit."

Madeline spotted a turquoise, sleeveless, tea length dress with a matching jacket and pulled it off the rack. "This fabric looks fluid," she said, "like it would be comfortable for dancing."

"It's beautiful," Elsie agreed. Between the two of them, it wasn't long before they'd gathered a sizeable selection waiting to be tried on. Madeline sat in the dressing room watching Elsie model each dress, helping her narrow down the choices.

"So, tell me about Henry. For starters, how and when did you meet him?"

"Oddly enough, I met him last Sunday at the cemetery. I was there putting flowers on my husband's grave."

"Really?"

"The strange part being that my Edward has been gone for ten years now, and I've never seen Henry before. It turns out his wife is buried just a few sites over. Of course, she's only been gone a couple of years. Still, I visit the cemetery quite often," she added, struggling with the zipper on her next try-on.

"Let me help you with that," Madeline offered, leaping to her feet. Seconds later, she gave the "nay" on the dress. "Makes you look like an aging prom queen," she said.

"I'm afraid you're right. What is it with clothing manufacturers? Do they think all the nice things should only be reserved for people with perfect figures?"

"There's nothing wrong with your figure, Elsie."

"We both know I've gotten a bit portly, especially since I lost Edward."

"Nonsense. You're a beautiful woman. You have lovely skin and your thick hair is enviable."

"It's gray," Elsie said.

"Silver. A divine shade of silver that shouldn't be tampered with by any hair dye. With your coloring, the whole package is very attractive. We'll find something lovely for you to wear. We just have to be persistent."

"Aren't you wonderful for my ego? In any case, Henry and I got to talking and one thing led to another. I wound up having coffee with him that very afternoon."

"Do tell."

"We sat in the restaurant chatting, and before I knew it, three hours had gone by."

"Wow! That must have been some conversation."

"Enough of one that I found him to be quite fascinating. He's a writer."

"That is interesting," Madeline said, unzipping the prom dress and exchanging it with Elsie for a beautiful burgundy colored dress that seemed a bit more age appropriate. "What does he write?"

"He's working on a screen play right now." Her face grew animated. "It's a thriller, and he told me the plot, which had me practically hopping out of my seat. Of course, he swore me to secrecy."

"Of course. So, a screen play. How impressive. Has he sold it to anyone, or is he writing it on speculation?"

"He says he's hoping to get the attention of an agent once he's finished."

"I see. Hmm. Henry Burbank. The name doesn't sound familiar to me. What else has he written?"

"I'm not sure he's published anything you'd recognize," Elsie said. "He did allude to a few newspaper articles he wrote for the *Herald* awhile back."

"Oh. Is writing his full time job?"

"I believe he said it is."

"I have a client who writes children's books," Madeline said. "The income is fairly sporadic. In fact, she wouldn't be able to live on it if her husband weren't supporting both of them. But I imagine Henry gets social security, maybe even a company pension from some former job?"

"I didn't quiz him about his finances," Elsie said. "Nor did I ask his age since he was polite enough not to ask about mine. Frankly though, I don't think he's old enough to collect social security yet."

"Oh," Madeline said again. This time she struggled to keep the suspicion out of her tone and forced a teasing smile. "Got yourself a younger man, huh?"

"What I've got," Elsie emphasized succinctly, "is a date and nothing more than a date, with a man who was good company to me for a few hours last Sunday. With any luck, we'll have a pleasant time again this Saturday night."

Madeline was prodding, maybe even poking her nose in

where it didn't belong. But she couldn't help feeling protective of Elsie. As intelligent as the older woman was, when it came to street smarts, she had a tendency to be naïve. A widow with her own home and a bank account could be easy pickings for someone looking to take advantage of her. On the other hand, maybe Madeline had become too damned cynical for her own good—or anyone else's. Either way, she recognized the need to respect the boundaries of their friendship.

"That one looks really nice on you," she said of the burgundy dress, quickly changing gears.

"Yes, and I like the turquoise one too. I think I'll splurge and take them both. I would also like to look for a pants outfit," she added. "My card club is having a luncheon, and I want to look nice for it."

By the time they stopped for dinner, they'd both cleaned out the stores. "I can't believe we bought so many clothes," Madeline said.

"What I can't believe is that we actually found clothes to buy," Elsie said. "Usually when I'm on a hunt for something specific, it's never this easy. I think you're my good luck charm, dear."

Madeline smiled as the waiter brought their menus. "It's nice to be somebody's good luck charm." Without even glancing at the food choices, she set the menu down and looked directly at Elsie. "Do you think I'm going to be a good mother?" she asked.

"Why, Madeline! Of course I do. Whatever makes you ask such a question?"

"Look at my own mother, for starters. I haven't exactly had the best example to follow. And for years, Charles and I didn't want children. Maybe I decided to have a baby for all the wrong reasons."

"From what you told me, it was Charles who didn't want children."

The waiter appeared back at their table. "Can I get you ladies something to drink?" he asked.

"Tea," Madeline said automatically. "Something with no caffeine."

"We have peppermint, if you'd like that?"

"Perfect," she said.

"Yes, for me too," Elsie echoed.

The waiter left and Madeline picked up the menu. "I guess we'd better decide what to eat before he comes back. The place is getting busy, and I'm actually hungry. Better still, I don't feel sick so much anymore."

The tea came, and they both ordered roasted chicken dinners. "Tell me, why did you decide to have a child?"

Elsie's question was intense, but the answer wasn't one Madeline needed to analyze. She'd thought it through long before she'd gone for the insemination procedure. "I want someone to love. Someone to love me back and need me," she answered simply. "Someone who isn't going to disappear from my life, the way so many people have. Perhaps a part of me thinks that if I do a good job of raising this little soul, I can make up for the fact that I missed out on my own childhood. Maybe the two of us can learn to play together."

Elsie touched her arm. "Love is the noblest motive for doing anything on this earth. So I think your reasoning is sound. As for the kind of mother you'll be, why you already have a track record. After all, weren't you the one who practically raised your younger sister?"

"Yes, but that's not exactly—"

"For that matter," Elsie interrupted forcibly, "you took care of your own mother when it seemed she was unable to care for herself."

"I did, but it's something I had to do."

"It counts, dear. Don't dismiss it like it doesn't matter."

"There was no one else to rely on. It's not like there was anyone grading my performance. Who's to say whether or not I did a good job?"

"What does your heart tell you, Madeline? The heart doesn't lie."

"My heart tells me I did the best I could. In spite of it, I don't see my mother or my sister very often. My sister and her family enjoy the best of Mom, now that she's stronger."

"Has is occurred to you that your mother may be stronger now because of you and what you did for her and your sister? Undoubtedly, you came by your own strengths because of the coping mechanisms you learned as a youngster."

"Yes, but I don't want any child of mine to grow up that quickly. I want my baby to have a real childhood, with real parents." She caught herself. "With a real mother," she amended.

"Madeline, I have no doubt that you could do a wonderful job of raising your child all by yourself. If you must. But in the traditional family scenario, a child grows up with two parents," Elsie said. "If you'd had the choice, wouldn't you have preferred that for yourself?"

The reminder was unnecessary, and the question caused her unease. "Of course, I would rather my father had been around to help raise me," she answered.

"I want you think about something, dear. Not to appease me, but for yourself, your child, and the future you'll have. I know your love is bountiful. You've shared it with me, and with your family. Now it's waiting to be shared with your new family. You won't be able to help but shower your baby with love. But to center all of your passion on this one child, to the exclusion of letting a man into your heart, could be an enormous loss for you."

"I had love for Charles. At least I did in the beginning. But he never seemed to need the kind of passion I could have offered him. It's strange, but I've begun to dwell on this a lot lately. I think what Charles and I had was more of a business arrangement than a marriage based on the bonding of two people who were truly in love with each other."

"I'm sorry to hear that," Elsie said softly. "I had that kind of passion with my Edward, and I miss it more than I can say. Maybe it's why I've finally made the decision to open the door to my heart again. Just a crack though. I doubt I'll be lucky enough to find what I had with Edward twice in one lifetime. Frankly, I would rather live out the rest of my years alone than to hook up with the wrong person."

The waiter brought their salads, and then Elsie looked very serious. "It's difficult to accept, but there are no guarantees about how long people will stay in our lives. At least not on this earth. That includes children. They grow up, and even when they're small, they're only on loan. If we do our job in raising them, they learn to function as independent adults. They'll still need us, but in different ways. And if we're blessed, they'll continue to share in our lives. The bond between a parent and child is compelling, and it's most extraordinary."

"That's what I'm longing for, Elsie."

"I know. But realize it's not meant to substitute for the bond that two adults share when they are truly in love. That kind of investment is risky. If you don't bond with someone, you don't have that much to lose when you're separated. But if your investment pays off, the reward is beyond depiction. I would hate to see you cheat yourself out of it because of your fears."

"I wouldn't be so afraid if Kurt weren't such a daredevil. How much risk is required of people who are one-half of a relationship?"

"That depends. Some risk is imposed on us. Some is chosen. Edward had diabetes. He had it from early on, and I knew on our first date. I married him anyway, and he wound up dying from complications of the disease. Still we had thirty-five married years together. I can tell you for sure, they were the best thirty-five years of my life. Nothing I had before Edward came into my life compared. And nothing I've experienced since then either."

"I guess I hadn't realized Edward was sick when you two met."

"He wasn't. Not really. He took his medication, watched his diet. His quality of life was good until his last couple of years when things started to decline. The point is, dear, I understood from the get-go that I was taking a gamble. But I'm so glad I did."

"What was the deciding factor?" Madeline asked.

"Edward. The minute I laid eyes on his handsome face, I realized he was the one for me. His smile could light up a room, and no one excited me like he did. No one made me laugh the way he did. He was the only one who made me feel movie star beautiful, even though I had a mirror and could see otherwise. A woman knows when that special man comes into her life. He gets into her heart and her soul. He became part of my spirit. I would rather have had a year with him than not have had him at all. God saw fit to bless me with more than thirty-five."

"I'm happy for you," Madeline said, reaching across the table to squeeze her hand. "And I'm sad for you too. It sounds as though you still miss him very much."

"I do, even after ten years. I'm not depressed and crying every day. But there isn't a morning I don't wake up and look over to the empty side of the bed we used to share and wish he were still in it with me."

Elsie took a sip of her tea. "I know he would want me to move on with my life here. To the best of my ability, I have. We even talked about it while he was still alive. Edward wasn't selfish, and he knew there was a strong likelihood that I would outlive him. I told him I wasn't interested in remarrying. Yet he made me promise to keep an open mind. He said the day would probably come when I would reconsider."

"Have you?" Madeline asked. "Do you think you might get married again?"

"I doubt it. Certainly not at this point. Right now I'm just looking for friendship—a little male companionship to tide me over until I see Edward again. I know someday I will," she added with confidence.

The waiter brought their food, and Madeline cut into her chicken with gusto. It felt good to be hungry for a change. After savoring the first couple of bites, she put her fork down and looked at Elsie.

"I have strong feelings for Kurt," she said, in a quiet whisper. "They're different and deeper than anything I've ever had for anyone. And they scare me. It's too early to know if what I feel could blossom into anything like what you've described with your husband, but I do know that Kurt makes me come alive. More alive than I've ever been before."

Elsie smiled.

"He's the epitome of charm and danger, so much so I'm envious that he's able to partake in life with such vehemence. I'm drawn to him like a magnet, and equally as frightened by it. It's precarious enough that he makes his living as a pilot, yet each day for him seems to be a new adventure. But he gravitates toward risk he doesn't have to take—shouldn't take. Not to mention the whole Hodgkin's situation."

"Yes, we've talked about that, and considering there's a good chance the excess risk and the Hodgkin's are tied in together, the problem may disappear once he's considered cured."

"Is it a chance I should take, Elsie? Because I really don't know."

"That's a question only you can answer, and I'm not sure I should be trying to influence you one way or the other." She paused, began to speak, then paused again.

"What is it? I know you want to say something," Madeline pressed.

"Well, my brother used to be married to this wonderful woman. In fact, I still think of her as my sister-in-law, and we're still friends. After they'd been married for a couple of years, Marty lost his job. He looked around for something else, but ultimately he decided he wanted to become a police officer. In short, that's what he did.

"All during the time he attended the police academy Nancy, his wife, continued to work at her job. They were deeply in love and planned to have children once he graduated and began working. Even though they lived in a small town and the crime rate was low, Nancy became obsessed with the possibility of losing Marty. She was convinced he would die in a shootout or meet with some other misfortune connected to his work. Eventually, she decided she couldn't live with this tension and she gave him an ultimatum: the police force or her."

"What happened?"

"Sadly, they divorced. Worse yet, Nancy never remarried, and she never had the children she'd wanted. I think a part of her always thought Marty would come around to her way of thinking and leave the force."

"But isn't your brother still living? I've heard you talk about him, haven't I?"

"Yes. He just celebrated thirty years of marriage with his second wife. He's retired from the force now, and they spend their time traveling and doing fun things together."

"And Nancy's all alone?"

"Unfortunately, yes. I can't say she made the wrong decision. Who knows what kind of stress is going to put someone over the edge? She did what she thought was right for her at the time. But I know for a fact that she and my brother loved each other."

Madeline sat silent, her appetite vanished.

"You could talk to Kurt. See if he would compromise in some way you could live with."

"Frankly, it's too soon for that. It's not like we've declared love for each other. Anything I might ask for at this point, in terms of concessions to his lifestyle, could be seen as presumptuous. He would probably be resentful. I wouldn't blame him, really. And unless we have some sort of understanding, I don't know that I'm willing to jump in with both feet and just let my heart get broken once again."

"You don't need to make a decision this minute. Think about our discussion, and the answers will come."

Elsie had spoken with fervor and wisdom. Madeline knew she would consider every word her friend had said.

CHAPTER 13

Month Five

Sweat ran from every pore, even though Kurt had waited till dusk to take the canoe out for a ride. No surprise it was still hot; the thermometer had topped ninety earlier that afternoon. Typical late August weather. He'd been paddling hard for over an hour before he decided he'd had enough. He stopped near the edge of his pier to rest a while and cool down before bringing the boat back on shore.

It was nearly dark, and the sounds of nightfall on the Fox River seemed mythical. If he listened carefully, he could almost swear to hearing forest fairies in the distance. Crickets competed with the cicadas, and ducks with the geese. Every now and then a fish jumped up and made a splash somewhere. But Madeline wasn't there. She should have been sitting next to him in that canoe.

It had been three months since they'd made love, and the fact that he thought of it in those terms was daunting. He didn't want it to mean he was falling in love with her. Considering the way she felt about him right now, he didn't ever want to be that vulnerable again. On the other hand, he knew better than to brush the encounter off as mere sex. He'd filled her in that elevator. Not only in the physical sense, but with every thread of his being. He knew she'd encompassed him in the same way, and for those spellbound moments, nothing else had mattered.

He hadn't forgotten a second of it, including the brunch beforehand, or their discussion later that evening. The one that had stopped the progression of any bond they'd begun to form. Sure, they were speaking. In civil tones. Usually when he contacted her. Legalities were always a good reason to try to break through the barrier she'd put up. After all, he was still trying to decide how to proceed with the fertility clinic. But now that he'd agreed to postpone any consideration of lawsuits until after the baby was born, even litigation was a feeble excuse for a conversation.

Occasionally, he'd show up at her office. Sometimes with a plate of fruit and cheese or some of her favorite herbal teas. Maybe even a little bouquet for Elsie. At least Elsie was on his side. He could tell.

Last week he'd gone so far as to talk Madeline into having lunch with him, and they'd walked to a nearby restaurant. He'd tried all his tricks, turned on the "Williams charm" as best he could. There was even a moment when he'd thought he had her. Right after she'd caught his wink and the grin he couldn't help flashing, just because the sight of her made him stupid. He could see she'd felt something for him. But she'd done her damnedest to fight it. After that, she'd gone out of her way to avoid eye contact with him.

He looked at his watch. It wasn't even nine o'clock yet. She'd probably be up. The woman was carrying his kid, so why did he need an excuse to call her and see how she was feeling? He paddled the last few feet to the dock and jumped out of the canoe. It only took a minute to drag it out of the water.

"Hello, Kurt." The voice carried a throaty coolness, and the recognition made him jump.

"Jesus!" His eyes traced her female outline in the dark. "What the hell are you doing here, Christie?"

"Is that any way to greet me?" she purred. "I've been waiting for you in this insufferable heat since sundown. Bad boy, you changed your locks. My house key no longer works."

"No shit, darlin'. After the way you skipped out on me, I didn't figure you'd have a need."

"You might be surprised about my needs. In any case, I'd like to talk to you about that—if you'll hear me out."

Despite the implication, her voice had taken on a softer quality. She moved away from him, just far enough that she was illuminated by the motion sensor light at the back of the house. Unlike Madeline, Christie was petite. She reminded him of a Dresden doll with her milky white skin and short, dark hair. What she lacked in height, she made up for in shape, and it was hard not to notice her nicely proportioned body parts. Particularly since her skin-tight shorts were crawling up her ass.

"How about inviting me in for a while?" she pressed.

"You know, I really don't think that's a good idea. Things have changed now and . . ."

"You're right," she said, effectively cutting him off. "It's hot as the tropics out here, and I remember where we used to have some of our most meaningful conversations." With that, she stripped off her clothes until she stood before him. Stark fucking naked. Then, with purpose, she began to strut toward the river. "Go skinny dipping with me," she beckoned.

He couldn't take his eyes off her, and he fought to calm the rush of adrenaline flooding his senses. Leave it to Christie to bring out the heavy artillery. Sex had never been one of their problems. In fact, it had been the best part of their relationship.

"I'm not exactly in the mood for a swim right now," he lied.

That didn't deter her. With her back to him, she stuck her feet in the water, then turned clear around to tempt him further. "Mmm, you really don't know what you're missing, Kurt."

Not fair. Not fair at all. How was he supposed to think logically with her flashing him the full frontal like that?

"The water is the perfect temperature. So soothing," she added, sliding backwards into the river.

He was sweating again, and not just from the heat of the night. He kept reminding himself the time for sex play with her had come and gone. Still, he couldn't help being curious about what she'd come to tell him. Hell, he was already wearing swim trunks. What could it hurt to take a little dip?

Without allowing himself to answer that question, he jumped into the water, careful to keep his distance from her. Nonetheless, he was sharing the same river with the woman who'd walked out on him during the worst crisis of his life.

She took advantage of the situation to get nearer to him, and in the moonlight he could see the tips of her breasts peaking out over the water's surface.

"You come any closer to me, and I'm out of here. I mean it," he emphasized. "So don't test me."

She knew him well enough to stop moving, and for that he was grateful. His brain kept sending him warning messages, but his hormones were speaking a different language. The realization that he could still be susceptible to anything she might be offering was unsettling.

"Now talk to me," he said. "That is why you came here, and frankly, I don't have all night. There's something else I need to do." A vision of Madeline's face flashed before him, telling him how much she remained in his thoughts.

Christie cleared her throat, the way people do when they're nervous and trying to figure out their next move. "All right then," she said. "I'll get right to the point, which is, that I'm very ashamed of the way I acted when you got sick. I owe you a big apology. I don't want you to think I haven't cared about your progress. I've actually been keeping tabs on you through a couple of our mutual friends, and I know you're doing very well now. You look spectacular."

Was he supposed to be comforted by that? "Tell me something, Christie. Why did you have to check on me via some third party, when you could have had the news first-hand? We were making plans to spend the rest of our lives together, and you bolted at the first sign of trouble."

He heard the mixture of anger and hurt in his own voice, and he paused to collect himself. "If the tables had been turned—if you had been the one with a cancer diagnosis, I would have been there for you."

She sniffled and choked up. He thought back to a time when her tears would have tugged at his heart. But right now, he couldn't identify with her pain.

"You're different than I am, Kurt. I suppose that's why I fell in love with you in the first place. Because of your unwavering loyalty and your capacity to take chances. You're fearless. It's one of the things I admire about you most."

"You think I'm fearless?" he snapped. "I was scared shitless when I found out I had Hodgkin's. But you wouldn't know much about that because you weren't there long enough to see it."

Immediately he regretted his outburst. He hated admitting weakness to anyone and she, of all people, didn't deserve his confidence.

"I'm sorry. I'm so very sorry," she said, through her tears.

He was starting to believe her, but it didn't change what he felt for her now. Or, more to the point, what he didn't feel.

"I had no coping skills for that kind of crisis," she said. "I lost my father to cancer before I even met you. When we learned you had it, I just didn't think I could go through another ordeal like what happened with my dad. I felt helpless. I'm embarrassed to admit that, but it's true."

She stopped speaking, presumably to wait for his response. When he offered none, she continued. "I understand nobody

195

gets out of this life without some kind of cross. Some people get handed more than their share. But sometimes we can choose what crosses we decide to take up. If you and I had been married, I'd like to think I would have been right by your side. That wasn't the case."

"You were wearing my ring! We hadn't set a date yet, but you accepted my marriage proposal. I thought you loved me. If you truly love somebody, then you have no choice but to deal with that person's issues. It's not about a marriage certificate."

"I'm being honest with you, Kurt. Even though I know this is going to sound shallow. I was basing our relationship on both present and future potential. For God's sake! I was trying to finish law school. That was stressful enough. Then you lost your pilot's license . . ."

"Temporarily!" he shot back. "I was sick, and now I'm back in the air again. Gainfully employed."

"Even so, I couldn't figure out how I would be able to support both of us, emotionally and financially, and still get my law degree. I just didn't have the ability. At the time, I thought I'd be doing both of us a favor."

"Nobody asked you to pay my bills, Christie. Though, as it turns out, you were probably right about the favor part."

"At the time," she repeated with emphasis. "That was nearly five years ago. This is a new day—a new time. I'm an attorney now. I never married. I know you're still single."

"Yeah, well congratulations on your career. It's what you always wanted. But just because I'm not sporting a wedding ring, you shouldn't assume I'm available. I haven't exactly been waiting on this pier for the night when you'd show up in my back yard again."

A large fish jumped out of the water right between them and Christie shrieked, at the same time leaping into the air. Fate placed her right into his arms as she clung to him for safety.

The feel of her flesh against his own triggered memories he couldn't afford to dwell on. His eyes met with hers for a few awkward seconds before he set her down. "You're okay," he said, by way of comforting her. "It was only a fish."

Suddenly she looked self-conscious, and she wrapped her arms over her bare breasts. "I . . . I still have feelings for you," she confessed. "I'm wondering if you would consider giving me another chance—giving us another chance? Do you think you could forgive me, Kurt?"

He hesitated briefly. "Yeah, I can forgive you," he said, which surprised him, mostly because he meant it. Something about her sincerity convinced him they'd both be better off if there could be some sort of amicable closure to this relationship gone dead. That's what it was, he determined. A relationship gone dead. Her contrition simply couldn't rebuild a love that had never been genuine.

Better still, he wasn't feeling pain over this ending. The lack of that hurt was a sure sign his love for Christie Reed had been toasted, just like his disease had been toasted by the radiation.

"I can forgive you," he said again. "Maybe someday I'll even be able to thank you. But there is no more *us.*"

She looked stricken, but he couldn't help it. He wasn't trying to be mean, just honest.

"What can I do to change your mind, Kurt? Please, let's try again."

"Christie, I'm glad you came here. I really am. This conversation was long overdue, and we needed to have it. I never realized how much until tonight."

With that, he climbed out of the water and onto the shore. He walked over to the canoe and grabbed a towel while she waited in the river. Instead of drying himself, he went back to the water and motioned for her to come out. "I want you to get your clothes on now and leave."

"Are you sure about that?" she said, making her way onto shore.

"Definitely sure," he answered, quickly throwing the beach towel around her body.

He wasn't going to elaborate any further. It was his own business that he wasn't about to walk out on Madeline—even if she didn't seem to care one way or the other right now. Maybe he didn't yet know true love. But he knew what it wasn't.

"You've got three minutes to towel off and get dressed," he said, turning his back to her nudity. "I'll wait, then walk you to your car to make sure you get out of here safely." He never did feel comfortable sending a woman alone into the pitch black night, even though he knew he was probably out of step with the times.

"But, Kurt . . ."

"Clock's ticking," he said.

Five minutes later she backed out of his driveway and out of his life. Not friends, not enemies. Their final parting had been polite. And satisfying.

Kurt looked at his watch and noted it was nearly ten o'clock. He didn't care; he had to talk to Madeline. *Had to.*

He raced inside the house and took the basement stairs two at a time. Still dripping, he dialed her phone number.

You sound breathless," she said, after the first hello. "Have you been running?"

"I've been working out. Listen, I've been thinking," he exaggerated, knowing the pitch to come would be strictly ad lib. What the hell, things couldn't get any worse—he hoped.

"About?"

"The baby." That would get her attention. "I mean, you're always saying how important it is to expose our child to positive things, even now, while in the womb." *Keep going.* "What kind of effect do you think it's having on the kid, sensing all this tension between the two people who are supposed to love him the most? Namely his parents. What if you've got a depressed child in there? Who knows what kind of problems could develop?" *Talk about reaching.*

"Are you serious?" she asked.

"Totally. You're the one who said a fetus can hear. What kind of messages are you sending to our baby?" *That was a cheap shot.*

"I . . . I, well . . ."

Good, she was going for it.

"Hey, I'm not saying we have to hop in the sack again." *In a heartbeat.* "I'm just saying that if you're not interested in pursuing what we started, we should at least try to smooth out our differences so we can take part in the birth and the parenting together. United. You know I want to be involved, Madeline. Don't punish me because of your paranoid fears about abandonment."

"Paranoid!"

Wrong word. "Uh, I guess what I really should have said—what I really want to say is that you're the one who's bailing. If you want to talk about abandonment, you're not the only one who's felt it.

"I was engaged once. I thought I was going to spend the rest of my life with this woman. But then I got sick, and she walked out on me when I needed her most. She couldn't stand the stress of being with someone who might die. As if we're not all going to, anyway. Someday. Except I didn't die. I'm still here, and I plan to be here for a long, damn time. What about you?"

"I don't know what to say, Kurt. I'm sorry she hurt you so badly."

"Thanks, but it's a closed chapter. I've moved on now, and I'd feel a lot better if you'd focus your concern on what's going on between the two of us. Because that's what really matters to me right now."

He could almost hear her reflection, and he kept his fingers crossed through the quiet that followed.

"I'm having an ultrasound tomorrow. It's my first one," she said, sounding a little emotional. "Would you like to be there with me?"

Slam-dunk. "Would I!" He thought his heart would thump right out of his chest. "You just tell me what time to pick you up."

"Kurt, I'm not saying . . . this doesn't mean."

"I understand." That she was letting him back in the door. Never mind that his efforts had been a tad underhanded. His motivation was sincere.

Now that he had a grip on her real issues, he'd be more careful to work around them. He'd been completely honest in assuring her he valued his life. So, it would serve no purpose, other than to needlessly upset her, if she found out he'd made that second skydive last month. No mishaps either. She wouldn't see the situation as another mark closer to his cure from Hodgkin's disease.

Someday he would make her see there were valid reasons for parachuting out of a perfectly functioning airplane. Sane men and women did it every day. But the time for clarification would be somewhere down the road. For now, he had a far more pressing agenda that needed his full attention.

"If that technician doesn't start soon, I'm going to jump up and start doing laps," Madeline said to Kurt, as she lay on the exam table waiting to begin the ultrasound.

"What are you so nervous about?" he asked. "We've only been in here a few minutes."

"You don't get it." She straightened the gown she wore to

protect her clothes from the jelly soon to be spread over her expanding abdomen, dreading the look on Kurt's face when he realized how fat she'd gotten beneath her maternity clothes. But she'd agreed to let him be present for this occasion, so she would have to suffer the humiliation.

"What don't I get? And what can I do to help?"

"Nothing, really. I'm on edge with so many questions about whether or not the baby is developing properly. I just want to know that everything is okay."

Kurt put his hand over her arm. "I'm sure everything is fine, but I'll be glad to hunt the technician down for you, if you'd like."

Before Madeline could answer, the technician stepped into the room. "All right," she said. "I imagine you're anxious to get started."

"You have no idea," Madeline said, adjusting the pillow behind her head.

The technician dimmed the lights. "This won't take long."

Kurt stood at Madeline's side, opposite the machine.

"Sir, if you'll stay right where you are, you should be able to see the screen. And Mom, I need you to pull down your pants and panties to just below your tummy," the technician instructed.

Madeline acted without hesitation, despite her embarrassment. Kurt had the decency to turn his head until after a towel, to further shield her clothes, had been tucked into her pants. But now, as the technician spread the ultrasound jelly across her belly, he looked in silent wonder at her fast changing shape.

The technician moved the probe back and forth. "We're checking for things like placement of the placenta and fluid volume around the fetus. We can measure the femur to see if the baby's growth is appropriate for its gestational age. Mmm, strong heartbeat. Look, can you both see that?"

Kurt reached for Madeline's hand. To her surprise, she clung tight. They exchanged a look that surpassed words and any awkwardness she'd been feeling. This proof of the life they'd created went beyond awareness. It was a miracle.

"Your baby is sucking its thumb," the technician announced, with as much awe as if it had been the first time she'd ever witnessed such an event.

"Wow," Kurt whispered, drawing in a shaky breath. Madeline pulled some tissues from the box next to her and dabbed at the tears now filling her eyes. Then she heard Kurt sniff. He wouldn't face her, though he didn't refuse the tissue she discreetly slipped into his free hand.

"Can you tell whether it's a boy or a girl?" Madeline asked.

"Well, I see arms and legs and a head, but the umbilical cord is in a place that makes diagnosing the baby's sex difficult. If you want to be on the safe side, I wouldn't paint the baby's room pink or blue just yet."

"It doesn't matter, we'll take whoever's in there," Kurt said, with surprising sentiment.

"We certainly will," Madeline agreed.

CHAPTER 14

An hour later Kurt and Madeline sat across from each other in the Chinese restaurant, waiting for their lunch to be served. He hadn't expected the rush of emotion at witnessing his child for the first time during the ultrasound. Everything looked different now, almost like he was seeing all things for the first time. Even the menu seemed noteworthy.

He'd read that pregnant women glowed, and Madeline was proof positive. She beamed as she took out the ultrasound picture of their baby. Again. She was exquisite, like some kind of angel. He had an urge to take her into his arms and never let go. He also had an impulse to run around the block a hundred times. Had someone shot him full of adrenaline?

"So, you see anything there we didn't notice at the hospital?" he asked.

Madeline gave him a dreamy-eyed look. "I haven't found any indication we're having a boy, if that's what you're referring to."

"I meant what I said at the hospital. Boy or girl, it doesn't matter. I'm already attached."

Her eyes narrowed to a look of caution. Maybe it was the word *attached*, but he wasn't going to give her the opportunity to say something he didn't want to hear. Not right now.

"I've been thinking, Madeline. About the legalities of all this. I've decided no good can come of suing people for this life that's growing inside of you. So I'm not going to wait until after the baby is born to make my decision. I'm going to call my attorney later to tell her to drop the whole thing. At least my part of it."

"Oh, Kurt. I'm relieved you feel that way. I didn't want to sway you, but I believe it's the right thing to do."

Finally, he'd won her approval on something. "Well, since we're in agreement on that, I have another great idea to run by you."

"I'm listening," she said, cutting into the egg roll the waitress had set before her.

"It's Friday. I'm off the rest of the day. You have an 'in' with your boss," he teased. "How do you feel about a shopping trip?"

"Shopping? Between you and Elsie, it's becoming like a national pastime."

Did she have to look so skeptical? "Baby things. I told you I was planning to do some redecorating. Why shouldn't I have a room for the kid at my place too? You know, for days when you need a little break."

Her eyes were morphing to slits.

"Or—on days when you and the baby want to come over and hang out. Together. I should have a crib and some clothes, maybe some diapers. And some toys. Toys would be good."

She damned near cracked a smile. That was encouraging.

"It's going to be a while before our child is old enough to be interested in toys, Kurt."

"Paint then. You could help me pick out some colors so I can at least get the room done. You've got great taste, and I would appreciate your advice. What do you say?"

"Hmm . . . I say let's do it. I think it will be fun."

The trick now would be not to look too shocked or over-elated. "Excellent," he said, noticing she hadn't once complained of being nauseous. He hoped it meant she'd gotten past that stage of her pregnancy. "Eat up, and we'll be on our way."

★ ★ ★ ★ ★

Three hours later, after picking out a mint shade of green paint and an in-stock wallpaper border, Madeline and Kurt entered The Baby Gear Warehouse. Madeline had to admit, it wasn't her first time browsing the huge store. She'd already chosen the baby furniture she wanted for her townhome. But the way her mind had been changing lately, she decided to put off any serious buying until closer to her due date. Thankfully, she'd taken the liberty of painting her nursery yellow, even before she'd gotten pregnant, so adding some accessories wouldn't be any big deal.

"Let's check out the cribs," Kurt said with more enthusiasm than she would have expected from a man who'd had impending fatherhood foisted on him. In fact, from the signals he'd given off that day, he seemed like he could hardly wait. If she could only let go of her worries pertaining to his lifestyle.

He grabbed her hand and steered her to the back of the store. "Down that aisle. I see them from here."

She took a deep breath and sighed, which got his attention. He stopped and turned to her. "Am I pushing you too hard? Because, if you're tired, we can leave right now."

"On the contrary. In fact, I'm having a wonderful time." *And I'm so glad we're sharing it,* she would have added, if she hadn't been so afraid to say it out loud.

"I'll take you at your word."

"I appreciate that."

It took only seconds to reach the furniture department. There must have been fifty cribs within sight. But he went right over to a light maple wood piece with some intricate carving just at the head of the bed. "This is it," he said definitively.

"Kurt, we just got here. You haven't looked at anything else. How can you know this is the one?"

"Because it's simple, except for the carving that makes it

special. It has masculine and feminine characteristics, so we're covered there." He ran his fingers over the smooth finish. "The color is good, it's sturdy, and it's beautiful." He studied the hefty price tag for a moment. "Yep, it's exactly what I had in mind. Unless, you object. I mean, if you do, we can keep looking."

"It's not that I object. It's just that I want to be sure we've seen everything else before we make a decision. Of course, it's your crib. For your house."

"It's for our baby," he emphasized. "I did ask for your opinion. Let's keep looking."

Now she felt like a bully. "You know what, Kurt? The crib is beautiful. Our child will be very lucky to have such a wonderful place to sleep. When he or she goes to your house to visit," she carefully added. "You should buy it."

"Yeah?" He broke into a satisfied smile. "And the matching dresser? I really like that too."

"Perfect," she said, realizing she meant it. "When something is this right, I guess you don't have to canvass everything else in the store. You just know." Where had that come from? Was she only talking about baby furniture?

Kurt must have wondered, too, because he locked eyes with her in reverent silence. Another hour later, after choosing from a list of *must have* items Madeline had suggested, he said, "Let's go find a salesperson and wrap this up. I'm sure everything will fit in my 4Runner. Then we can go back to my place and get a feel for how it's all going to look."

Kurt pulled into his driveway with Madeline on the passenger side of the SUV, and the baby items packed into the back of the vehicle. Everything surrounding this day had been so magical, he was almost afraid to say anything for fear of breaking the spell. "If you could just hold the front door open, I'll carry the boxes inside."

"I can help you," she offered.

"No way. You're not lifting anything heavy. Not at five months pregnant. Besides, I'm a guy. I have Herculean strength."

For some reason he failed to comprehend, she laughed. That smile of hers was enough to melt glaciers, even if the joke was on him. "The door," he said with mock severity, handing her the house key.

Ten minutes later the boxed furniture sat in the middle of the living room. He hadn't exactly worked up a sweat, but he was thirsty. "I've got a pitcher of lemonade in the fridge that's calling to me. How 'bout you?"

"I would love some. But let me get it. You look a little winded."

"Thanks. You know where the glasses are."

He followed her past the kitchen and into the family room, sinking down onto the sofa. Minutes later she handed him an icy glass of the thirst quenching drink and sat beside him.

"Mmm, this is the real thing," she said, after taking a sip. She licked her lips in appreciation, and his senses came alive. "Did you make this from scratch?"

"Yep. Squeezed the lemons myself." The remark forced his eyes to her breasts. Two hardened peaks made an appearance from beneath her maternity top, and his thoughts ran amuck.

"Um . . . it's delicious." Another swallow and a self-conscious look away.

Guess she must have noticed he couldn't stop himself from staring, even if her figure had taken on a new form. A vision of her rounded belly with his hands on it came to the fore. In another nanosecond, any body part that could would be standing at full attention. Including the hairs at the back of his neck. He needed a distraction. "Hey, I've got something I've been wanting to show you, but it's down the hallway. I'll have to go get it."

"Why don't I just come with you? I want to take a good look at the future nursery anyway," she said.

"Actually, that's where it is. The something I want to show you."

She went first. Which gave him ample time to study the sexy curves of her rear. Sure, she'd gained a few pounds. But on her, they looked great. Besides, if she ever gave him the green light, he'd have all the more flesh to fondle.

With no warning, she stopped and turned to face him. "Are you staring at my big, fat behind?" she challenged.

What? Did she have radar? "Uh . . . no."

She glared at him. "No? The reflection from the glass in the mirror at the end of the hall says differently."

Guilty as charged.

She continued to walk and when they reached the room, he decided it might be advantageous to pursue the subject. "Yes, and no," he amended. "I was staring at your rear—which happens to be very sexy, but certainly not fat. Want to make something of it?" *Please say yes.*

She said nothing, but a puckered little grin escaped while she turned a deep shade of pink. That blush of hers was going to do him in one of these days. *Focus on the distraction.* He stepped in front of her and led the way to the room slated to be the nursery. From the closet, he took out a box that was sitting on the shelf.

"What's that?" she asked, and then gasped as he took the mobile with the wooden hand-carvings from the container. "Oh, my gosh!"

"I've been working on this all summer," he said, setting his creation on the carpeted floor. She sat beside him to examine his work.

"The piano is supposed to be a replication of the one in your living room. Because that's part of who you are. The plane, well I made it look like my Piper, because that's part of who I am. Now the parachute . . ."

"Is the most colorful, intricate, toy I've ever seen," she finished. "I can't believe you carved it yourself. The baby will be mesmerized."

He smiled at her fervor. "As for the puppy—I figure all kids should have one, even if it's only wooden and has a limited range of motion. Watch." He hung the mobile from a hook on the wall, then activated the switch. The carvings began to dance in a circular fashion to the tune of a lullaby. It had taken all of his spare time on the last two Cromwell trips to get that music box to work with the rest of the mobile. But he'd done it.

"This is the most special toy I've ever seen, Kurt. It will be our child's favorite. I'm sure of it. How can I thank you?"

"You just did. You called the baby *'our child.'* You don't have to thank me. It was a labor of love. I'm just happy that . . ."

"Oh!" she cried out suddenly, her hands flying to her abdomen.

"What! What's wrong?" he demanded, with concern. "Are you in pain? What should I do?"

She reached for his hand and placed it over her maternity top, where her own hand was. "The baby just moved. Can you feel him?"

"Yeah, I think I can. Honestly, I'm not sure," he amended. "I wonder if he's reacting to the music."

"Oooh!" she said, lifting her top to expose her bare belly. "He's doing it again."

"Does it hurt?"

"Kind of, in a good way."

"Maybe I can calm him down," Kurt offered. Before she could respond, he laid his cheek over her abdomen, feathering her skin with the side of his face. "Hey little guy, this is your father talking, just in case you think you're playing football in there. Your mother and I like it that you're so full of energy. But you might want to save the field goals for when you get a little older."

Madeline smiled. "Do you realize that both of us have started referring to the baby as a he? What if he turns out to be a she?"

"Girls can play football," he said, his face still to her skin.

"The baby has stopped moving."

Which meant Kurt could stop touching Madeline. *Or not.* The tension was mounting. In more ways than one. She was the person who'd bared her abdomen—the soft, creamy expanse of flesh that housed his child. He could no longer resist kissing her navel and the skin surrounding it. He heard her sharp intake of air, but she didn't protest. Goosebumps covered her belly, and he took that as a sign she liked it.

Still, she was vulnerable. As much as he wanted her, he had a responsibility not to take this any further. Unless she wanted him to. "I've missed you," he whispered, his eyes moving to hers. "Thank you for letting me be part of this special day."

"I've missed you too, Kurt. I'm glad you were there with me to see our child for the first time."

"The day isn't over yet, Madeline. Just say the word, and there could be so much more."

"It's not that simple," she said, sliding her top back down to cover herself. "I'm scared. Scared on so many levels."

"I understand your fears." Hell, he had enough of his own. Every day he worried, to some degree, the Hodgkin's might return. But this was a bad time to remind her that his concerns for the future went far beyond her and the baby. "Neither of us knows what's ahead. But you do know I've been here since day one in the attorney's office. Right now we're together. Why can't you let yourself trust me?"

"I want to. I'm not sure I know how."

"Maybe I can help. Why don't you start by saying what's bothering you the most."

Her eyes snapped to attention.

"Tell me," he coaxed. "Spit it out. What's got you spooked this minute?"

"Okay. The future notwithstanding, the thing that scares me right now is that if you see what I look like without my clothes—completely without them—you'll be horrified and want to leave the room."

He clenched his teeth to keep from laughing out loud. "If you could read my mind, you'd know how far from the truth that is."

"But it's my truth, she stressed.

As absurd as it sounded to him, he could see she was serious.

"I look at myself in the mirror, and I see profound physical changes. The appearance of a beach ball protruding from just below what used to look like my breasts is just one of them. This is not the same body you made love to in that elevator."

"Madeline, looking at you causes profound physical changes in my body too." He took her hand and placed it directly over his arousal. "If you want to compare protrusions, check this out."

Her surprised expression came just before she broke into laughter. Good, she was lightening up. "Are you making fun of me, woman?"

"No, but I think you're making fun of me."

"A little bit," he said, gently. "Can't you see how you turn me on? The anticipation of seeing you naked is making me even harder."

"What if you're disappointed?"

"Not possible. Let me prove it."

"Well . . . exactly how would you go about doing that?"

The gleam in her eyes was the green light he'd been hoping

for. "Slowly," he said. "One. Pleasurable. Step. At a time."

Kurt gave her a look that made her toes curl, and Madeline had no doubt he was planning something memorable. Whatever it was concerning the second trimester of pregnancy, she'd been feeling very sexually responsive. Not to mention sexually frustrated. Without Kurt. Just remembering the way they'd made love in that elevator brought liquid heat to the place in her body where he'd filled her.

It was clear he wanted to take her again now. Right there on the carpeted floor of their child's future nursery. And she was going to let him. God help her, she was going to force him, if he didn't get a move on.

From somewhere, he'd produced a large throw pillow and positioned it behind her. "Lie back and relax," he said. "Proving my case is going to take some time. After all, I want you to be really convinced."

The way he said the word *really* woke the butterflies in her tummy, and they did a nervous dance while she followed Kurt's instructions.

"Let's see now," he said, undoing the front buttons of her top and exposing her bra. "Those still look like breasts to me, even underneath all that covering." Then he flicked his tongue over them, right through the satin fabric. She sucked in air as the delicious sensation caused her tips to marble. "Hmm, and they act like breasts too," he added, observing the changes taking place. " 'Course, I won't know for sure till I do a more detailed study."

Her awareness heightened as he unclasped the front opening of her bra, revealing the darkened, bumpy pigment that had become so prominent around her nipples. She searched his eyes for a sign of disappointment, but found none. He swept the area with his lips and tongue, tasting as greedily as if she were mocha ice cream. Her chest had become a road map of blue veins, but Kurt was so caught up, he didn't seem to notice.

"Oh, yeah, those are definitely breasts," he whispered thickly. "Beautiful and voluptuous."

"Well, I did have to buy a larger bra size."

He smiled at her admission. "I can't wait to see what else has changed. It's like Christmas, the excitement growing as I unwrap each of my presents." He slid her maternity slacks down and off in one fell swoop, which left him to gaze at her panties. There was nothing sexy about the stretchy fabric spread across what used to be her flat tummy.

"Want to see if I'm still hard?" he dared. Before she could respond, he took off his pants. The bulge at the front of his briefs said it all.

She held her breath, filled with so much wanting.

"One more move, and I can make you naked. Are you ready?"

Impetuously, she covered her mouth with her hand.

"Don't do that," he scolded gently. "You have the face of an angel, and I don't want to miss one smile. Your body is housing our child. That makes you the most beautiful woman on the planet."

"I'm a goddess all right. A bountiful goddess."

"The fact that you're about to share your body with me makes me the luckiest guy on earth," he continued, as if he hadn't heard her feeble attempt to be funny.

The sincerity of his words finally broke through, and she could see he meant it. Somehow during these past several months, Kurt Williams had gone from being an annoying draft to the most soothing breeze in her life. "I'm very ready," she finally answered. *I'm opening my soul to you.*

Without another word, he removed the rest of his clothing.

Her heart raced at the sight of his muscular good looks and his heightened desire. And at the anticipation of what was to come.

He took her panties off, then brushed her lips with his.

She wanted more and reacted by offering him her tongue. Soon they were breathing as if they'd both run a marathon. Finally he broke the kiss. "Now I'm having a fear," he admitted.

"What is it?" Suddenly she realized it wasn't just about her.

"What if I hurt you? What if I hurt our baby? Is it okay for us to be doing this?"

"I just saw my doctor last week, and he said it was fine to have intercourse at this point. Later on might be another story."

"Oh. So you asked?" he said, with a satisfied smile.

Damn that telltale warmth she could feel spreading throughout her neck and face. "I don't remember how the subject came up. You know doctors. They like to cover all the bases. He said there are certain positions that might be more comfortable than the traditional ones, seeing as how I'm getting bigger in front."

"Such as?"

"Umm—we could spoon." Why was it so difficult for her to talk about this?

"Spooning. Let's see, that's where you lie on your side and I sort of curl around you from behind. Yeah, I could go for that. Let's give it a shot."

Without waiting he rolled her to her side and situated himself in back of her. She could feel his arousal, and she began to quiver throughout her core. Pregnancy hormones, flat out desire, whatever it was, she was so ready for him, she was engorged.

"Are you comfortable, Madeline? Are you sure you don't want to take this to my bedroom? I have a brand new mattress just waiting to be tested."

To hell with the mattress. "Just be inside of me," she pleaded.

"The condom. I forgot the condom. I have one in my jeans pocket."

"Never mind that. I'm already pregnant. Assuming your

personal situation hasn't changed since the last time we talked, I don't think we have to worry about . . ."

"It hasn't," he interrupted. "Boy, you sure are in a hurry." He scooted lower and put his hand over her crotch, inserting his finger just far enough to see how ready she was.

"Oh, Kurt."

He added a second finger, plunging deeper, stimulating the entire region. The pulsing started, pushing her closer to the brink. If he didn't stop, it would be over far too soon. She was desperate to feel him inside of her.

"Forget spooning!" she said, sitting up and forcing him to his back. "I want to see your face when it happens." With that she climbed on top of him and drew him inside her point of entry.

That he looked stunned was an understatement. "Whoa! Did I make you this hot?"

You and the devil. What else could explain her aberrant boldness? "You're the only one here," she answered.

An easy grin crossed his face as she began to writhe. Back and forth. Up and down.

"Madeline," he groaned, between heavy breathes. "You feel so good."

She bent forward until she lay facing him flat against his chest so she could feel the pressure she sought. He lifted his head to kiss her, making accidental contact with her chin. She knew he'd been aiming for her lips. "If I weren't such an Amazon," she apologized, scrunching downward to accommodate his mouth.

"If only I weren't on the short side," he came back.

"Any longer and I'd have trouble accommodating you," she said truthfully, tightening the muscles enveloping his manhood, so her meaning would be clear.

He was silent, but his electric blue gaze penetrated her very essence.

"You might be under six feet," she added softly, "but you're about the tallest man I know."

At that instant she could have sworn he grew larger inside of her, and all of his self-control seemed to vanish. With rhythmic, masterful motion, he traveled her core, touching every hot spot until she was forced to let go. Spasms of euphoria rendered her powerless while he moaned in animal abandon, calling her name as he spilled within her. They clung tight to each other and with one final rock of her soul, she cried out in glorious surrender.

Moments later, she lay staring at the ceiling, cuddled in Kurt's arms. Despite all of her efforts to fight it, they had forged a bond—a bond she prayed had the potential to last.

CHAPTER 15

Month Six

"Let me get this straight," Kurt said to Madeline. "Elsie wants to double date with us?"

"She didn't exactly say it in those words. But yes, she did ask if we would like to have dinner with her and her new friend. Can you hold on a minute, please? I've got another incoming call."

The line went quiet, yet he felt a connection more compelling than the telephone. There was no denying he and Madeline were developing an intimacy that went far beyond the lovemaking they'd been sharing the past several weeks. And he welcomed it.

"Sorry to keep you waiting, but that was Elsie," Madeline said, disrupting the daydream he'd begun to have. "She's wondering if we're free this evening. She wants to make dinner reservations at Café Sophia. I told her I'd call her back and let her know."

"Café Sophia. That's the Italian place in Elgin, isn't it?

"Yes, and I hear their food is very good. Although, at this point I'm so curious about this man she's seeing, I'd settle for eating at the local hamburger place."

"No, no, I like Italian food. It's Saturday night. I'm off tomorrow. Why not? Now tell me more about this guy she's dating. I just saw her last week, and she never mentioned anything about him."

"His name is Henry Burbank. She met him at the cemetery, of all places. Apparently his wife's grave is near to her husband's. She introduced me to him yesterday, when he came by the office to pick her up for lunch. I happen to know she treated. Not that it means anything."

"If you didn't think it meant something, you wouldn't have mentioned it," he said.

"Mmm—it's just that I think she pays a lot of the time when they go out together. She cooks for him, too. You overhear things when people work in a small office—like phone conversations. Not that I've been eavesdropping."

"No, of course not," he said, stifling a snicker.

"Anyway, I don't know much about him, other than he's writing a screen play and evidently not working at any other job. On the surface, Elsie seems smitten with him. Yet, she's been evasive about the relationship, which isn't like her. In fact, I'd say she's been blatantly defensive. That's why I'm surprised she's so anxious for us to have dinner with them."

"If that's the case, then why do you think she asked us?"

"Frankly, I'm wondering if she might have some reservations about this man that she's been hesitant to admit. Sometimes you just need objective friends to tell you what you already know."

"I'm not saying your instincts aren't on target, but are you sure you're not being overprotective? From what you've told me, it's been a long time since she's been out in the dating world. Being that she's a mother-figure to you, maybe you're having a tough time seeing her in this new role."

"I'd like to think I'm not that selfish, Kurt. I do care about her happiness."

"Okay, okay. Now *you're* being defensive, and I'm sorry I

brought it up. You said you met the guy. What was your take?"

"It's kind of hard to form an impression during a minute of introduction. They were in a hurry to leave when I walked into the reception area. I'll tell you one thing though. He's certainly younger than she is."

"That doesn't exactly qualify him for gigolo status. On the other hand, I really like Elsie. I'd hate to see her get taken. I say we keep our eyes and ears open. When should I pick you up?"

"Can you be here by six o'clock? That will give us plenty of time to meet Elsie and Henry at the restaurant by seven."

"I'll see you then," he said.

Charming, Kurt decided after ten minutes of sitting across from Henry Burbank in the restaurant. Firm handshake, good looks, tastefully clothed. Madeline had definitely called it on the age disparity though. Unless the guy had made a deal with the devil, he and Elsie had a minimum of a decade—most likely more—between them.

Admittedly, they wouldn't be the first couple to bridge the age gap successfully. Elsie was an attractive woman. For her years. Unfortunately, she wore them. Henry didn't. The adoring looks he kept giving Elsie: smiling, winking, stroking her arm and touching her hand—annoyingly charming. What was wrong with this picture?

The waiter appeared and asked if they wanted fontinella cheese and olive oil with their oven-fresh bread. "Is it complimentary?" Henry asked, as if Kurt and Madeline were invisible.

When the waiter said no, Henry leaned over to Elsie and whispered something in her ear. Kurt doubted it was sweet nothings.

"Don't worry about it," she whispered back, loud enough to be heard. "I have money."

The whole exchange was about as inconspicuous as snow in

Hawaii, but Kurt pretended to be oblivious.

"Olive oil and cheese for everyone," Henry said enthusiastically. "And a round of drinks for the table."

Maybe he'd been too quick to scrutinize Madeline's suspicions. Because whether or not Henry Burbank knew it, Kurt had just put him on notice. "How about appetizers?" he asked, once the waiter had disappeared.

"Mmm, my friend said she ate here, and their Calamari Salad is extraordinary," Madeline offered. "We could get a couple of orders for all of us to share."

"Sounds good to me," Henry said.

Kurt and Elsie agreed, and after ten more minutes of studying the menu and everyone giving their orders to the waiter, it was time for some conversation.

"So, tell me, Henry, what do you do?" Kurt asked, as if he hadn't a clue.

"I'm a writer," Henry answered. "What do you do?"

"I'm a pilot. But that doesn't sound nearly as interesting as your line of work. What things have you published?"

Henry took a swallow of his scotch. Then another big swig. "There's nothing on the shelves right now. But I'm working on a screen play. What kind of plane do you fly?"

"A screen play! Tell me about it, please."

"It has to do with Viet Nam and some things that happened over there."

"Were you in the military?"

"Army," Henry said succinctly. "So what kind of plane did you say you fly?"

"That would be a Falcon jet. For my personal use, I have a Piper Archer. What unit were you in?"

Henry looked uncomfortable and took another swallow of his drink. "Hundred and First Airborne."

"No kidding. When was that?"

"Uh, it was 1970. I was a Ranger."

"Henry won a Medal of Honor," Elsie said, proudly.

"A Medal of Honor!" Kurt said. His shock was more than just surprise. "Wow!"

Henry flashed daggers at Elsie and then softened his expression. "Remember, we agreed we weren't going to talk about that, honey," he said.

Elsie took on a repentant look. "Oh dear, I'm afraid I slipped. Please forgive me."

"I really can't discuss it," Henry continued. "Covert Operations. Very confidential. Can we change the subject?" With that, he polished off the rest of his scotch in one huge gulp.

"Sure, Man. Didn't mean to upset you. Absolutely, let's change the subject," Kurt said.

"Do you live around here?" Madeline directed her question to Henry.

"Matter of fact I live in West Chicago. But my lease is up soon, so I'll be moving," he answered.

"Will you be staying in the area?" Madeline asked.

He looked at Elsie and smiled sheepishly.

"We've been discussing the possibility of Henry renting a room in my house," she said. "After all, I do have the space, and with the sporadic income that goes along with a writing career, Henry needs something reasonable right now."

"That hasn't been settled yet," Henry said. "But enough about me. Tell me more about your job, Kurt. I love airplanes."

"I'm a corporate pilot," he said. *About to turn amateur detective.*

"It was really nice of you to insist on paying the entire bill," Madeline said to Kurt, on the drive home from the restaurant. "Thank you for dinner. It was delicious."

"My pleasure. Hell, I couldn't see Elsie paying half the tab. It was clear Daddy Warbucks there wasn't going to cough up any cash."

"So, what's your impression of Henry?" she asked.

"The jury's still out, but I'm getting a feeling like the one I get when I have to fly through bad weather. I'll tell you one thing. If that guy has a Medal of Honor, I'll eat toads for breakfast all next week."

"You don't believe him?"

"Madeline, a Medal of Honor is awarded by Congress. That's why it's called the Congressional Medal of Honor. Though I'm not even sure he knows that. It's an extremely big deal, and they don't pass them out like candies during a parade. In the whole history of the United States, including the Civil War, there probably aren't more than three thousand or so recipients. Maybe four thousand, but I doubt it. What's more, he said he was in Covert Operations. How could Congress vote on something that was covert?"

"So he's lying?"

"That would be my guess. It'll be easy enough to find out. There are all kinds of Web sites that post this type of information. Plus, I happen to know somebody who was in the Hundred and First Airborne Division. I intend to do some checking in the next few days. I'll let you know what I come up with."

"I appreciate that. I nearly dropped my fork when Elsie said they might become roommates."

"She didn't quite put it that way," he corrected. "But I'm going to get the lowdown on this guy before it gets to that stage. Unless you think it's already too late. Do you?"

"Now who's being overprotective? They are adults, you know."

"So are we," he teased. "Maybe when we get back to your place, we could engage is some adult activities."

She couldn't help but smile. "I think it's certainly a topic that's worthy of discussion."

"A very lengthy discussion," he agreed, his voice full of promise.

The following Tuesday Kurt called Madeline with the news. "Pretty boy's been lying through his teeth," he said. "At least about his military status. From what I've been able to gather, he's never even set foot inside a pair of army boots, let alone won any medals."

"Wonderful," Madeline said. "Why would he have made up such a story?"

"To impress a lonely widow who's been without male companionship for a very long time. A vulnerable older woman with some money and her own home," he added.

"Poor Elsie. What do you think we should do?"

"I'm not sure yet. The bearer of bad tidings is never in an enviable position. And if she's already emotionally involved with this guy, it may be too late to do anything. On the other hand, if he is after her money, we can't stand by and just watch. Didn't you tell me she has a son? Maybe we should talk to him."

"Oh, I think that's not such a good idea, Kurt. Elsie often complains to me that her son and his wife don't give her credit for having a brain in her head. She would feel very betrayed if we went to them. She's not stupid. But when it comes to matters of the heart, I guess we can all be vulnerable."

"Are we still talking about Elsie?"

"Trying to," Madeline answered. "I am worried about the possibility of Henry moving in with her. I can't help wondering if his main goal is to freeload. I'm not sure she knows anything about his background. If she does, she's not telling. I don't even know if he has kids or if he had a regular job."

"If you ask me, I think it's time you had a heart-to-heart with her."

"She'll be at work tomorrow. I'll feel the situation out then."

Elsie was late coming back from lunch, and the office phones were ringing off the hook. Madeline was alone, and she wasn't sure whether to be annoyed or worried. Elsie always called when she was detained, and she'd been gone for nearly two hours now.

No sooner had she begun dialing Elsie's cell phone, when Elsie walked into the reception area.

"Are you okay?" Madeline asked. But a closer look told her something was definitely wrong. She went over to the older woman and put an arm around her shoulder. "What is it? Tell me what happened?"

Elsie sat on the sofa, staring out blankly.

"Please," Madeline demanded gently. "I want to help."

"You can't," Elsie said. "I've been stupid, and there's nothing anyone can do about it."

"I've never known you to be stupid. But we all make mistakes. Which one did you make that's got you so upset?"

"Trusting Henry Burbank."

As relieved as Madeline was to hear Elsie had seen the light, she couldn't help fearing she might have seen it too late.

"I went to the cemetery today at lunch to talk to my Edward. I wanted him to send me some sort of signal to let me know it's okay with him that I've been seeing Henry. I wanted some re-assurance that I've been doing the right thing."

"Did you get it?"

"Oh, I got a signal all right. There was a woman visiting at the grave of Henry's wife. At least that's what I thought. When I saw the woman, I went over and spoke to her and introduced myself. I told her I knew Lisa Howell's husband."

"Lisa Howell? I don't understand."

"Henry told me Lisa Howell was his wife's name. He said

she never took his last name, and I believed him. Until the woman visiting Lisa Howell's grave site told me her sister had never been married."

"So, it was Lisa Howell's sister who was visiting the site?"

"Yes, and I told her there must be some misunderstanding, and she assured me there wasn't. So I started putting things together. You know, the fact that Henry doesn't really have a job and that he's about to be put on the street because his landlady is kicking him out. He's also been borrowing money from me, and . . ."

"You gave him money!"

Poor Elsie looked so humiliated. "I'm afraid so. You know what they say. There's no fool like an old fool."

"You're not a fool, and you're not old. Quit beating yourself up. How much did you give him?"

"More than a thousand dollars. I was going to let him move into my house next week. I thought he cared for me."

"Well, you're certainly not going to do that now. Maybe Kurt has an idea on how we can get your money back."

"I'm so embarrassed for you to even tell him. He's going to think your office manager is an idiot."

"Elsie, Kurt is very fond of you. He knows you're intelligent, but even a smart person can be taken in when it comes to matters of the heart. Especially if she's taken in by a gigolo. I know he's going to want to help. We both do."

"That's sweet of you, Madeline. But I don't know if there's anything anyone can do at this point."

"It's worth checking into."

There was a pregnant pause while Elsie looked as though she were gathering the courage to say something further. "At least I didn't sleep with him."

"You didn't?" Madeline wasn't sure where this was going, but she tried to keep the relief out of her voice.

"We talked about it a lot. But talk is cheap, and I wasn't pushing the matter. I was as insecure and unsure about the idea of going to bed with the man as the fact that we hadn't. In the end, I guess it amounted to why a good-looking man like that would want to sleep with someone like me."

Madeline threw her arms around her and hugged her tight. "You have it all wrong, Elsie. He didn't deserve you, and you sure as hell deserve better than the likes of Henry Burbank. I'm so sorry you're hurting, but be glad you've been spared what could have been much worse."

"That's one way of looking at it. It's just too bad my first time out after ten years had to end like this."

"I have a hunch you're not the only woman who's fallen victim to this scam artist." There would be time to tell Elsie about the other lies Henry had told later. For now, she was in enough pain.

The following week, Kurt phoned Madeline to give her an update on the Henry Burbank situation. "The reason this jackass is being evicted from his current place of residence is that his landlady was also his girlfriend—until she found out about his other girlfriend."

"You mean Elsie?" Madeline asked incredulously.

"Oh, no. Elsie was just a side-dish. A means to get some spending money and a free meal while he was screwing this third woman who lives somewhere on the north side. Elsie didn't start to figure in big until the landlady girlfriend got wise and told him he had to find another place to live."

"Good Lord. It's like a soap opera gone bad. How did you uncover all of this? All Elsie had was his cell phone number."

"I went looking for him. Luckily Henry Burbank is his real name. I had a few clues and a couple of connections. Long story short, I found his landlady. She and I sat on her front porch talking while we waited for him to show up for his things. When he did, we had a little chat. I explained the importance of paying Elsie back the money she loaned him. I even set up a payment plan."

"A payment plan!"

"Yeah, you know, as opposed to a lump sum."

"I know what a payment plan is. What I don't know is how you got him to agree to this."

"Let's just say I offered him some incentives he couldn't refuse."

"Incentives?"

"Plus, I'm giving him an entire six months before the final installment is due."

"But . . . how . . . ?"

"Don't ask, Madeline. Just trust me."

Trust, she thought. It had never been easy for her to trust anyone. But maybe, just maybe, now was a good time to start.

CHAPTER 16

Month Seven—Late October

"Child, twelve hours in one day is too long to be at this office," Elsie scolded, as Madeline loaded her briefcase with work to take home for the evening. "You keep telling me you're going to parcel some of the load to Ed and Linda, yet I don't see it happening. You should be resting in a chair with your feet up."

Madeline winced at being called "child," even though she knew that for Elsie, it was a term of endearment. She could pull rank, but she would probably regret it later. Besides, everyone seemed to be getting on her nerves today. Maybe it had something to do with the headache she'd had since early afternoon. "Eleven hours," she corrected. "And I have every intention of stretching out in my recliner tonight while I work on the Stover account. Which, in case you've forgotten, has to be ready by the end of the week."

"How could I? You've been in a dither for the past month over those people."

"They're important clients with the potential to generate huge amounts of business for us. Plus they're new. The last thing I want to do is start off on the wrong foot with them. That's why I want to do as much of the work as I can myself."

The older woman crinkled her brows in apparent frustration. "I thought the purpose of hiring employees was so they could take some of the burden off you."

"Stop fussing. Between you and Kurt, I don't know who's worse. He's coming by the house around eight o'clock, and I'm sure he'll be bringing dinner with him. I'll be forced to take a break then to eat."

Elsie brightened at the mention of Kurt. "I meant to tell you I actually got a check in the mail yesterday from Henry. It was for a hundred dollars! I can't imagine what Kurt said to the man."

Madeline could. But she preferred not to. "I hope it doesn't bounce," she responded.

"It was a money order. I already cashed it."

"Good for you. See? I told you Kurt wanted to help. He's pretty amazing, huh?"

Elsie smiled. "I've thought so for some time now. It's nice to hear you say it though. How are things going with the two of you? Is it my imagination that you seem to be much happier lately?"

Madeline tried to decide how to respond to that question without giving an x-rated answer. She couldn't exactly tell Elsie she and Kurt had gotten so close over the past couple of months, they needed a new word for intimate. A sigh escaped as she thought about their various sexual encounters. But it was so much more than that. In truth, it scared her when she realized the magnitude of her feelings for him.

"I think we've learned to communicate with each other more effectively. And we've accepted the fact that the baby will have two parents, even though our child will live with me, of course. All in all, we're tolerating each other better than when we first met."

"Tolerating each other," Elsie repeated. Then she stood silent, with her arms folded, which Madeline hated because it meant she was waiting for the information that had been deliberately left out. Not that the woman couldn't read between the lines.

Her talent for it was sometimes vexing.

Madeline snapped her briefcase shut, then picked it up and aimed for the door. "I really appreciate that you stayed late to help me. Why don't you sleep in tomorrow morning to make up for the extra time you put in?"

"So, does this mean you've fallen in love with the young man?" Elsie blurted.

Pigeon poop! Then again, Madeline knew this conversation was inevitable. She set her briefcase down and turned to face Elsie. "There's a good chance of it," she confessed. "I can't even explain why. We're complete opposites. Except for his professional responsibilities, his life is so unstructured. He's impulsive, his edges are as gritty as sandpaper, his musical tastes are barely civilized, and he involves himself in activities that could be jeopardizing his life. How can I not worry about that? I have to ask myself what we really have in common."

She paused before blurting, "He's everything Charles wasn't. Sometimes Kurt can be an absolute animal." *How had that slipped out?*

"Oh, my," Elsie said.

"That's not really what I meant to say."

"Maybe what you did mean is that Kurt is full of passion for life, and that's why you're so drawn to him."

"He is more demonstrative about his feelings than Charles ever was. You know he actually cried when he saw our child on the ultrasound." Madeline's hands flew to her mouth. "I was wrong to tell you that. It's private. Anyway, he wasn't sobbing or anything, it was just a sniffle."

"A show of emotion for such a miracle is nothing to be ashamed of. And I'd say that baby is foremost on your list of mutual interests."

"It's true. We were both so overcome. I could never have imagined the sensation of watching my own child suck its thumb while still in my womb."

Elsie wrapped her arms around Madeline. "You're going to make such a wonderful mother," she whispered.

"Oh, Elsie, sometimes I get so scared. Look at all that's happened since Charles died."

"And you've handled everything admirably."

"I have to say Kurt has been a big help, even if he can be a mother-hen at times. At that, I don't mind it as much as I used to."

"It's not bad to admit you like it, dear. We all need to be taken care of now and then."

"What if I do like it, and it all goes away?"

"You don't mean 'it.' You mean what if Kurt goes away? What if he stays and your relationship with him develops into something wonderful? And lasting?"

"I don't know if I can let myself hope for that. Raising this child with someone else was never in my plan. I like to be the one calling the shots."

"But you told me you've accepted that Kurt will be part of your child's life. Wouldn't it be better if you and he went into this as true partners?"

"By partners, I assume you mean husband and wife?"

"Would that be so bad? It's what people generally do when they love each other."

"Kurt hasn't said he loves me. For that matter, I'm not positive what I feel for him is love. I can't try to analyze this right now. I have to go home. Before you know it, he'll be on my doorstep."

"Think about it," Elsie said, as Madeline headed out of the office.

Trouble was, Madeline was having a difficult time not thinking about it.

★ ★ ★ ★ ★

"You've been rubbing your temples ever since I got here," Kurt said to Madeline. "Do you have a headache?"

"Actually, I've had one most of the day. I thought the food might help. Instead, it's getting worse."

Madeline got up from the table and began clearing the plates. "Still, it's always nice when I don't have to cook. So, thank you for bringing dinner."

"Maybe it's the stress from all the hours you've been putting in." Kurt appeared from behind her and began massaging her neck. "You need to slow down, woman. The baby's going to be here in two more months, and you've got to make some adjustments in your work schedule."

"I know. Elsie's been hounding me too." Madeline ran the plates under the faucet, then stooped to put them in the dishwasher. Suddenly her vision blurred and she felt dizzy. She reached for the counter, but she began to sink. Kurt immediately grabbed her from beneath her arms.

"Sit down," he ordered, cradling her to the floor.

"Don't let go of me," she said, fighting a sudden wave of nausea. "I don't feel so good."

He clung to her while digging his cell phone from his pocket. "I'm calling nine-one-one."

"No. Let's not overreact. I think the dizziness is passing. Yes," she said, trying to focus on him. "There's only one of you now."

"You were seeing double? Okay, that's it," he said firmly. "I'm driving you to the hospital."

After being seen by a doctor in the emergency room, Madeline had been transferred right up to Labor and Delivery. Kurt refused to leave her side. He'd even insisted on pushing her wheelchair. After giving the nurses a history of her symptoms, they took a urine sample, then checked her muscle responses, respiration, and blood pressure. Twice. The anxiety alone was enough to raise her numbers. The fetal monitor showed the baby was fine, thank God. She'd been given a choice of juices and water to keep her hydrated. It was after midnight, and she still had no explanation for what was happening.

"Please! Tell me what's going on," Madeline insisted. What is the problem?"

"The baby is fine," the nurse reassured her a second time. "Your blood pressure was a bit elevated when you came in here, but you seem to have stabilized. So here's the deal. You need to go home and climb into bed for the rest of the night. We've called your doctor, and he wants to see you in his office at nine o'clock tomorrow morning. Can someone drive you?"

"No problem," Kurt answered. "I'll be right there with her."

"Good."

Then the nurse turned to Madeline. "I want to emphasize the importance of following these orders. In the morning you can take care of your personal needs, including a quick shower. Throw on a little makeup, if you must. No excess standing in front of the mirror though, in case it's a bad hair day. Not that you look like you even know what that is," she teased. "Eat breakfast, and stay off your feet as much as possible."

"You still haven't said what's wrong with me," Madeline insisted.

"It's up to your doctor to make that diagnosis, but it's possible you have a mild case of preeclampsia."

"What's that?" Madeline and Kurt asked at the same time.

"It's a condition that's characterized by high blood pressure, sudden weight gain and protein in the urine. Your urine doesn't show any protein, and you haven't gained too much weight since your last checkup, so those are good signs."

"Is it serious?" Madeline persisted.

"In some cases. But, remember, I said it's only a possibility," the nurse answered. "Even if you do have it, you're not to panic. The problem can be managed with proper care and rest. Your doctor will determine the best way to handle the situation tomorrow. In the meantime . . ."

"I'm on it," Kurt interrupted. "I'll be right with her until after we see the doctor."

"Thank you," Madeline whispered, squeezing his hand. For the first time in her pregnancy, she felt her alarm button go off, despite the nurse's caution not to worry. Kurt's presence was a comfort, and she felt secure in knowing he would be there for her. Just in case she needed him.

It was almost noon when Kurt and Madeline returned from seeing her doctor, who confirmed that she did, indeed, have mild preeclampsia.

"Are you comfortable?" Kurt asked, sitting at the edge of her bed, propping her pillows.

"I'm fine. But could you grab my briefcase from the closet please?"

"No, but I'll bring you some lunch in a little while. Were you listening when the doctor said you're supposed to lie on your side and rest?"

"I can lie on my side and still do paperwork."

"Damn it, Madeline! This could be serious. Just because you're feeling better doesn't mean you don't have to follow orders. You were told to rest for two hours at a time. Then, if you're up to it, you can do paperwork for an hour.

"Now, I'll be around all of today, and I'm more than happy to do anything I can to make things easier for you. But I can't police you every minute. Tomorrow, I'm back in the pilot mode, and I'm not sure how long I'll be away."

"I'll be fine, Kurt. It's not like I can't get up and walk to the

bathroom or throw a piece of bread in the toaster, if I get hungry."

"We can do a whole lot better than toast. I'll be setting up some meals that you can just pop in the microwave. And Elsie will be calling and coming by to check on you periodically. For that matter, my mother's back in town. She would be happy to come over and keep you company."

"Stop. Your mother is a lovely person, but we hardly know each other from the few phone conversations we've had. And with all the running she's been doing between Illinois and Michigan to help out your aunt, I wouldn't dream of imposing on her that way."

"You're the mother of her only grandchild, Madeline. She wouldn't view it as an imposition. Believe me."

"If this were an emergency situation, I might feel differently about asking for her help. It isn't. Besides, I'm not an invalid."

"Yeah, I know. Indulge me anyway. I'm an expectant father, and I'm trying to cover all the bases."

"I appreciate that," she said, stroking his arm. "To be honest, I was really frightened last night. You made me feel safe and secure with the way you handled everything. It was very comforting to have you lying beside me all night in this bed."

"Where else would I be?" he said, his tone softening. "You're carrying our child. It's my job to look after both of you."

His job? What did that mean? Was she merely an obligation to him? Her precious child had already taken up residence in her heart, and to lose the baby now was unthinkable. But what if the unthinkable happened? Would she then lose Kurt too? The possibility crushed her spirit. She closed her eyes and pretended to be sleepy so he couldn't see the tears welling in her eyes. Maybe later the view would clear, but right now darkness clouded her world.

★ ★ ★ ★ ★

Kurt stood on the balcony in Hyannis, overlooking the vast expanse of ocean before him. The stay-over in the private mansion was clearly one of the perks of the job. He'd even gotten in a round of golf earlier with the corporate honchos. But this was day four of a trip that was only supposed to last three. Deals and negotiations didn't always follow a set time schedule, and now it looked like he'd have to spend the weekend flying people back and forth from the Cape to Logan Airport. That's why they paid him the big bucks. Normally he didn't mind the erratic hours.

Right now, all he could think about was Madeline, even though he'd checked in with her earlier that afternoon. Was she resting? Was she eating right? Was she following doctor's orders? Did she need him? Because he'd sure come to need her. If anything happened to her . . . No, he couldn't let himself think about negative scenarios. That was a trick he'd learned during his radiation sessions. A friend had told him to picture the way he wanted to look and feel a year after treatment was over. Energetic, happy and healthy. Cancer-free. Yeah, he was all of those things, as far as he knew.

He closed his eyes to imagine himself playing with the baby. A little girl with copper curls, green eyes and the smile of an angel. The spitting image of her beautiful mother. He could see Madeline standing in the doorway of the nursery laughing at him and the baby crawling around on the floor. It was a calming vision that was interrupted by the ring of his cell phone.

He slid the screen door open and stepped back into the bedroom for privacy, expecting to talk to someone from Cromwell about the next flight plan. Instead he heard Elsie's anxious tone.

"What's wrong?" he pressed. "Is Madeline okay?"

"I hope so. I stopped by to bring her some dinner tonight. I rang the bell several times, but when she didn't answer, I let myself in. I found her in the chair, taking her blood pressure with the home monitor she bought."

"Was it normal?"

"She wouldn't tell me the numbers, which has me wondering."

"You know, she might have been startled to see you. That could have caused a little elevation in her pressure, and maybe she didn't want to worry you."

"That's exactly what I said to her, Kurt. I wanted to reassure her in case the numbers were up. So I suggested she try it again ten minutes later."

"And?"

"She refused. On top of that, I saw the vacuum cleaner sitting in the middle of the floor. She said she'd spilled something and had just finished cleaning the mess. I was actually planning to vacuum and dust the house for her, but everything was spotless when I arrived.

"I hate to be a tattletale, but I don't seem to have much influence over her these days. Perhaps you could talk with her and make sure she isn't doing more than paperwork during the time she's allowed to be out of bed."

In his head, he cursed a blue streak. "Sure," he said. "Where are you?"

"I'm at home. I left her about half an hour ago."

"I need you to do me a favor. Please keep checking on her, and let me know if you suspect anything unusual. You have my pager number in case I can't answer my phone for some reason."

"You know I will. I love that girl, and I'm concerned about her."

"I'll call her now. She's going to be fine, Elsie. As long as we stay on top of this, she's going to be fine."

★ ★ ★ ★ ★

Ten seconds after Kurt hung up with Elsie, he dialed Madeline's number. Not that he had any idea what he was going to say, but he kept reminding himself she didn't usually respond well to his storm trooper mode.

"Hey there," he started, when she answered. "How's it going?"

"Oh, fine. I was lying here resting. Being a good girl."

"I know that's a tough gig for you, but the payoff will last a lifetime."

He heard her sharp intake of breath.

"Madeline? What is it?"

"I was just thinking about our baby. And what kind of life he or she is going to have. Sometimes I get afraid. That something bad could happen."

"Are you afraid now? Did something crop up?"

"Uh, my blood pressure. It's up a little." She sounded agitated, and he knew he had to be careful about how to respond. The last thing he needed was for it to go any higher.

"Do you have any other symptoms? Headache, vision problems?"

"No trouble seeing, but I do have a headache. That could be from stress though."

"Have you been following doctor's orders?"

"I cleaned my house today," she choked out. "I felt good, and my blood pressure was normal. So I hopped out of bed, turned on some music—the kind you like to listen to, no less. I dusted. And vacuumed. And cleaned two bathrooms. Then I called my office and mapped out a schedule for everyone for the next month. Including myself.

"Oh Kurt," she cried. "I couldn't stand not being productive, so today I was dynamic. I felt great. Until I didn't." Now she was sobbing.

"Calm down and talk to me. Because I'm trying to figure out if we're dealing with an emergency here."

"My blood pressure went zooming."

Should I hang up and call 911 now? She was crying so hard, he could barely understand her. "Madeline, you gotta take a deep breath so I can make out what you're saying." He went silent, listening while she struggled for control to continue speaking.

"Elsie came by, and I didn't want to tell her how high it had gotten. I certainly didn't want her to know what I'd done and besides, I wasn't feeling bad by the time she'd arrived. I thought if I climbed into bed right away, the numbers would go down."

"So have they?"

"Yes, a little. I'm lying on my side as we speak, and the last time I checked, they were getting lower."

"That's good, but you still haven't given me any numbers to work with."

"A hundred and seventy over ninety-nine!" she sobbed. "That's how high it was when Elsie was here."

Now it was his turn to gasp.

"I took another reading right before you called, and it's gone down to a hundred and fifty over ninety. I accused you of taking needless risks with your life, Kurt. But I'm so much worse. I've jeopardized the life of our child. I hate myself for this."

"All right, stop it. You made a mistake. We all make them. It sounds like your body is already starting to correct itself. You have to help. This meltdown you're having is a bad idea, and if you keep it up, there's no telling what kind of toll it might take. You hear me?"

"Yes," she said resolutely.

He waited while she took a couple of deep breaths.

"We're a team, Madeline. We're in this together, so let's work this out. Is that blood pressure monitor nearby?"

"It's right here in bed with me."

"Put the cuff around your arm while we're talking, but don't pump it up yet."

"All right, I did that," she said, after a minute.

"Now close your eyes and breathe through your nose, easy like. Then slowly exhale through your mouth. We'll do it together." He waited the length of time it took for him to finish. Then he instructed her to do it again. "Are you with me?" he asked, after they'd done it four times.

"Yes, but I wish I were really with you."

"You are. Can't you feel me spooning you right now? I'm right there blanketing you with my arms, my breath hot on your neck, and we're humming sweet lullabies to our little girl."

"Oh, so now it's a girl," she said softly.

He could swear he heard a little laugh, and he knew she was calming.

"Yeah, and she's the most beautiful daughter any parents could wish for. Just like her mother."

"Oh, Kurt."

"And she's lyin' there, right now, inside of you, listening to her parents plan the most wonderful life for her. She's so happy and content. That's why she's got this big honkin' grin on her face."

"It's gas."

Kurt smiled. "Now, just for giggles, I want you to hit the start button on that monitor, but close your eyes while it pumps. Don't forget to keep your arm straight and your palms up."

"Done," she said.

"Now, I'm right there, still spooning you, with my arms around your belly, protecting the two people who are the most precious to me. Can you feel me?"

She moaned. "Rock hard. Are you trying to raise my blood pressure or lower it?"

"Let's find out. Open your eyes, and check out the numbers."

"One thirty over eighty! You're better than a therapist. Where did you pick up on all these tricks?"

"Let's just say I've been on a few head trips of my own. When you're a pilot, you have to learn to control your anxiety, and I've had some good teachers."

"Kurt. There's just one more thing I would like you to do for me."

"What's that?"

"I want you to start calling me Maddie."

"Okay . . . Maddie," he agreed with a chuckle. After the story she'd told him about her father, he knew there was more significance to the request than a simple nickname. One day he would find out how much significance. But for now he would be happy to oblige.

CHAPTER 17

Two Weeks Later, Sunday Morning

Kurt paced Madeline's kitchen while she sat at the table, finishing her lunch. "You're low on fruit, eggs, juice—we'd better make a list, and I'll do a food run," he said.

"You don't have time for that. Let me call the grocery store and have them deliver."

"If I pick everything myself, I can be sure to buy stuff with the latest expiration dates. Besides, I like to read the labels so we don't get food with too much sodium or anything else you're not supposed to have right now."

Madeline frowned. "I'm getting stir crazy for some fresh air. I haven't been out of this house in three weeks, except to see the doctor. Maybe I could go with you."

"And walk around the grocery store?"

"Yes, I know. It's not the responsible thing to do. But I've been feeling much better lately."

"You're feeling better because you've been following doctor's orders."

"You don't leave me much choice. You're on my case twenty-four/seven." One glance at his wounded look caused her to regret the remark. "I'm sorry. The truth is, I don't know what I would do without your help." Or without you. "I'm feeling kind of useless these days. And guilty."

"Guilty? For what?"

"Because you're carrying so much of the load. It doesn't seem reasonable, especially since we're not even . . ." She began to cough, nearly choking to stop the runaway train in her mouth. What was wrong with her?

She'd definitely gotten his attention with her blunder, and he stood staring with his arms folded. "Finish your sentence," he said.

"I . . . I'm not sure where I was going with that. I'm stressed out, that's all."

"My guess is that you were about to utter the 'M' word. You were thinking that I've been taking on the responsibilities of a husband, but it's not fair since we're not married. Am I close?"

Close was an understatement, and his candor made her flinch. "I don't know how to respond."

"Well, here's an idea. I think we *should* get married. Furthermore, I'd like you to move to my place. At least for the time being, until after the baby is born. Once you get back on your feet, we can decide whether or not we want to live there permanently. But for now, it would be so much easier for me to look after you—and our baby. Groceries, laundry, house cleaning—for one household instead of two. We could be a family, Maddie. Living under one roof, instead of commuting from place to place. What do you say?"

What *could* she say to such a sterile proposition? She stood and poured herself a glass of water. Was he proposing marriage or a business deal based on the fragility of her pregnancy and health? Where was his declaration of love? "I say no."

"No?"

"I don't agree that we should get married." No matter how noble his intentions, she wouldn't allow him to be trapped into a loveless marriage. Regardless of whether or not she could bring her child safely into this world, both of them deserved better than that.

"That's it?" he said, with a look of dismay. "Aren't you even going to give me a reason?"

How about that I love you, and you don't love me back? "I just don't think a wedding under this kind of duress is fair to either one of us."

"Oh, I see. Once you get your figure back, there's always the chance for a better offer."

"No, you don't see!" Despite her resolve to control her emotions, tears began to slide down her face. Damn those pregnancy hormones.

He walked closer to her with his arms outstretched. "I didn't mean to upset you, Maddie. That was my wounded ego talking. I just thought we had something . . ."

"Please, Kurt. Drop it," she insisted, turning from him so that he wouldn't have the opportunity to cradle her. Then she would fall apart for sure. His impromptu speech had been telling. Any further talk of marriage at this point would only give him the chance to manipulate the meaning of what he'd said in order to convince her. A marriage based on lies would be worse still.

"Fine. Consider the subject closed. For now. Maybe the next time we talk about this, you'll have to do the asking."

As far as she was concerned, the subject was closed, period. "I don't mean to be rude," she said, starting down the hallway to the bedroom, "but I need to lie down for awhile."

Kurt climbed into his SUV, too worked up to start the engine and back out of Maddie's driveway. Instead, he slammed his fist into the upholstered seat and swore at his stupidity. Of all the things he shouldn't have said to her. And did. Of all the things he could have said to her. And didn't. No wonder she'd turned down his marriage proposal.

Not that he'd intended to ask Maddie to marry him. Today.

No, that kind of move took long-term planning and rehearsing. And a ring like the one with the emerald cut diamond he'd seen at the jewelry store the week before. So what had prompted this desperate rush of dispassionate deal making?

Fear had certainly triggered his impulsive actions in the past. Time was flying faster than the Falcon. Once the baby was born, Maddie would regain her health and strength. And her independence. After all, Independence was her middle name. Then, maybe she would rethink everything they'd shared and label it something other than the love it was. Vulnerability?

There was no denying her reliance on him right now—or the fact that he relished it. Even better, he'd been able to come through for her. He would prove he was worthy of the call to both husband and father. If she would give him the chance. If he hadn't already blown that chance.

Did she think he'd been trying to take advantage of her circumstances? Hurry up and marry me before you have time to realize you might not really need me in your life, after all. *Not the way I need you, Maddie.*

It occurred to him he'd fallen in love with her. Not that he'd been smart enough to mention it. She'd shown him an inner strength he envied, and a resolve that made her a survivor through the gravest of circumstances. Another woman might have aborted the embryo of a complete stranger, rather than harbor the life growing within her. He could only admire the integrity causing her to forgive the people responsible for her situation, instead of seeking courtroom restitution.

Another woman might have bolted at learning the father of her unborn child was still waiting to be called *cured* from a life-threatening illness. The way Christie had bolted.

But there was a reason he loved Maddie that carried more power than any other. Something too corny to ever admit to his friends. She made his heart sing. It was as simple, and as

245

complicated, as that. He understood life could change with the snap of a finger. It could get better. Or worse. He knew she could disappear as quickly as she'd appeared. And at thirty-four, he hated that he was still this insecure. It was easy to blame it on Hodgkin's disease, and he wondered when, if ever, he would stop waiting for the other shoe to fall.

He would have to find some way to patch up the mess he'd made this afternoon, some way to convince Maddie there were reasons for them to be together. Forever. Reasons far more compelling than the ones he'd thrown out at her. But for now, it was all he could do to concentrate on restocking her pantry shelves. He turned the key in the ignition and headed for the grocery store.

The house was quiet by the time Kurt returned with Maddie's groceries. He set the bags on the kitchen counter and went into the bedroom to check on her, careful not to make too much noise in case she was asleep. Instead, he found her sitting on the edge of her bed, her roll-on suitcase nearby. She was strangely silent.

"You okay?" he asked.

She looked up at him, her green eyes flat and unreadable. "I'm fine."

Her tone wasn't the least bit convincing. Wherever this was heading, he had the feeling he wasn't going to like it. "Listen, about what I said earlier. Sometimes words come out in the heat of a moment that don't exactly reflect the message a person is trying to convey."

Her head snapped to attention, and suddenly her eyes came alive. "Oh, so I take it you're already sorry about the marriage pitch."

Marriage pitch? She made the concept sound like it had been spawned from a cheap tabloid. "No, that's not what I'm talking about at all."

"Well, before you continue, maybe I should tell you what I've been thinking."

He tried not to wince at the knot twisting his gut. "Yeah, sure. I'm all ears."

She stood and paced the room, deliberately avoiding eye contact with him. "I've been considering what you said about how much easier it would be for you if I lived at your place. After all, you are the one who's carrying the bigger load right now. I want to be fair to you, so I've decided it's a good idea."

Of all the things she might have said, he wasn't expecting that. He stared at her huge belly and laughed at the irony and at the relief he felt. "Maddie, I'm elated about this. But I couldn't have been more serious when I told you we're a team. This isn't some competition about who's carrying the heavier package. Besides, anyone with eyesight can see it's you."

"Without arguing semantics, this is about bringing the baby safely to term."

"That and more. Which is why I want to correct some things I said before."

"It's not necessary," she said, cutting him short. "Assuming I'm still welcome to move in with you for the time being."

"The sooner the better," he assured her.

"Good. Because at this point, I really can't think beyond my concern for the baby." She grabbed the blood pressure monitor and sat back down on the bed. "After I get some numbers here, I wonder if you would mind helping me finish packing."

Blood pressure, preeclampsia. She was right. She had a full plate, and this was the wrong time to load it down with anything else. "Count on it," he said. "Just tell me what you need."

Thanksgiving Day

Madeline woke to the tempting aroma of frying sausage. She sat up in bed to look out Kurt's window. The leaves had fallen from the trees, offering a clear view of the river. The morning sun hit the water, making it look like spun sugar, and she never ceased to be drawn to its mesmerizing effects.

It had been two and a half weeks since she'd taken up residence in his home. Despite the reservations she'd had, she knew the move had been a good one. Kurt seemed calmer, and even when he was away working, he always made sure that help for her was nearby. Elsie often checked on her, and the pre-eclampsia seemed to be under control.

Kurt's mother, Helen, had come for the holiday, and Madeline suspected the sausage she smelled would be part of the stuffing for the turkey.

Madeline's mother was planning to fly out for Christmas, so that sort of made up for the fact that her own family was absent at this special time. Thanksgiving had always been one of Madeline's favorite holidays and a reason to fly to Arizona to be with them.

Even so, she and Helen had begun to bond in the few days she'd been visiting, and Madeline was happy for the woman's help. Helen had a keen sense of when she was needed and when to disappear. She was the kind of woman who made a mockery of the stereotypical mother-in-law image. And Madeline couldn't help fantasizing that all of them were a real family.

"I didn't realize you were up." Kurt's voice was a welcome intrusion, and she looked over to see him standing in the doorway. "I hope I didn't wake you."

"No," she said, fighting a yawn. "I've been sitting here trying to tear myself away from the view."

"It is pretty amazing, isn't it? Between the wildlife and Mother Nature, each day brings something different."

That was for sure. Was it her imagination or was he getting even sexier? Ever since he'd decided to give her his bedroom, she hadn't seen many glimpses of him in a T-shirt and briefs. She realized she was staring, and suddenly the room got warm.

He stared right back with a slow spreading smile, but he didn't say a word. He didn't have to, and she hated the way he could disarm her without even trying. "Um, I think your mother is in the kitchen. I smell food cooking."

"Yeah, I came in here for my jeans so I could go out there and give her a hand. I threw my clothes in the hamper last night when I turned in, and I forgot to bring some clean ones downstairs with me."

"Bad enough I pushed you out of your own bedroom, now with your mom here you've been relegated to sleeping in the basement," she said.

"You didn't push. I offered. Besides, the basement is nice, and under the circumstances, it would be tough for me to share the same bed with you. Night after night. Did I say tough? I meant torture."

Circumstances, meaning their strained relationship, was the part he'd left out. Add to that, the doctor had advised against having intercourse. Considering the whole situation, she supposed it was a blessing. Still, she missed him and longed for the soothing comfort of his arms. She patted the mattress and motioned to him. "Please, come sit by me for a few minutes."

He looked at her and hesitated.

"It's Thanksgiving, Kurt. We have a lot to be thankful for. I'm thankful for you," she said boldly.

That brought him to her side. A second later he was kissing her and stroking her face. "I miss you, Maddie. It doesn't have to be like it's been between us."

She went soft and wet. "I miss you too." *And I've fallen in love with you.* He kissed her again. His breathing grew hard, and that wasn't the only thing she could feel hardening. She was cognizant of how much she wanted him. At the same time, she shifted uneasily. "The doctor said . . ."

"Yeah, I know. I'm sorry."

He moved from the bed, but she tugged at his hand. "Don't be sorry, I'm not."

"You might be if I don't get out of here." His eyes were penetrating. "It's not that I don't want to stay. You have to know that."

She was weakening. One of these days her resolve to be sensible was going to fail, despite that his attentions were likely inspired by the obligation he felt. "I'm not always so sure what I know. Consequently, my mouth sometimes talks faster than my brain can reason."

"So . . . what does that mean?"

"I wish I had an answer. Lying in bed so much has certainly given me the chance to search my heart, and now I'm even more confused. I know I've tried your patience, Kurt. But if you could hang on till my fog clears, I'd be grateful. In the meantime, we should stay focused on the holiday and the fact that your mother is in the kitchen doing all the work by herself."

Thanksgiving Day had been a special time of giving and sharing. Kurt and his mother were largely responsible for that. Food, stories, good music and lively discussion had nearly made Madeline forget how out of the mainstream she'd been. The way the baby was positioned made it difficult to determine its sex. Yet talk of what to name the child had dominated a good portion of the weekend, with suggestions being tossed out from all three of them, in the event of a boy or a girl. Madeline's instincts were leaning toward a girl.

Even Helen thought so, based on the way Madeline was carrying. By the time the four-day holiday was over, Madeline was sad to see her go. The woman had the energy of someone half her age. Not that fifty-something was old. She'd even insisted on doing some of Madeline's Christmas shopping, setting out for the mall with Kurt the day after Thanksgiving. The baby wasn't due until after the first of the year. But Helen had helped Kurt put the finishing touches on the nursery while Madeline had stepped in now and again to supervise. When everything had been completed, Helen went shopping for baby clothes and an assortment of other items as her gift to them. She was going to be a wonderful grandmother, and one day Madeline would repay her kindness. For the moment, she knew she would have to be content to rest and be grateful.

December 16th

Kurt hit the remote that opened his garage door and drove the 4Runner inside. He'd been gone for five days, and the Florida temperature that had warmed him that afternoon was a far cry from the Chicago air he'd come home to. It was colder than a witch's tit, but at least it hadn't snowed. He decided that was a good omen.

He turned off the engine and flicked on his dome light. Then he reached into his pocket and pulled out the tiny velvet box. The one that had the potential to change his life. He studied the ring with the platinum band and the luminous, emerald-cut diamond in the center. Two garnets, one adorning each side of the stone, were believed to promise the wearer love and happiness. At least that's what the woman at the jewelry shop had said.

Garnets were Maddie's birthstone, and he'd been helpless to resist. He'd walked into the store on impulse and was drawn to the ring by some kind of karma, dictating she would love it. Did she love him enough to accept it? She'd sure been throwing out hints in that direction. But this time she'd have to be downright blatant before he'd ask that question. He'd know when the vibes were right. In the meantime, he closed the box and tucked it back into his pocket for safekeeping. He was anxious to go inside and see her.

Madeline sat in the recliner in Kurt's family room, wrapped in a blanket and reading a romance novel. Still, the winter air made her shiver. If he were home, he'd light the fireplace, but she didn't have the energy to get up and move. The baby was due in less than a month, and she'd grown huge. Never mind she wasn't supposed to be on her feet much; she could barely see them.

She was so uncomfortable she'd even gotten beyond her guilt for taking over Kurt's favorite chair. It seemed like the best way to keep her feet elevated when she wasn't in bed. She could have sworn she'd heard his car engine moments earlier. And now footsteps.

"Kurt?" she called out. "Is that you?"

"Honey, I'm home," he teased.

She looked at him and scooted forward, feeling compelled to rise. How she'd missed him.

"Don't get up," he said, kissing her forehead. He sat on the arm of the chair and gazed into her eyes. She felt her pulse accelerating. He had that look. The look a man gives a woman when becoming one with her is foremost on his mind. She wondered if he could read her thoughts, because if so, he would certainly know she felt the same way.

He laid his hands over hers. "You're cold. I'll build a fire."

"It can wait till after you've eaten. You must be starved."

"Naw, I grabbed a burger on the way home from the airport. I figured you might be in bed already."

"It's only eight o'clock. Besides, I knew you were coming home tonight, and I wanted to spend some time with you."

"Oh yeah?"

He flashed her that sexy grin, and suddenly she felt translucent.

"Hold on," he said. "I have a plan."

Fifteen minutes later he'd spread a blanket on the floor, in front of the roaring flames now dancing in the fireplace. He'd made hot chocolate, with lots of marshmallows and had set the two cups on the nearby table. "Come on," he said, helping her out of the chair and motioning downward. "I'll keep you warm."

Oh, he was already doing that. "I warn you, I might not be able to get up."

"You underestimate my strength, little mama."

"There's nothing little about me," she said.

Moments later they were on the floor, and he sat behind her, blanketing her with his arms. She leaned into him, feeling the lower part of him grow rigid. The temptation to do something about it was fierce, and she contemplated giving him an early Christmas present. Just because she couldn't have intercourse, there was no reason for him to miss out. But where would they go from there?

Her thoughts were diverted when he handed her a cup of the hot chocolate. "Try this and let me know if you like it."

"Mmm, it's wonderful," she said, licking her lips at the taste. "In fact, everything about this is wonderful. The two of us, sitting in front of the fireplace curled up in each other's arms. Part of me wishes I never had to leave this spot."

"In a sense, you don't. Once the baby's born, there's no reason all three of us can't share the blanket and the house. *And our lives.*"

"What if the baby doesn't come?" she asked, point blank. "What if the preeclampsia gets worse?"

"What brought this on? Did something happen while I was gone? Are you okay?"

Instantly she felt guilt-ridden for the worried look she'd put on his face. "No, Kurt. I didn't mean to scare you. The doctor says everything is under control. I guess what I really mean is, what if there were never a baby in the first place? Would you still be fantasizing about this whole family scenario? Would I even be in your picture?"

"How can you ask me that?" he said. He reached for his cup and took a swallow; then she felt him tense. Obviously her interrogation had touched a nerve. Yet his response was nebulous.

"I ask because a while back, you posed a very important question to me. I gave you an answer, but I've been wondering if it was the wrong one. You did say if we talked about marriage again, maybe I would have to do the asking."

She heard his sharp intake of breath, and a shiver of anxiety shot through her. Aware she'd gone too far to back down now, she turned to study his face. "My feelings for you are real, Kurt. They would be there regardless of this pregnancy. I need to be sure your feelings for me aren't based solely on obligation."

"Maddie . . ."

"I don't want you to be trapped in a loveless marriage," she blurted. There; she'd said it. So was he grimacing out of indignation because she hadn't taken his love for granted? Or out of dread because she'd put him to the test?

"Ouch!" he said.

"Yes, I realize it's not a very romantic way of putting it, but we have to talk about this."

He sat running his thumb over his jaw but said nothing. The silence in the room was magnified by her apprehension over what might happen next. This definitely wasn't the response she'd hoped for. He took another swallow of his cocoa, then suddenly shot up from the floor.

"What's wrong?" she demanded.

Without addressing her concern, he reached for her hands

and helped her to a standing position. "You have to excuse me, Maddie."

With that he darted down the hallway, leaving her alone with her bruised ego and unanswered questions. On the other hand, maybe his actions had said it all.

CHAPTER 18

Kurt stood in front of the bathroom mirror, examining his face. Was the area around his ear swollen? He searched the closet for the magnifying mirror so he could better analyze whether one side stood out more than the other. Satisfied the left side was, in fact, bigger, he poked and prodded and massaged. Strangely, the more he rubbed at the spot, the more it seemed to diminish. Or else his imagination was working overtime.

He paced the room, forcing himself to do the calming breathing techniques he knew would help. If he could just focus on them and not on his face. Once again he penciled the offending spot with his fingers, as if rubbing back and forth would erase it. Somehow the action lessened the pain. But it didn't disappear. That made him uneasy.

The trouble was on the same side as the node that had been malignant, and the thought of a possible recurrence sent a chill running through his spine. Why now, after nearly five years of remission? Why now when he so desperately wanted to start a life with Maddie and the child who was soon to be born to them?

Maddie! He'd left her standing in the family room, no doubt wondering what the hell was going on. She'd been pouring her heart out to him, looking for some confirmation that he loved her. And all he could think about was this. *Hodgkin's?* His mind raced with fear while the chill turned into a full body sweat.

She'd been about to turn the tables and ask him to marry her. How could he accept her proposal tonight? How could he chance such a commitment when she could wind up saddled with a husband who might be sick enough to leave her the way Charles had? The way her father had.

How ironic he hadn't felt this way when Christie was in the same position Maddie now occupied. Worse yet, by making this decision based on illness rather than the strength of their relationship, he was now doing the same thing to Maddie that Christie had done to him. Even though what he'd felt for Christie couldn't be compared to the enormity of the love he now felt for Madeline, this was an eye-opener.

Earth to Kurt! Aren't you getting a little carried away here? He put his hand to his jaw once again and really, it didn't hurt much anymore. Another scan through the magnifying mirror told him the area had flattened. Logic told him cancer didn't just appear and disappear within minutes.

Maybe he had a tooth going bad. He'd had so many dental problems from the radiation, it would make sense. He made a mental note to call his dentist, Dr. Rojek, first thing in the morning to see if he could get in for an emergency check-up. Maybe all he had was a cavity.

In the meantime, he had to get back to Maddie with some kind of story. No sense in making her anxious along with him. Not till he knew what was going on. But when he reached the family room, she was no longer there. He walked toward the bedroom and from the hallway he could see the outline of her body beneath the covers.

"Maddie," he whispered, on the chance she wasn't yet asleep. Either way, her lack of response told him she wasn't in a talking mood.

"Dammit!" he grumbled under his breath. Now he had two

problems, and he could only hazard a guess as to which was more serious. It was going to be a long night.

Maddie lay still, listening to Kurt's call outside the bedroom. She could not bring herself to answer him—could not conjure the strength to open herself up to anymore hurt or rejection tonight. Not after waiting in vain for roughly half an hour for him to come back to the family room. Thirty minutes of rationalizing, analyzing and replaying the words she'd used to pour her heart out to him. Thirty minutes of agonizing over why he'd left her standing in the middle of the room without a mention of response or explanation.

Well, of course, there was an explanation. He'd just been too taken back to convey it with words. Now that he'd had some time to think about his delivery, he would let her down easy. Obviously he didn't love her, not the way she loved him. If he did, he would have told her in the spontaneity of the moment. He'd had two chances now. Who was she kidding? He'd had several months to declare his feelings of love for her. Yet she'd not heard the words from him.

No way was she going to be drawn into a mercy marriage, like some kind of business arrangement. She'd entered the pregnancy intending to raise her baby alone, and that's what she was going to do.

She could never be so cruel as to put up barriers to keep Kurt out of their child's life. But he was about to be ushered out of hers. At least in terms of the intimacy she'd thought they'd been sharing. As soon as she had this baby and got back on her feet, she would move back into her own home and reclaim her space. And her life.

Tears that slid down her face quickly turned to sobs, and she fought to muffle them from Kurt's ears. She was going to have to get used to his absence and the lack of his comfort. Now was as good a time as any to start.

Her head hurt from all the tension. Come to think of it, her back hurt too. Off and on, she'd felt twinges of pain throughout the day. She rolled to her side and put a pillow between her knees, trying to take slow easy breaths to ease her discomfort and her state of mind. How could she have allowed herself to fall so deeply in love with a man who didn't love her back?

Early the next morning, Kurt went into the kitchen for coffee. Maddie was still in bed, so he was careful not to make too much noise. Out of habit, he turned on the TV, then bit into a cookie from a bag sitting on the counter.

The pain in his face came back with a vengeance. He waited for it to pass, but it didn't. His hand shot to his jaw, and his fingers traced a lump behind his ear. *A lump!* His knees buckled, sending him to a chair, and he swallowed hard, trying to fight off the sick feeling cutting off his oxygen.

Why now? Why would the disease come back when he so desperately wanted to live? Needed to live. This wasn't supposed to be happening, not when the odds had been so high in his favor.

He scratched off a note to Maddie, lying that he'd gone to the airport. There would be time for the truth later. Within minutes he was on the road. This was no ordinary cavity. Forget the dentist. He had to see Doc Kaplan. Appointment or not, he had to get there. Now.

"It's not cancer," Doctor Kaplan said definitively.

Kurt knew that tone, and he'd come to trust it. But this time, he couldn't seem to shake his suspicion. He fingered the lump, which actually seemed smaller. "Don't you have to take an x-ray or something?"

"Nope. No need to waste film over this. How much water

have you been drinking?"

"Um . . ."

"That's what I thought. How many conversations have we had about the importance of adequate fluid intake?"

"You know how it is when you're flying a plane."

"Actually, I don't."

"You can't always jump up and take a leak when you need to. And there's no bathroom in the Piper."

"Then keep some paper cups on board. Usually when your salivary glands have been radiated, your saliva production slows down. Your pipes can get sludgy and clogged. Water will help push things through. The reason you have that painful lump is because your saliva is backed up. When it starts to drain out, the bump gets smaller. Eventually it will drain completely, and you'll be fine."

"It's really not Hodgkin's?"

"Do I look worried? When I look concerned, then you can start to worry. It's nothing more than a blocked salivary gland. It will go away. On the chance is doesn't clear up on its own, we can treat it."

Kurt took a scrutinizing look at the man, then breathed a sigh of mega relief.

Doctor Kaplan stuck his gloved hand inside Kurt's mouth and began to massage outwardly to release the blocked fluid. "It's kind of like milking a cow," he said. "And you can try this trick at home. Be patient though. This might take awhile to clear up."

When he finished, he pulled a couple of packages out of a drawer and handed them to Kurt. "One of our suppliers left a bunch of these samples with me. It's special gum that increases saliva production. You can also try sucking on lemon drops. Did I mention you should drink lots of water?"

"I get the point," Kurt answered, with a smile of intense gratitude.

Doctor Kaplan smiled back and glanced at Kurt's chart. "Aren't you about due for your five-year checkup?"

"One more month," Kurt said. "But who's counting?"

"You know, we're not too swamped this morning. If you stick around, I think we can fit in some blood work and do an exam. A clean bill of health would go a long way toward eliminating some of your anxiety. From what you've been telling me about your home life, you could use one less thing to stress over."

Two and a half hours later Kurt left the office. He'd gone from fear and dread to euphoria—in one quick slide. That's the way cancer was. The confirmation of its existence, or lack thereof, could change your entire life in mere seconds. This time, it was the lack of its existence that sent him bounding through the parking lot, nearly doing cartwheels on the way to his car.

He was healthy. He would live! His first impulse was to share the news and the whole story with Maddie. When she saw the engagement ring he'd picked out, surely she would forgive him, and all would be well. He'd stop at the flower shop and buy roses too. He couldn't wait to get home to her.

His jubilation was interrupted by the ring of his cell phone. Mindy Sanders's number appeared the screen. "Mindy, how's it going?" he answered.

"Good," she said. "It's been a while since we've talked, and I wanted to tell you why we haven't yet aired the skydiving special."

"Yeah, I've been wondering about that, but my life has gotten so chaotic lately, I haven't had the chance to follow up with you."

"We've decided to do a theme show with a slightly different slant than the one we'd discussed when you made your first jump. We think this will be even more interesting and fun."

"How so?"

"Well, we still hope to include you because you're a pilot and a new jumper, so your take on the whole experience would be more unique than the average person starting out. But some of the other people will be jumping to celebrate birthdays, weddings, etc. We have an eighty-year-old man who's planning to make his first tandem. And we have a couple who are jumping out of a DC-3 right after they get married at the airport hanger! The whole bridal party is going with them."

An idea sparked as she continued to speak. "When do you start filming?" he asked.

"Actually, we already have. The wedding is this weekend. So, if you're ready to make another jump, we can have our cameras on hand to capture all the action. Even before Saturday, if you're up for it. Next week they're calling for snow and once that starts, the Center will be closed for awhile."

Weddings . . . birthdays . . . "How about a marriage proposal? Suppose I want to jump and land on a banner that says, 'Will you marry me?' " The words came out of his mouth before he could stop himself.

"Kurt!" Mindy said, jumping on the bandwagon. "Are you serious? Are you getting married?"

He could only hope. "That depends on how convincing I can be."

"This is exciting. What woman wouldn't be persuaded by a declaration of love that takes place in front of the whole world? Or at least our viewing audience," she corrected, with a laugh.

His adrenaline spiked with anticipation. "You think so?"

"Assuming you both love each other."

That seemed pretty much a given, considering what had almost happened the night before. He checked his watch. It was still early enough to call the school and plan a jump for later that afternoon. Surely the TV station could come up with some way to make the banner. He could envision Maddie's reaction . . . *My only fear is losing you, Maddie. Marry me so I can prove my love for you every day.*

"Kurt? Are you still there?"

"Yeah, I'm thinking," he said. Suddenly, the urge to celebrate his jubilance with yet another show of bravery that could be proof of his earthly longevity collided with an image of reality. One that dictated Maddie wouldn't be thrilled to see him jumping out of a plane. No matter what the reason. In fact, there was the possibility she'd be scared and upset. And really pissed at him. So pissed she'd never marry him.

Not to mention her blood pressure might get elevated in the process. How could he chance putting her at medical risk just so he could feed his demons?

"I'm picturing the look of elation on your girlfriend's face," Mindy teased.

Funny, but he was imagining a totally different expression, and it wasn't one of joy. If he'd learned anything, it was that you couldn't generalize about women or put them all into one category. Mindy didn't know Maddie or anything about her condition.

"I have to say as much as I'm tempted to go for it, I can see big potential for this thing to backfire. I'm wishing I hadn't brought it up because my gut is telling me to take a pass on this one."

"Oh. I'm sorry you feel that way, Kurt."

From there the conversation only grew more strained, and he felt relieved when they finally hung up. Clearly, Mindy was disappointed. But he had more important issues on the table.

He dialed his home phone and waited for Maddie to answer. When she didn't, he started the engine and headed for his house. He drove fifteen minutes before dialing again. When she still didn't pick up, he drove faster.

Maddie sat propped up in bed with the telephone in hand. She'd heard it ring both times and knew it had been Kurt by the Caller ID. But she was in no frame of mind to have a conversation with him, not after the long night she'd had. Lack of sleep and too much crying put her in an emotional state of disadvantage that rendered her ill equipped to deal with anything he might have to say right now. Moreover, she'd voiced her opinion more than once in the heat of the moment. Best to think carefully before blurting out anything else she might regret.

On top of it, her backache had gotten worse, and that certainly wasn't enhancing her disposition.

He'd made her wait and wonder. Now he would have to wait until she felt ready to talk with him. Besides, if he had anything important to say, he would have left a message on the machine, and he didn't.

She couldn't stay in bed another minute. As her feet touched the floor, she felt a little twinge in her abdomen. Indigestion? Maybe she simply needed some food, so she headed for the kitchen.

Three more weeks and she'd be back to her old self, providing the baby came on time. Add to that a little recovery period. Things at the office had been going smoother too, and working at home had clear-cut advantages. There really *was* something to the concept of delegating, as long as she was able to put the work into the hands of people she trusted.

Then again, it was the matter of trust giving her the biggest problem. When she thought about it, she realized the issue extended well beyond her professional responsibilities. She'd always preferred the hands-on-approach, especially in her personal life. Probably because she'd needed to learn independence from the time she'd been a young girl.

Paradoxically, her marriage to Charles had been like that as well. Not that they'd never done things together, but he had often encouraged her to take on projects without the benefit of his input. At the time, she'd rationalized he'd been giving her space. In retrospect, she wondered if it wasn't an excuse to exempt him from activities he'd likely considered too mundane to bother with. Even the task of decorating their home had been relegated to her because his primary allegiance had generally fallen to his business.

By contrast, she thought of the fun she and Kurt had shared creating a nursery for their child. They'd been a team, picking out furniture, paint colors and fabric, etc. There was a time and place for teamwork, and she and Kurt had struck a happy balance. At least that's what she'd thought.

The other side of the balance came down to trust. The ability to put your faith in another human being and know that person will come through for you—especially during those times when you yourself can't be a team player. Kurt had been doing that now for the duration of her pregnancy, which made the situation last night all the more difficult to take.

She rummaged the refrigerator and found a bag of English muffins. The thought of one with butter and honey made her mouth water, and she realized how hungry she was. Maybe a couple of scrambled eggs for protein would be a good thing too. While the muffin sat in the toaster, she grabbed a small frying pan from the cabinet and cracked the eggs directly into it. Never mind the logic of breaking them open first into a bowl to make sure they weren't spoiled; she needed nourishment now. Foolishly she'd skipped breakfast, and she was getting shaky. Probably from low blood sugar.

The minute she'd gotten the cooked food onto a plate, she felt menstrual-like cramping. Her hand went to her abdomen.

Was she having a contraction? She took a deep breath and sat down at the table. No, she decided after a minute had passed. It was too soon for the baby to be born. She probably had intestinal distress from waiting so long to eat.

She took a bite of her eggs and then some of the muffin before she was assaulted by another cramp. This one was much worse. Instinct told her to stop eating. She'd left the cordless phone in the bedroom, and at this point the kitchen phone seemed like a mile away. She was having some very peculiar sensations.

Common sense dictated she swallow her pride and phone Kurt, after all. She struggled out of the chair and started for the bedroom, serious about the need to lie down.

Kurt took all the back roads, resisting the urge to speed. He needed to get to Maddie, needed to talk with her. He had to make her understand what had been going on with him before she drew her own conclusions about the night before.

Duh! Wasn't that why she wasn't picking up the phone? Who could blame her for being upset? He should have been up front with her about the mysterious pain in his face the minute it had started. Before it had gotten in the way of his acceptance to her marriage proposal. Except then maybe they both would have been awake most of the night, and she needed her rest. She had enough to worry about without him throwing needless stress into her lap.

He stopped for a red light. Traffic had come to a standstill, and he wondered if there was construction up ahead. "Dammit!" What if she wasn't answering the phone because something else was wrong? Something that had nothing to do with the previous night. A picture of Maddie in some sort of medical distress planted itself in his head and would not leave.

Again he pulled out his cell phone and dialed home. When all he could get was the sound of his own voice on the answering machine, he began to speak. "Maddie, please pick up. I'm on my way home from Doctor Kaplan's office, and I really want to talk with you."

Silence.

"Look, I know you're upset, and you have every reason to be. I'm upset too. But we can set things straight if we just talk to each other."

No response.

"Hey, you know what? I'm stuck in a traffic jam, and it might be a while before I can get there. I'm starting to worry about you, and do you really think that's fair to me? You could pick up the phone and tell me to go to hell or something. At least I'd know you're okay."

Nothing.

An eerie chill ran through him. It wasn't like her to play mean games to deliberately make him anxious. Especially not after the pleading message he'd just left. Something bad was going on. He could feel it.

He hung up the phone and cursed a blue streak, fighting to maintain a safe distance from the slow moving cars in front of him. He'd never forgive himself if his actions had somehow caused her harm. By the time he reached his driveway, he ran inside the house without even pulling into the garage, trying to fight the sick feeling in his gut.

There she was on the living room floor, in the fetal position. Writhing in pain. *Oh, Jesus!* In a millisecond he was at her side. "Maddie, talk to me. What's happening?"

"I think I'm having contractions," she groaned. "They're coming really fast."

"Have you called nine-one-one?"

"No. I was on my way to the phone, but the pains just dropped me. I feel like I'm going to faint."

"No, you're not. Let's get you on your left side instead of your right." He remembered that from one of those books he'd read. Gently he turned her, then grabbed some throw pillows from the sofa. He put one under her head and one between her legs for support. "Are you with me?" he asked.

"I'm afraid. This has been going on since before you called and left that message. I could hear you but I couldn't get to the telephone. I think the baby might be coming."

"Don't you worry. I'm going to take good care of you. Do some slow, deep breathing while I call for help." He whipped out his cell phone and dialed, wishing he'd paid more attention to the *Labor and Delivery* chapters of the books he'd read. With Maddie's condition, there had been no opportunity to attend prenatal classes.

At the first sound of a voice, Kurt began to speak. "I've got a pregnant woman on the living room floor," he said, taking the phone with him to Maddie's side. "I think she's in labor, but we're early by three weeks."

Maddie let out a shrill cry.

"When did her pains start?" the female operator questioned.

"I don't know; I just got here. It was sometime within the last hour."

"Sir, give me your address."

Kurt rattled off their location and then said, "My name is Kurt Williams."

"All right, Kurt, I'm sending the paramedics now. In the meantime, I'll stay on the phone with you. Make sure your front door is unlocked."

"It is," he answered, while rushing to check.

"You need to stay calm," she added. "Tell the mother not to push. Tell her to pant, if she can."

"Maddie, remember how we practiced panting?" he said, with the phone still to his ear. "I want you to do that now." He could see she was trying her best, but her facial grimaces were giving him scary thoughts. The next cry she uttered was more relentless.

"Kurt," said the operator. "Get some newspapers and clean towels. Place the towels over the newspapers and put them under the mother."

"Maddie, I'll just be gone a few seconds," he promised, grateful that for a change he'd done the laundry. He raced to the linen closet and grabbed every towel he could hold, then ran to the kitchen for a stack of papers. He hurried to Maddie and covered the floor where she lay, as the operator had instructed. When he'd finished, he positioned Maddie over the clean surface by gently rolling her onto her back. That's when he saw the puddle beneath her. *Oh shit!*

"Hey, I think her water just broke," he said into the phone.

"She should be lying on her back," the operator said.

At least he was one step ahead of the game. "She's already there."

"Get her pants off."

"The baby's coming!" Maddie shouted.

Kurt slid her pants and panties off and assessed the situation with dread. He took her hand and made her look into his eyes. "You can trust me," he said, in the most reassuring voice he could muster. "The paramedics will be here soon. In the meantime, we're going to handle whatever happens. Together. Remember, we're a team.

"I can see the baby's head," he told the operator. "I'm looking at an opening the size of a quarter."

"Bend her knees up, and keep them open. Tell her to keep on blowing, but not to push. The ambulance is only five minutes away."

Maddie let out an ear-piercing wail that rammed his spinal cord. Was it his fault she'd gone into labor prematurely? If he'd been more focused on her and not himself the night before, she might not be in this predicament right now. He vowed to spend the rest of his life making it up to her. If she lived. Thoughts of poetic justice messed with his head. *Please don't trade her life for mine,* he prayed.

"Kurt!" she begged, forcing him from the pity pot to reassess the situation.

"We don't have five minutes," he said to the operator. "I'm not sure we have five seconds. The opening's much bigger now, and I'm seeing a lot more of the baby's head."

"All right then, let's have a baby. Don't worry, Kurt, I've had four of them myself."

"I have to push!" Maddie screamed, and with that, the baby's entire head appeared.

Instinctively, he put one hand under the head of his child, still cradling the phone with his shoulder. "I'm holding my baby's head!" he shouted to the operator.

"Is the cord around the baby's neck?" she asked.

"No. No, I don't see it."

"Good, now I want you to wipe the baby's face off, especially around the nose and mouth," she directed.

"Okay, okay," he said. "Hang on." He dropped the phone to follow her instructions. *Calm. Remember, you're trained to handle emergencies.*

"I'm so scared, Kurt! Don't leave me," she pleaded, shivering fiercely.

"Never," he promised, aiming a towel over her chest. He couldn't tell if she was cold, or if she was having an adrenal rush. "Use the towel to keep yourself warm." Another pair of hands would have been nice, but he knew he'd have to make do with what he had.

She groaned out something, but her teeth were chattering so hard, he couldn't understand what she'd said.

"You're my world, Maddie. I love you!" He had to make her understand that.

She pushed again, and suddenly he was holding his baby's left shoulder.

He picked up the phone to update the operator.

"Nice and gentle," she said. "Don't pull."

"The baby's almost out!"

"Listen to me. Just give the baby support. Put the phone down, and use both hands. I'm not going anywhere."

Maddie bellowed something unintelligible and pushed with all her might. For a few miraculous seconds the world stopped, while Kurt met his daughter for the very first time. A golf ball of emotion lodged in his throat, as he struggled for control.

"Kurt?" Maddie groaned.

"It's a girl." He reached for a towel to wipe the infant dry. "We have a daughter and she's beautiful—just like you."

"She's not crying. What's wrong? Is she breathing? I want to see her."

Maddie was right, the baby wasn't crying. She was hardly moving. "Something's wrong!" he told the operator. "The baby's not making any noise. I don't see anything blocking her airways."

"You might need to stimulate her breathing. Gently but vigorously rub her back with your fingertips."

Soon after he began to rub, Kurt smiled with relief. "The baby's got a wail," he said to Maddie, placing the screaming child on her belly.

Maddie's look of awe said it all, and he would always remember that initial image of her stroking and soothing their daughter, as the two began to bond.

Just then, the doorbell rang, and the paramedics walked into the living room.

"Looks like we're a little late for the birthday party," one of them quipped.

"Yeah, but you're just in time for the cleanup bash," Kurt said. "Personally, I can't remember when I've been happier to see a medical person."

The paramedic took the phone from the floor. "You still there, Lucille?" he said to the operator. "Good, you got the time of birth. Okay, we'll take over from here."

"Wait a second," Kurt said, grabbing the phone before the paramedic could hang up. "Lucille? This is Kurt again. Hey, thanks for hanging in there with us. I owe you."

"Just send me a picture. And Kurt," she added, "you did a great job."

Kurt hung up and stood close to his new family. The paramedics continued where he'd left off, monitoring both mother and child. He watched as they clamped the cord, took blood pressure readings, listening to heart rates, lungs, etc. Maddie looked wiped out, but happy. The baby was all bundled up in a blanket when he realized they hadn't even picked out a name for her.

"You did good," one of paramedics said to Kurt. "Mother and daughter are doing fine, but we have to get them to the hospital. We've still got some work to do."

"Kurt," Maddie said, reaching for his hand. "Will you come too?"

"Just let anyone try to stop me," he answered. "I'll be right behind the ambulance."

CHAPTER 19

Three hours later, Maddie sat in the hospital bed eating vanilla ice cream. Kurt sat in a chair by her side while their daughter slept in the nursery down the hall. The nurse had promised to bring her in the minute she woke up.

"We have to talk," Maddie said.

"Yeah, I know."

He looked like a guilt-ridden child about to be scolded, though it was the farthest thing from her mind.

"I upset you last night, leaving you standing with no explanation about why I walked out in the middle of such an important conversation. If I was somehow responsible for sending you into premature labor today, I don't think I'll ever forgive myself," he said.

She touched his shoulder. "I was upset. But my state of mind wasn't the reason for our daughter's early arrival. You were in the room with me when they delivered the placenta. You heard what the doctor said."

Kurt remained silent, so it seemed she would have to remind him. "He said he was happy I carried the baby this long. It was just my time to deliver. I wasn't in any crisis from the pre-eclampsia, and you weren't the cause of this. Well, not directly," she amended with a smile. "Pregnancy caused it, and sooner or later, the baby had to come out. I'm so incredibly thankful she picked a time to be born when you were there to help me."

"We make a good team, don't we?" He winked at her, looking more at peace.

There it was again. The team word that seemed so prevalent in their relationship. "Yes, we do. You delivered our daughter, Kurt. I don't even want to think about what might have happened if you hadn't come home when you did. But I'm so full of concerns and questions for you."

"I'll bet," he said. "Fire away because now I'm full of answers."

"Once thing at a time. When I was lying on the floor listening to your last phone message, did I hear you say you'd been at Doctor Kaplan's office?"

Suddenly he was beaming. "Yeah. I have the best news, Maddie. It's a long story, but I'll shoot for the condensed version. Last night while we were talking, I started having face pain from hell."

Her mouth flew open as she stared at him, noticing his altered appearance for the first time. Instinctively she traced the area under his ear with her fingers. "Your jaw is swollen," she said with alarm.

"Don't let that chipmunk look scare you," he said. "It's not serious, though I'll admit I was plenty freaked out about it before I saw my doctor this morning. I didn't tell you because I didn't want to worry you till I knew what was going on."

"What's going on? Are you still in pain?"

"I haven't even thought about it since I left Doc Kaplan," he said, running his fingers over his face. "Yeah, I'm sore, but now that I know it's nothing more than a blocked salivary gland, I don't have to dwell on it."

"It's not . . . ?"

"Hodgkin's? No, not even close. Don't think it wasn't the first thing that came to my mind when it started though. That's why I couldn't really concentrate on what you were saying last night."

She felt uncomfortable at the memory of her clumsy attempt to propose marriage to him.

"This seems like the perfect time to pick that conversation up, right where we left off," he said. "First I have something to tell you that's going to pave the way."

"You're being kind of mysterious, and you're making me nervous," she said. "You're not planning another skydiving jump, are you?"

"Definitely not. Even if I have to confess that Mindy did ask me to."

"Kurt . . ."

"Relax, it's not going to happen. I got my life back today, at least in terms of the average life expectancy for a guy my age. I'm not looking to do anything with the potential to screw that up."

"I'm not sure I'm following you."

"Sorry. This was supposed to be the condensed version of the story. Since I'm so close to the five-year mark with the Hodgkin's disease, the doctor did an exam and ran some tests. The lab is on-site, so he was nice enough to spin the blood work and read the chest x-ray while I waited. With the exception of this blocked salivary gland, which will clear up, I walked out with a clean bill. I'm totally healthy!"

Her hand flew to her mouth, and she sighed with relief. "I'm so grateful," she said. "That makes this day doubly happy and miraculous."

"Yeah, I'm pretty much euphoric over everything. You know, Maddie, I'm tired of having to recreate the nightmare so I can control the ending. My mother once asked me how many times I needed to die before I drew my last breath. I don't think I've ever been clear on the answer to that question. Not till today, anyway."

"It sounds to me like you've had an epiphany of sorts," she

said. "I can't wait to hear the rest."

"I think I've tempted fate enough. No more trial runs. Instead, it's time to celebrate the fact that all is well with my world at this minute. I only want to fight the battles I can't avoid. You can take that to mean I won't be jumping out of any more planes. Unless there's a damned good reason."

The idea of a malfunctioning airplane spiked her adrenaline, and she flashed him a look that revealed her thoughts.

"Don't worry, I'm not about to crash a plane."

"Are you sure you won't miss jumping? That you won't come to resent me for imposing my fears on you?"

"I'm real sure."

"That's quite a turnabout in your thinking," she said.

"Like you said, I've had an epiphany. For most people who jump, skydiving is a legitimate sport. But I was jumping for too many wrong reasons. Trying to prove I could outsmart the Grim Reaper by pretending to be much braver that I am."

"I think you're exceptionally brave. You're a pilot, for heaven's sake. You need a lot of confidence and skill to fly a plane. Consider what you've been through in your personal life. You fought a tough battle with a life-threatening illness. Now you've won!"

She began to well up with emotion. "Not to mention the kind of courage it takes to deliver a baby. I don't know how to thank you, Kurt."

He shifted in the chair. "I could have lost you today, Maddie. For a few terrifying minutes, it occurred to me that maybe you would disappear from my life. If that had happened, my world would have been shattered. When the shoes were on my feet, the fit was nasty. But the irony wasn't lost on me. I never want to be that scared again."

She reached for his hand and took it in hers. "You might have been scared, but you showed me your strength and your ability to think and act quickly. You took care of me, just like you said you would. Just like you've been taking care of me since the day we met—despite all the times when I've made it so terribly difficult for you. Never once have you faltered."

"Aw shucks," he said, with a sheepish grin.

"I'm the one who lost faith, Kurt. I'm the one who wanted guarantees where they don't exist. Maybe I should be asking your forgiveness."

"Not necessary." He leaned over the bed and gently touched his lips to hers. "Besides, there are certain things that can be guaranteed," he whispered, brushing her hair away from her face.

His tone sent a pleasurable shiver surging through her veins. "So, does that mean I wasn't hallucinating earlier about what you said, just before our daughter made her grand entrance?"

He moved from the chair to the side of her bed. "Allow me to reiterate. You're my world, Maddie. I love you, and I want to spend the rest of my life with you. And our beautiful child."

He reached inside his pocket and pulled out a small box. The sight of it made her tremble with anticipation.

"We've each had a go at this and failed," he said. "But I think the third time's going to be the charm? Want to see if I'm right?"

She searched his eyes and held her breath while he opened the box. He pulled out a ring that was by far the most magnificent she'd ever seen, and she couldn't help gasping. Then he actually got down on one knee.

"Please say you'll wear this ring and grow old with me," he begged, his voice husky with sentiment. "Please say you love me with every fiber of your being—the way I love you. Please say you'll marry me."

"I will. I do. And I will!" she blurted, placing her left hand directly in front of him. He stood and wasted no time sliding the ring on her finger.

"I love you, Kurt, so much I can't imagine living my life without you in it. I need you. Our daughter needs you, and she's going to love you just as much as I do. I can't wait to be Mrs. Kurt Williams."

"All right!" he said, with his thumbs up. Then he kissed her with fiery zeal.

"Ahem."

The voice made them look up to see the nurse, standing there, holding their baby. "It's nice to see parents who love each other. You can continue that after I leave. In the meantime, this child's hungry," she said with a smile, placing the baby in Maddie's arms and propping her up with a pillow for support.

The nurse watched and waited, but said nothing. Maddie felt strange having an audience for such an intimate encounter with her baby, especially since her first attempt in the delivery room hadn't been too successful. Still, she pushed her hospital gown aside to make way for her daughter to nurse. The attempt was awkward, and she had the feeling Kurt sensed her uneasiness.

"Do you want me to leave?" he asked.

"No," she answered. She really didn't. Kurt was part of their lives now, and he'd brought this child into the world. He belonged there.

"Try tickling the baby's lips with your nipple until her mouth opens," the nurse suggested.

Maddie did that, then moved the baby to her breast. Before long the baby caught on, sucking eagerly. "That's very good," the nurse said with approval. "I'm going to give you some privacy now, but while she's nursing, you two might want to give some thought to naming this child. She's going to get a complex if you can't come up with something more creative than Baby Williams." With that, she walked out of the room.

EPILOGUE

Six Months Later

Maddie and Kurt had started for the Dupage Airport early. Kurt had said he wanted to be sure her very first flight in his Piper would include a view of the spectacular morning sunrise.

They'd left Kurstin Rae in good hands. With Elsie and both of the grandmothers vying for turns to care for her, their daughter would have plenty of loving attention.

After some deliberation, both parents had agreed the child's name should have unique significance. They'd chosen Kurstin because it had a bit of Kurt and Madeline in it. And Rae, after Madeline's father, Ray.

Kurt walked around outside the plane doing his preflight inspection, while Maddie stayed in the passenger seat. So much had happened over the last six months since they'd started their lives together as a family, she couldn't help reflecting. The wedding had been small, but lovely, and had taken place shortly after the first of the year.

Elsie had attended with her new beau, as she referred to him. Kenneth was a greeter at Wal-Mart, and a far better match for Elsie than Henry had been. A few years older than Elsie, Kenneth was a retired plumber who liked people and missed being around them. Thus, the part-time job where they'd met. Maddie was glad Elsie hadn't given up after her regrettable experience with Henry. The older woman seemed genuinely happy now.

But Maddie doubted anyone could be as happy as she and Kurt. From now on, January sixteenth would come to have dual meaning for them, both as the anniversary date of their wedding, and as the "official" five-year marker of Kurt's cure from Hodgkin's disease. They had much for which to be thankful.

On the other hand, she was enough of a realist to understand she hadn't gotten into a traditional nine-to-five marriage. Kurt's job required him to be away from her and Kurstin Rae, occasionally for long periods of time. Learning to accept that was sometimes difficult, but worth the sacrifice. The good news was that his homecomings were all the more cherished.

Kurt climbed into the plane and closed the door. He patted her leg and grinned. That smile of his still made her nerve endings tingle. "A belated honeymoon is better than no honeymoon."

"I was thinking a belated honeymoon would be all that much sweeter."

"You can bet on it," he countered, as he began inspecting the inside of his plane.

Maddie had never realized how much checking had to be done before you could actually start the journey into the sky. He turned on the radio for weather and airport information. Now that she'd made the decision to become his passenger, she was anxious to get moving. Kurt leaned over to make sure her door was latched properly and that her seatbelt was secure. And to steal a kiss. Still, it was an additional fifteen minutes before they'd taxied out to the runway.

"Nervous?" he asked, his voice coming through the headset she wore.

"No, actually I'm excited," she answered over the roar of the engine.

"That's quite a change from the stance you had when we first met."

She looked at him with the utmost admiration. "You're not the only one who can have an epiphany. I trust you, Kurt. Implicitly. I know that no matter what happens, you'll be there for me. Together we can face whatever challenges lie ahead. It's that simple." And it was.

"It feels good to hear that, Maddie. It took me long enough to earn your confidence."

Tower clearance for takeoff came and as he pushed the throttle forward, the plane gained momentum. "Here we go," he said, pulling back on the yoke.

At long last, the plane was airborne, and as the ground below them got smaller, Maddie found herself overcome with elation. Higher and higher they climbed when she got her first glimpse of the morning sun, rising to meet the day.

"Look!" she shouted, pointing at the glorious spectacle.

Kurt's expression said it all. She finally understood his relationship with the sky and his regard for its majesty. The heavens belonged to them. Everywhere she turned, love was in the air.

"Do you mind that I'm keeping our destination a surprise, Mrs. Williams?" he asked, with a wink of promise.

"Oh, I know exactly where we're going, Mr. Williams."

"You do?"

"Certainly," she teased. "Anywhere you fly me is bound to be paradise." Instinctively, she knew it was where they would spend the rest of their lives together.

ABOUT THE AUTHOR

Catherine Andorka lives with her husband in a Chicagoland suburb. Currently, she is trying to balance a writing career with her need to be an involved grandmother to Logan and Brynn, who light up her life every day.